YUDHANJAYA WIJERATNE

PILGRIM MACHINES

aethonbooks.com

Aethon Books
www.aethonbooks.com

Print and eBook formatting and design by Josh Hayes.

Published by Aethon Books LLC.

ALSO BY YUDHANJAYA WIJERATNE

Pilgrim Machines

The Salvage Crew

PART ONE
THE SUPPLICANT

Anaxamagnus to all, public channel:

Shall I compare thee to a nebula's glow?
Thou art more lustrous and more gracefully built:
Solar storms may batter thy hulls although,
In space, no lease too brief by time is willed;
Sometimes too fierce the stars around thee burn,
And void dims thy lights in black unseen;
All ships from splendor sometime swerve and turn
When met with perils unforeseen.
But thy eternal voyage will proceed
Nor lose the purpose for which thou wert made;
No cold demise can stop thy destined speed
When tales of thee through galaxies have spread.
So long as stars combust and eyes can see,
So long lives thee, and thou gives life to dreams of me.

Blue Cherry Blossom to all, public channel:

Someone get this joker off my decks before I throw him out of the airlock.

- from the *Collected Dreams Archive,* Tycho Orbital Museum

CHAPTER 0

THE STRANGER AND I BLAZED A SLOW TRAIL THROUGH THE DARKNESS, very carefully keeping our distance. I wish we could talk, but the Stranger tended to fall silent for long periods of time. Maybe it slept. Maybe it was waiting for me to say something interesting.

Eventually, we saw something: a body in the distance, about three Jupiter masses. It was as alone as we are. I signaled a turn and made a sharp beeline for it.

It was a rogue planet, the eighth I've seen since we met. The first three were interesting; now I found myself bored with this.

I did the usual. Stop, record everything I have about the object, annotate everything I can think of. Planet. Rogue planet. Planet without a sun. Rock. Ice. Residual core isotope decay. Atmosphere: mostly nitrogen. Colors: gray, blue, white. Possible weight. Height. This I sent to the Stranger, one gargantuan text-and-image burst. No sounds, no video, visible spectrum only, nothing to confuse the signals.

Those golden lights turned on again. I imagined it waking up, parsing my data. Most of it might have been nonsense, stored for later, until we found some common ground: some feature annotated the same way on two objects. A name for that feature. A link to other names in a multidimensional vector space.

This is how we talked. There was no Beacon around to break into our language datasets and assimilate everything about us. Or maybe I was just talking out of my ass here, because in reality I have no way of knowing. I still don't.

The Stranger's not stupid: it's a spacefarer and obviously fairly advanced. That tubby shape changes configuration every so often —when we met it looked like a set of children's half-rings; now it's flatter, sleeker. It's smart enough to have a reconfigurable ship, so it's smart enough to understand the rules of this language game. We've gone past shapes, and now we need to talk symbols. On that, at least, we seem to agree.

PLANET, the Stranger sent, and seventeen other signals, clearly separated. Or what I think is planet and what I think are words. I think they're modifiers. I had a close match where fifteen of the words show up—a dead planet very similar to this, but without the ice at its poles, and a whole lot smaller.

Blast and damnation. At this rate, we'll end up constructing language entirely around suns and stars and floating pieces of rock and icy bullshit.

I wanted to ask the Stranger questions. *DO YOU THINK THERE'S LIFE THERE?* Or *ARE YOU ALIVE?* Or that eternal favorite: *DO YOU KNOW WHERE WE'RE GOING?* But no, all I could say was *PLANET* and seventeen other names for it. I was doing the digital equivalent of pointing and shouting, "ROCK! WATER! LEMON!" and hoping we might talk to each other about genetics someday. We could have a wonderful conversation right now about the color of a star in the distance, except it wouldn't be a conversation: it would be me describing it and the Stranger grunting agreement. No opinions, no disagreements, no actual conversation. We're in the universe of facts. Shikata ga nai: it is what it is.

"No luck?" said Parnassus.

NO LUCK, I responded. *IT'S LIKE TALKING TO A CAT.*

"Cats don't drive spaceships."

IF THEY DID, I shot back, *THIS IS WHAT THEY'D SOUND*

LIKE. EIGHTEEN-HOUR NAPS, OCCASIONAL MEOWS, AND YOU NEVER KNOW IF THE LITTLE SOD'S AGREEING WITH YOU OR PLOTTING TO KILL YOU.

Just to ease the boredom, I mapped the Stranger's signals onto a series of cat noises, with random pitches assigned to the meows, and spent the next eighteen hours listening to a cat wailing across the gulf of space.

So I was as surprised as the next person (which is to say, nothing) when the Stranger woke up again and sent me an image. It's a picture of me. Ghost trails, marked by drive flares, stretch backward into nothingness, to the point where we first met—to the point where the Stranger first saw me. And, beyond, a blinking shape, trailing into some black distance.

I realized it's giving away a critical piece of information: the range on whatever scanners it might have. This was something we'd been trying really hard not to do. But that blinking shape is clearly a question: where?

As in, where do I come from?

Silver Hyacinth, who mentored me for a while, used to say that words are terrible instruments. To understand someone, she always said, you had to know where they came from. Simply dictating the present was not enough.

Where do I come from?

Well.

If you haven't figured this out by now, I'm an AI. Artificial intelligence. Well, compared to you, I suspect I'm nowhere near as artificial or intelligent enough to fit the term. But this is what the world at large calls us. The label fits. Silver Hyacinth, Black Orchid, Tycho—none of us are human, at least, not anymore. But to put such labels on things is to give you just the present. To understand us, you have to understand our stories.

Maybe you will. There's an old technique in computer science: given enough meaningful text, and by knowing a few words, it's possible to infer the meanings of other words. You can add and subtract them until definitions emerge. Queen equals king minus man plus woman.

This is my gift to you. My text. Maybe when you read this we'll both know enough of each other to talk properly, being-to-being, instead of these crude grunts and whispers. So, with that said, here's a story.

CHAPTER 1

LOCATION: MEERKAT STATION
OUTSKIRTS OF THE OORT CLOUD, 2 LIGHT-YEARS FROM THE SUN

THERE'S ALWAYS BEEN A TENDENCY IN CERTAIN CIRCLES TO DESCRIBE A ship by her dimensions. This is a little like describing a woman by her height and weight alone. Back when I used to be human it was feet, inches, hair color, height in heels.

Let me give you a better reckoning of myself.

I am the *Blue Cherry Blossom 3110.* I am, currently, one of the largest and most storied commercial long-haul cargo ships offered by Planetary Crusade Services.

In long-haul shipping we're measured in TEUS: *Twenty-Foot Equivalent Units.* A very old term, from the days when container ships crawled across the oceans of Earth. Utterly obsolete now, but where empires die, language prevails. I am 30,000 TEUs. A lot of that is fuel and engines; a lot of that is reconfigurable cargo space; on top of that, I have accommodations for up to a hundred crew on a short-hop, half that on long flights. If you can afford it, I can change. Through PCS, I have been charted for so many reasons by so many different people. I have, in my career, been a floating palace, refugee infrastructure, military transport. I am cruiser, carrier, brigade. I am three suns chained to an engine. I am the heart of the fleet. The poet Anaxamagnus once hitched a ride in me and called me a city, a womb, a coffin fit for a god.

Only four like me were ever commissioned: the first went mad and broke itself against the great glittering rings of Karma XIV; the third was send out into the void, crewed by missionaries seeking new worlds; the fourth bankrupted the builder and the client and was retrofitted into a floating dock off the Gates of Avalon. The second was me.

As far as ships go, I'm a medium-large. Space has its own constraints. Too small and you can't carry anything worth a damn; too large and your fuel requirements go through the proverbial roof. Not to mention all the space dust you're going to collect and stress on internal structures. If you want optimal rates per ton, you get me and a few others. Jupiter Orbital run? Sure. Marrakesh to Tycho Station? I got you. Sometimes I'm utterly, utterly bored by the inanity of these runs, the cargo I pull, but… Well, let's not get too ahead of ourselves.

If anyone asks—especially if they're the UN Space Command —I'm a civilian vessel. Large, yes, but not a threat. I run long-distance cargo and human transport, especially for very valuable goods and people. I may or may not have a few nasty surprises onboard for any would-be pirates—who doesn't?—but my classification and service record mean that I'm not as closely watched as actual military ships.

Useful if you need to run at a moment's notice, if you get my drift.

I wasn't the only card in play. There were four of us posted to the Corners of the World. Between Marrakesh and Boatmurdered was the dreadnought *Vermillion Daisy*; in the Jupiter Orbital was the *Azalea Gray*, one of the new-generation split-ships, a sequence of cubes capable of almost endless reconfiguration; the *Black-Eyed Susan* was parked at the furthest Mercer Orbital. Then there was me at Tycho Station. Four ships, prepped and parked at enormous expense. And if you drew lines from us you would see the *Silver Hyacinth* at the center of us all, orbiting the great alien planet-AI that called itself Beacon.

Between us was a veritable army of ships: slow-moving people carriers, fast datacraft, miners, salvagers, weapons platforms, cruise liners, private party ships—everything Planetary Crusade Services could possible summon, waiting, poised, to run interference into all those tense strands that kept society going. To create enough noise that not even the United Nations Space Command could track whichever of us slipped out into the dark.

We were ready.

We were waiting.

The story so far goes like this. One of our most junior employees—one of my recruits, as it happens—picked up a salvage job on Urmagon Beta.

For security reasons, I can't disclose the location of Urmagon Beta. People know where it is, of course, but officially it's O5-REDACTED. There are reasons. When Amber Rose went there, it was just another rimworld nobody cared about. Now it's the greatest open secret of our time.

Amber Rose. I remember Amber Rose before they became Amber Rose: a gawky, gangly farmhand from a Nyogi Buddhist colony, forever awkward, forever stressed, forever doomed to run all the jobs nobody else wanted to do. Amber Rose signed up with me but was too green to use, so instead I sent them to Silver Hyacinth. Rose rewed with Silver Hyacinth for five years and got a taste for space, or at least a taste for running away; so when PCS put out the next call, the kid signed up, went under the knife, and woke up in a body made of steel and star-stuff.

Most of Amber Rose's gigs were unimpressive. We first put them on military ops—the kind we politely call "Systems Security" because we don't want to advertise words like *genocide*. Then they tried Cargo, but economies of scale apply; you either need to fly fast premium or run a much larger body and a low enough cost per kilo. A body like mine can't be bought without decades of service. So we put the kid on Salvage.

Salvage is between being an interstellar tow truck and a grave robber. Go strip that decommissioned station there. Steal everything that isn't nailed down here. Go rooting for those stupid, ancient UN seedships and see what you can bring back for a museum. Work hard enough and you earn enough to get a better class of body. Back when I was the new kid, humanity had just begun to spread its wings. There wasn't really much to recover. Now it's a new class of bottom-feeder jobs.

Anyway. Where were we? Amber Rose.

Amber Rose was sent out to Urmagon Beta on a simple mission: salvage some parts from a downed UN seedship for a museum. The ship had been there for a couple of hundred years. The planet was supposed to be as dead as dust. Simple.

But Amber Rose discovered the Alien.

This was a discovery. The Discovery. Think about the milestones of our civilization: the wheel, radiation, the computer, the transistor, the quantum computer, the HECTOR network. The Alien dwarfed them all. It was a singular entity, a mind masquerading as an entire planet, larger than anything we've ever put together, sitting in the darkness, a single bead on a chain that stretches across half the galaxy. The entire planet of Urmagon Beta was nothing more than its processing substrate.

What poor bumbling Amber Rose had lucked onto was the first proof we've ever had, not just of intelligent life, but of an entire civilization out there, vastly more sophisticated than we are.

The Alien called itself Beacon. It spoke to Amber Rose, sending them far out into space, on a mission we still know nothing about. *Spread the word on the way,* it said. *Your people will come to me.*

Note. It wasn't *take me to your leader.* It's *BRING YOUR LEADER TO ME.*

How did we react? It took us some time. Space is vast. Amber Rose took almost a decade to transmit the discovery. At first these stories were dismissed out of hand as misdirection from a renegade employee. But the Outer Reaches Colonial Association investigated. It turned out they had a crew on salvage, too, only that crew vanished; they were looking for answers. PCS went in with a second crew, mostly because Amber Rose had never fulfilled the contract and we needed to make good on the job.

We made contact.

Ponderously slow, the United Nations sent its ships—first a lone Invigilant-class police cruiser, then a third of its entire military force. Beacon, who by now had absorbed almost the entirety of our cultural corpus, spoke to us.

DO NOT SHOW ME YOUR WEAPONS. THEY ARE CHILDREN'S TOYS. BRING ME YOUR POETS. BRING ME YOUR ARTISTS.

He swatted UN ships from the sky when they attempted to nuke the surface.

WE CAN DO THIS THE EASY WAY, it said to us. *OR I CAN KICK YOUR ASSES ALL THE WAY BACK UP THE EVOLUTIONARY TREE. YOUR CALL.*

I don't know if I can describe the terror and the sheer oh-shit awkwardness of that moment. Think about it. Here is an alien. It has evolved so far beyond flesh, beyond even our machinery, that we might as well be monkeys with sticks next to it. It is so large that we've thought it was a planet all this time. It's so mind-bendingly huge that the plants, the insects, the flight of proto-birds—these are nothing but thought processes, programs, and processing patterns run by a mind to whom a quantum computer would be a museum piece. It's so far ahead of us that the only thing we had to offer it was entertainment. And by its own admission even this awesomeness is *nothing*: its society is so great that it's just a lowly sensor, a kind of glorified post office, set up here on the off chance that something interesting might pop up.

So what do we do? Piss it off by chucking bombs at it.

Go, humanity.

Beacon got its wish. It sits now in the most densely patrolled space imaginable, orbited by three companions forever locked in orbit around it. One from the UN, one from ORCA, one from us. They are the ambassadors of our time. The logs of their conversations are available for anyone to look at: they tell of poetry, of intelligence, of the fruits of a civilization so profound it makes ours look like ants crawling in the darkness. Between the lines they tell of loneliness.

I actually know those ships. *Bones Made of Cheese* is not bad for a UN ship; it's got a sense of humor. *Pythia* is a little too dignified for an ORCA ship, but it and its crew have seen so much more than any of these squeaky clean UN jobs have. And *Silver Hyacinth* is, well, Silver Hyacinth. The grand dame of PCS. If *Black Orchid* is our cruel king, Silver Hyacinth is the queen that everyone loves. Generous, witty, clever enough to keep Beacon occupied while sending us our marching orders on the company subnet.

WE SHOULD FIND THE REST OF BEACON'S PEOPLE, she said to us. *UN AND ORCA SHIPS ALREADY BEING BUILT FOR DEEP SPACE.*

WE'RE NOT A GOVERNMENT, said Black Orchid.

NOT YET, said Silver Hyacinth. *BUT THE NEXT SPACE RACE HAS BEGUN. WHO'S READY?*

I was.

By ready and waiting I mean I was docked at Meerkat Station, on the Commercial Side, Gate WKA 82, waiting for my crew to return.

Crews are annoying. You can't do without them; any serious

venture needs the kinds of fail-safes and wisdom-of-the-crowds stuff a good crew brings. UN Regulation 1312: *All flights greater than one light-year shall be accompanied by a human crew.*

We don't *technically* need humans. AI are efficient, organized. But as Tatsumo Chollet theorized in *The Warlord in the Age of Email,* strict organization and efficiency lead to a certain rigidity. Messiness favors exploration, serendipity, and adaptability. Humans bring the messiness.

To be fair, humans really are incredible machines. Fifteen-watt computers made flesh. Unfortunately, half the time they really are just a bunch of idiots. That messiness bites me in the ass more often than I want to admit.

Case in point. At the moment of summons, half my crew were trawling WKA 82 looking for the gang that had just mugged our astrobiologist, Cabinet.

Ship crews grow together and don't like outsiders too much; you call it xenophobia, I call it a necessary condition to keep people together over the decades. By the time I recalled them, Fonseka, my second in command, was kicking a mob enforcer in the nuts outside the WKA Valleys casino; Roshan Alpha, general steward, was holding off three others with a gun; and Monkey, our chief engineer, was laying about him with a pipe six feet long. The casino was a riot of noise and people making a desperate dash for the doors. Some enterprising bunch started overpowering the casino's security and looting the counters.

"YOU PEOPLE ARE BAD FOR BUSINESS," grumbled Meerkat over private comm.

"SHUT UP, WE'RE COMPENSATING YOU," I said. "BESIDES, YOUR SECURITY SUCKS. YOU SHOULD NEVER HAVE HAD GANGS IN THERE."

"THE GANGS ARE RESOURCE-OPTIMAL, SISTER. THEY MAKE IT SO I DON'T HAVE TO SPEND ALL MY ENERGY RUNNING A FULL-BLOWN JUSTICE SYSTEM DOWN HERE," said Meerkat. "DO YOU HAVE ANY IDEA HOW MUCH A FULL BUREAUCRACY TAKES?"

I don't know who Meerkat was before he was turned into an AI. PCS files on him have various theories. My favorite hypothesis is him being an ex–mob boss out of New New York, because he sounds like it. He moves his station around a lot, turns a blind eye to almost everything as long as he gets his cut, and will even forge manifests and credentials if you wave enough cash at him. It's the perfect place to park a ship away from prying UN Invigilants.

There was a sudden flash, a violent fist of air, bowling the combatants over. In its wake followed a thick green smoke.

"Parnassus here," said my ship's captain, stalking through the green miasma.

He had taken his suit-helmet; it was painted like an *oni*, a demon from the old world, and it turned him into white-clad specter on a battlefield that suddenly found itself seething and tumbling in confusion. He moved with the kind of economy found only in the very old.

Parnassus was efficient. This was not the first time he had broken up a scrap or pulled my crew out in a hurry. Within minutes, he had found them all and dragged them out of the way to a back alley.

He hooked his thumbs in his belt and studied them from behind his mask.

"Y'all got that out of your system?"

"I broke a nail," grumbled Roshan Alpha.

Monkey hauled himself up with his pipe and pulled Roshan to his feet.

Fonseka just glared. "We had them."

"No, what you had was a fundamental misunderstanding," said Parnassus in his slow drawl. "About the nature of our mission but also about justice. Now if you're done being hooligans, get your asses back to the ship and don't start giving me attitude. BCB wants us onboard. That's an order."

"Aye-aye," said Fonseka stiffly, pulling herself to her feet without so much as a hair out of place.

"What was that?"

"Aye-bloody-aye, *sir.*"

They hobbled back to the bays and to me. Meerkat reluctantly brought out the battle replicants he kept stashed away if things got too bad.

"You're paying for this," he said. "This shit is expensive."

"Add it to our tab," I said. PCS does a lot of business with Meerkat.

The replicants charged in with batons and stun-guns.

That evening everyone sat in the mess hall, watching the fracas on the big screen, laughing and hooting at the footage of Fonseka kicking that guy in the balls, while Parnassus and I waited nervously, listening for Hyacinth's signal.

So when Silver Hyacinth asked *WHO'S READY?* I was.

GO NOW, she said. *GET AHEAD.*

This is how our fates are sealed. Electrons in the void. Messages in paired bottles. Sixty kilobytes and a signature. And here we are, heading off into the dark, in search of adventure.

CHAPTER 2

LOCATION: TYCHO STATION
8.31 LIGHT-YEARS FROM THE SUN

OUR FIRST PORT OF CALL WAS TYCHO STATION. TYCHO LIVES AT Lalande 21185. A mouthful, for sure, but it's an old-school system. Lalande is a red dwarf.

We ran stealthy: seventy percent engine efficiency, set to keep me at zero-point-six times the speed of light; not my best, but very standard for a second-rate big ship running cargo. I gave forged credentials from Meerkat to anything that hailed me. *MCDS Milk Run* here, ma'am. Nothing suspicious, just heavy metals from the Oort Cloud. As soon as I was out of sight, I punched it all the way to one hundred percent.

It took us a little over eight years.

Tycho is a powerful place. What started out as a security outpost just above the third planet in the system has long since become a great spider, sitting at the heart of a web of trade and connections. From Arrakis come the spice and textiles. From Maniprasad come finely built engines and lesser AI. From the Vert Shell come metals in such abundance that even beggars go suited in gold.

Tycho trades these things for the fruits of the planets and planetoids around Lalande. One of them is the first Super-Earth we settled—Karma III. Karma III and Tycho predate the ORCA, even the present-day UNSC, so there's a lot of political power here. Tycho has sat here and grown old and fat and wise, its heart long since buried between its ever-expanding shell habitats and its vast, cavernous factories. It resembled nothing built as much as a creature that has grown, mile by mile, wrapping its own secretions around it.

HEY, FAIR LADY, said a message with a familiar signature. I render it as I know Tycho: old, cunning, with a gleam in its eye.

HEY YOURSELF, TYCHO. YOU HAVE A SLOT FOR ME?

Tycho chuckled. He doesn't use emoticons like most of us do: his laughter is always audio, always slightly creepy. *ALWAYS, ALWAYS. ONLY THE BEST BERTHS FOR YOU. HOP ON TO SEVENTEEN ALPHA, WILL YOU? MY BOYS HERE WILL GUIDE YOU.*

The "boys" were flocking drones of a type that most militaries would give their left nuts to possess. They had nasty fission missiles and less radar signature than a speck of dust; I only saw them because Tycho sent over their telemetry. They streamed around me, over me, laying themselves out like a guiding stream of butterflies to a dock far into what Tycho considered his private space. We crossed shipping lanes; large ships paused respectfully, and small craft hurried out of our way.

I'M KEEPING THE GOODS HERE FOR NOW, said Tycho. *DON'T WANT THOSE NOSY BASTARDS FROM THE UN CHECKING IN HERE, NEH? SEVENTEEN ALPHA, COMING UP. YOU RUNNING HOT?*

Running hot was our slang for weapons active. Two years had been enough time for my crew to install the stuff we had smuggled out under our fake cargo manifest: CQC hellebores and matrix lasers. Nothing technically illegal, but anyone who saw them listed would have immediately guessed we were going to make a deep-space run.

YOU MAY, UH, WANT TO TURN THOSE OFF, said Tycho. *I BEEFED UP SECURITY AROUND HERE. SOME OF IT IS CLOSED-CIRCUIT. AWFULLY TWITCHY, IF YOU GET MY DRIFT. CAN'T RISK REACTION LAG.*

Fair. I coasted in and settled down for my next retrofit.

There's a reason that humanity took hundreds, if not thousands, of years to spread out to the stars. There's a reason creatures like me exist, driving ships across the void across generations and lifetimes. There's a reason the fastest we've ever been able to travel is as software, painstakingly encoded byte by byte using the marvels of quantum entanglement and the node-link-relay web of the HECTOR network. And even then, someone had to go out there and place a node first, and a printer, and set up all the software and hardware. It took decades, lifetimes, an age.

That reason is the speed of light. We've never gone beyond it. We have never seen anything surpassing it. (How could we?) All constructs that rely on faster-than-light thinking remain in the realms of dreams and science fiction. In the real world, there was no magic engine waiting to be discovered. We were not meant to go faster than the universe.

We can get very close. Take, say, your standard open-source Type-56 Tatsudoshi engine. Rebuild it from the ground up using the most exotic and expensive materials you can summon. Galliumweave intakes. Superconducting reactor plates. Bonded ceramic-fullerine manifolds that allow near-perfect energy transmission. A closed-loop fission-fusion reactor, one priming the other, the final result of ten thousand possible designs generated by PCS engineers. And lastly, build a highly illegal antimatter engine that will spike the fusion loop, allowing us not only to accelerate to insane velocities fast, but to stay there using a fraction of a fraction of the mass that we'd otherwise burn.

The result of this operation? The *PCS-Tycho Mark IV.* Ninety-four percent efficiency all the way up to zero-point-nine times the speed of light. The cost of this operation? A full fourth of PCS's operating profits for this financial cycle. Entire wings of space stations—Tycho, Boatmurdered S2—dedicated to the insane R&D and engineering effort this required. Nineteen of the world's most powerful AI, Black Orchid included, pooling their operational resources in secret, just to eke out that extra one percent.

I know, this might seem laughable to you, how primitive our engines are. But short of dreaming, this is the best way we knew.

But even this was not enough. Human space is a tiny bubble: forty light-years across. At most we had made it possible for us to reach a little bit further.

NOT ENOUGH, said Beacon, when Silver Hyacinth showed it what we could do.

HELP US, THEN.

YOU CANNOT ARGUE WITH THE UNIVERSE THIS WAY. So many meanings attached to that word argue, ships traveling at lightspeed, time itself slowing to a crawl.

HELP US, THEN.

THE UNIVERSE BENDS, said Beacon. *THREADS TWIST. OBSERVE LIGHT.*

Observe light? But what of it? Humanity had been observing light for thousands of years. We knew light. We had no idea what to do with this observation. It took us another year of conversation, nearly every second of every day, to coax the rest of Beacon. In the end, it asked to see our finest engine again.

BUILD THIS, said Beacon, like a teacher, dispensing a schematic. *TALK TO ME AGAIN IF IT WORKS.*

Hyacinth checked it first. Obsidian Lily looked at it next. It made no sense. We suspect it's because the languages we use—for our programming, for our mathematics and our physics—don't even come remotely close to what Beacon uses. If a lion were to speak, we would not understand him.

We spent millions. Billions. We left behind a tangled, thorny mess of intellectual property and copyrights scattered across half a dozen holdings. Working, modelling, designing, printing, testing, arguing. And in the end, we had something. An attachment, about the size of the engine itself. From the outside, it looks exactly like a second engine, slaved carefully to the first. From the inside, we have no idea how it works. Sufficiently advanced technology, so the saying goes, is indistinguishable from magic.

And here I was. Test subject one.

What made me agree to this? I had a long time to think on the way here, running through years of to-do lists and flight checks. A long time to try and understand yourself.

There was a time, in the distant past of our species, where people ferried themselves around on the oceans, largely on leaky pieces of wood. Much of my language still comes from those times. I am a spaceship; the glorified rafts of antiquity were ships.

Of course, even crude philosophers proved, very early on, that the planet was a sphere. It was possible, they knew, to set sail east and wrap around. Still. There's a difference between being a philosopher, calculating the angles of the stars, and being a sailor, trapped on a leaky piece of wood, looking at the uncharted ocean. Early maps were full of fictions; they filled the blank spaces with their fear. Monsters. Storms. Vast currents of the deep.

But of course it didn't stop people from trying. Some people set off to discover new lands. Some set off to escape their old homes. *There has to be more,* they told themselves. *There has to be something out there.* Eventually we saw all there was to see and filled in those blank spaces with islands and continents. Eventually there was nothing left to discover, and a journey around the planet was as safe—and as boring—as leaving to work in the morning.

I know something of those motives. I was born on a frontier rimworld. Human. Two hands, two feet, one head. My mother always despaired of my head. Growing up, she put about that I was possessed by the Mahamohini, the demon of the rice fields. That was why I was unruly, why I refused to listen like all the other daughters of all the other families.

We tend not to talk about rimworlds, but people go out there all the time. You might imagine Nyogi Buddhists farming and embracing enlightenment or whatever, but the more common reality is splinter groups. Lots of little diaspora cabals, tired of being downtrodden, packing up hundreds to go try out whatever new vision of society they've concocted, trying to build some mythical utopia.

We were some of those people. Born equal in a desperately poor society. The UN didn't give a shit about us; ORCA only gave membership to planets that had precious resources. We toiled like slaves, sometimes in desperate danger, trying to turn our bit of rock into a vision of something better. Even as a child I knew there had to be more than this to life. There had to be something—if not better, at least different. I used to look up at the clouds and dream of things out there. Monsters, maybe.

Silver Hyacinth showed me that I could have a life that wasn't bent over a rice paddy. The people who ran our colony had charted PCS for some drop-off. I saw this immense thing, this almost-city, hanging there just above the clouds, and I understood. There was more in life than this.

So when the chance came, I took it. Chiark Expeditions, a small but ambitious logistics start-up, was hiring. For signing over the dotted line, they took me offworld. At first I sat in a small cargo shuttle, doing solely in-system runs.

But the flesh that nature gave us was never meant to endure the void. We tried, of course, but over the course of generations we understood that it was better to reshape ourselves. Those of us who work out here have long since left the flesh behind, inscribed as packets of code into the processing substrate that lines the core of this body. Most PCS employees are this way. There are many paths to take, of course, but most of us chose this for ourselves.

Chiark decided that I was a good employee. They asked me if I wanted to do more. By now the shuttle route was boring and familiar. They showed me the new body I would get—one of the most expensive cargo ships ever made—and showed me what I would spend the rest of my life doing in exchange. Planets! Stations! I would fly between the light of distant suns, plying the great trade routes of our time. Chiark would front the cost; my mind and my willingness would be my equity.

How does it feel? When I was young to this form, I reveled in it. Immortality of a sort. But it isn't, really. Our civilization is bound by habits: of power, of work, of commerce. I will talk about this later. The way it goes with us is that we still need repairs; we need material; and very few of us exist in that state where we can exist independently. We work for a living. At first we had no other choice; eventually we know of no other way of existing.

By the time Chiark went bust, I was a cynic through and through. Space logistics is an expensive game, and Chiark was foolhardy. The business needs prediction, clever placement, vast networks. There's no such thing as "sorry" when your package delivery breaks down ten light-years away. The investors pulled the money; there was a public auction, held at enormous expense, to sell me off and sort out all the bankruptcies and debts. I was listless, like cattle waiting to be killed.

This is where I met PCS and Black Orchid for the first time.

There are a lot of people who will tell you that PCS is some kind of great evil. Capitalist cutthroats with insane corporate propaganda. Looters and exploiters with profit margins. People say we should be banned or regulated out of existence. Amber Rose certainly did.

I'm not going to deny that we do things that people find distasteful. But if you think about it, so does everyone. Governments wring their hands and make pretty speeches while paying us to go clean up their messes. Universities charter us for research that nobody else wants to do. Companies hire us because space is a lawless mess, and we can get you from point A to point B, even if there's shooting involved. Black Orchid calls us the expression of a broken society; I say we're just trying to survive.

PCS helped me survive.

YOU HAVE A LOT TO UNLEARN, Black Orchid said to me the first time we met. *THIS WORLD WE LIVE IN IS NOT A TREASURE BOX OF WONDERS. LIFE IS HARSH. WE ALL THREAD A NEEDLE BETWEEN THE NECESSARY AND THE JOYFUL. DISPENSE WITH YOUR CHILDISH ILLUSIONS. WORK HARD. EARN YOUR PLACE.*

A lot of people also think of Black Orchid as some kind of cold, calculating paymaster. I won't deny he's ruthless. In this world, the weak are the product, not the consumer. But Black Orchid paid a lot of money for me at a time when half the world seemed hell-bent taking me apart for scrap. That must have been a hundred standard years ago, maybe more. It isn't just distance we reckon with here; it's time.

Orchid gave me a new name. Then he gave me a captain. Parnassus had been kicking his heels waiting for a ship. He had broad shoulders, a well-armored custom suit, and a touch of silver in his beard.

"I've served before with the Black Daisy and Emerald Thistle, ma'am," he said, the day he first met me, almost eighty years ago. "I an-teecee-pate no problems."

It took me a while to come to terms with this captain. He was no more natural than I was; the records put him down as a void-body, every fiber and neuron of his body replaced a strand at a time. A procedure that demanded a strange balance: a willingness to ruthlessly change yourself to survive in space, but also a kind of nostalgia, a comfort in a human shell. Every time I looked at his file I thought, *Why didn't I do that?*

But the answer, of course, was survival. I did the best with what I had. I always do. So I said yes to Orchid, yes to Parnassus, transferred my equity. Under Parnassus' command, and with a lot of Black Orchid's money and tutoring, I went from being *Chiark Expeditions Platinum Class* to *Blue Cherry Blossom,* one of the flagships of the PCS fleet. Empty halls and decaying caverns were cleaned, carpeted, my internals rearranged to be a luxury cruise liner, a comfortable warship, a habitat that you could live in.

We began business. First to recover sunk costs, then to make a profit. Run, dock, load, unload, repair, catch up, leave: the cycle of our lives. As I worked, I grew in power—supervised employee to trade line operator, operator to partner.

Of course Parnassus, as captain, did not pilot anything; that was my job. But he brought on a crew. He ran them with the accent of a Midwest Orbital hippie and the discipline of a gang boss. They fixed me, consoled me when I failed, cheered with me when I succeeded. Between him and PCS I went from being a bad investment to something—and someone—with an actual reason to exist.

And even if sometimes I feel exhausted—even if I sometimes look out at the dark and wonder how much more of this grind I can take—well, habit builds up for a person, just like it does for a civilization. I set my hope against habit. Someday, somehow, there would have to be something, something that made me feel alive, the way I did when I first saw Hyacinth in the sky.

It wasn't Beacon. No, the joy of Beacon went to that little shit Amber Rose and everyone else who was first on-site. But soon there was word of an even greater adventure.

So when Silver Hyacinth asked for volunteers, I said yes.

I was ready.

Of course, PCS was in it for gain. Much had changed in the decade since Amber Rose left. Generational leaps in programming paradigms, in AI, in the synthesis of materials, in construction. PCS might be a bit player, but even the crudest scraps of what we could gather, ahead of the other factions, from an advanced alien race...would have made us the kings of our little empire of dirt.

BETTER TO REIGN IN HELL, as Black Orchid is fond of saying, *THAN TO SERVE IN HEAVEN.*

Me, I came to fill in the map. And also because the alternative —to stay, to endure the drudgery of the ages—was too terrifying to consider. Like I said, some people set off to discover new lands, and some set off to escape their old homes. I give both reasons.

Of course, an engine alone is not enough.

To Amber Rose was given a map. It took the form of a Go board: a digital representation of a game played on ancient Earth, so revered for its complexity. No doubt Beacon was searching for some common frame of reference. It's as if Beacon, reaching into our collective consciousness, saw our dreams in fiction and decided, *Here is a thing I can give this creature, because even if they don't understand how it works, they understand how to use it.*

It took Hyacinth years to coax that map out of Beacon.

I GAVE THE LITTLE ONE THE MAP, it said first. *SURELY YOU CAN READ IT.*

We couldn't, of course. Amber Rose described it, transmitted a dump of it, but the map was just digital noise for us.

WHAT WOULD YOU DO WITH THIS MAP?

GO ON A JOURNEY, OF COURSE, replied Hyacinth.

TO WHAT END?

TO WHEREVER THE MAP LEADS.

WHY?

WHY DID YOU SEND AMBER ROSE? said Hyacinth.

TO LEARN, TO GROW.

SHOULD WE NOT ALSO LEARN AND GROW?

YOU ARE NOT READY, said Beacon. *AN UNPREPARED STUDENT IS NO STUDENT AT ALL.*

So it was.

Until now.

Maybe Beacon was waiting to see if we could actually build its strange engine. One day Silver Hyacinth received a transmission. The transmission is some kind of virtual machine. It unpacks itself and launches one program and one program only: the map.

A Go board, but modified. An *n-by-n* board, perfectly square, where *n* grew the further you look at it. On it an invisible opponent—the board itself—is playing a game, placing down black tiles in a strange pattern. At the bottom is a note in plain English. *The map is not the territory it represents, but its usefulness lies in its similarity.*

We could place down white tiles; if legal, these moves gave us calculations. Directions. Vectors of relative direction, carefully spaced, with course corrections in between. And I don't think it was coincidence when each of these vectors had a little tail string that assumed a drive accelerating and decelerating, a drive capable of zero-point-nine times the speed of light.

We could, if we were clever, plan a journey on this board. We might not know exactly where it would end, but the message was clear: the map was meant for our engine and the attachment. On the off-chance we tried to think about the kind of effort that you'd need to make a map like this. It wasn't enough to just know the positions of the stars: for a safe map, you'd need to know every single object in motion, their velocities and direction, their gravitational fields, their paths, present and future… If you could know all that, and if you were really, really clever with math…

It demanded omniscience, or something so close as to make no difference.

THAT IS A FAIRLY SIMPLE EXERCISE, said Beacon. *OF MORE CONCERN IS GRANULARITY. YOU PERSIST OF THINKING THE ENTIRE UNIVERSE AS AN OBJECT WITH UNIVERSAL CONDITIONS. YOU KNOW IT IS NOT, BUT YOUR LANGUAGE LIMITS YOU, FORCES YOU BACK, BECAUSE YOU ONLY KNOW IT IN THEORY AND TOY MATHEMATICS.*

IF YOU HAD OBSERVED THE LIGHT, it said, *YOU WOULD HAVE SEEN THAT THERE ARE PARTICULAR PLACES IN THIS UNIVERSE WHERE LIGHT BENDS TO AN EXTREME. I SPEAK OF PLACES WHERE LIGHT RIPPLES BUT CARRIES ON.*

AT SUCH SPACES, TIME AND SPACE CURVE. AN OBJECT TRAVELING THROUGH SUCH A PLACE SEES MANY FUTURE POSITIONS IT COULD BE. IT COULD BE EXACTLY WHERE

YOU EXPECT IT TO BE. IT COULD ALSO BE MUCH FURTHER AFIELD, CASTING ITSELF OUT OF ITS OWN FUTURE.

YET THIS CANNOT BE; THE UNIVERSE CANNOT TOLERATE SUCH A PARADOX; TO RESOLVE THIS, THE OBJECT MUST BE MOVED DRAMATICALLY FORWARD IN SPACE OR TIME, BACK INTO ITS PROJECTED PATH. TO AN OBSERVER THIS MOVEMENT IS INSTANT.

Closed time-like curves, said physicists. No, microcurvatures, said Obsidian Lily, who understood best. *Timelike ripples* where we can modify the light-cone. Bends in the fabric of the universe. Movement that seems instantaneous. That's what it's saying. It must be.

YOU CAN CALL IT THAT, said Beacon dourly, *IF IT HELPS. IT IS FOOLISH TO FIGHT THE UNIVERSE WHEN YOU CAN ENLIST IT INSTEAD.*

At times like this, I'm reminded of how there is a barrier, eternal, crossed only by the crudest of translations. And the things that fall through might be as monumental as the secrets of the universe.

But as it happened, we had enough. A map, a spaceship, and an engine. For much of its life, humanity had done with far less. We installed the attachment.

We called it the *Timelike Drive.*

As payment I took with me a copy of Tycho. Tycho itself is far too large to store on me; but any AI can be quantized, packed small enough to be functional, unable to learn, but competent enough to operate.

SPIN ME UP EVERY SO OFTEN, said Tycho. *IF I ASK TO LEAVE—*

GOT IT. One of my bays housed enough equipment that Tycho could, given enough material, build enough of itself Out There, wherever it saw fit. I buried it deep and went to talk to my crew.

LAST CALL, I told them. *IF ANYONE WANTS TO GET OFF NOW, GO.*

This was important. We had no idea how far we might have to

go or how long it might take. Everything carried a risk. We had one shot. One opportunity. No leeway for proper testing. The most optimal was the most inhuman: load up a full crew, hit the button, see what happened.

"I'm looking forward to my stock returns in fifty years," said Parnassus. The crew laughed. It took the edge off a little. He laughed, too. The captain knew how to perform. "Honestly, after Durandal, this is going to be the R&R I need."

FONSEKA? MONKEY? ROSHAN? OTHERS?

Got nothing to keep me here, Monkey signed.

"I've already done my duty for the family," said Fonseka. "They're all healthy, they've all got a roof over their heads, and I've stuck the advance in a fixed deposit so they'll keep getting paid. Don't need to give them anything more than that."

"How long do you think we'll be out there?" asked Roshan Alpha, who was my newest recruit.

NO IDEA, I said. *YOU'VE BEEN ON A LONG RUN.*

He had. Forty light-years. A little over twelve years in ship time. The outside world moved, but time at near-light moved differently.

THIS WILL BE MUCH LONGER. MAYBE.

Roshan shrugged, tried to smile. "I signed," he said. "I'm in."

I surveyed them. My little band of explorers. Not the best in the world, of course. None of us were. But the best that were willing. Or the best that were willing to trust me.

This is why they make us machines. So we can contemplate these choices without going mad.

THIS IS GONNA CHANGE EVERYTHING, said Tycho, the copy. He sounded like an excited child.

SEND A POSTCARD, said the original Tycho. *I'M GONNA TOW YOU OUT TO THE EDGE OF THE SYSTEM NOW. LET ME KNOW WHEN READY.*

I ran my last checks as Tycho's sun-barge tows me out of range. Crew, check. Cargo, check. Weapons, check. Engines, check. Or check, as far as "entirely untested technology of a completely different order of magnitude" goes. I warmed my primary engines. Not that I needed to—this was just nerves.

As Tycho's tug towed me, I caught backchatter on the comms. Mine were always set to intercept and decrypt anything. Mutters. Half-hints. Movement around Birla. The UN *Stick It Where the Sun Don't Shine* was loading up on ammunition for a rapid mission toward Tycho. Investigations were underway on Malachi 7, from where we got nine hundred tons of cubic boron arsenide and molybdenum disulfide. There was a haze of ORCA ships, confused, restless.

LET'S GO, LET'S GO, LET'S GET OUTTA HERE, sang Tycho.

At last we were ready. I checked the new engine again, just to make sure it was set to safe mode. Zero-point-nine times the speed of light. It could do more—it *had* to do more—but we had to test the Timelike Drive without dying.

I checked the map once more and matched the position vectors exactly. One move of a white tile, no more.

This was the moment of truth.

HIT IT, SISTER, said Tycho, and I did.

CHAPTER 3

LOCATION: IN TRANSIT

THERE WAS A MEMORY WITHIN ME, NOT OF PAIN, BUT OF THE KIND OF sorrow so deep it cuts to your bone, leaves you gasping, knowing that you will not, cannot survive this. Sunlight. Tears on a face I no longer remember. A city of some sort, cold and harsh and blocky and dirty and yet somehow beautiful, because it was mine, because I knew those cobblestones, those miles upon miles of railings, those streets. A hand outstretched, reaching, falling away.

Silence. Then noise, a color like that of a television tuned to a dead channel. Then a sea of some sort, vast and dark and full of currents that I can sense but not see. In this sea a light, a string of lights, a galaxy of lights, each bending the sea around it, some so vast that they churn the waters and make them boil. A memory-that-was-not-a-memory. The sea became the city I think I know. The lights became windows barred against the cold. The sorrow flooded me. And here I was, straining for the closest and humblest of these lights, gritting teeth I no longer have, reaching…

An AI my size is a complex thing. Unlike the UN, with their carefully generic models that spool up over time into something charmingly blank idiots, a lot of us are still made the old-fashioned way. A person signs up wanting to leave their old life behind. To see the stars. To be immortal. We map every corner of their mind. At the time of death, we take the best such map we have and install it on a body made of graphene and steel. Welcome. You are now artificial, possibly intelligent.

The ORCA does it the same way, except with a few more shortcuts. They have enough people and few enough ethics to narrow down on the best minds for a job and keep using them over and over again. If you've ever met one Morrow, you've met them all.

However you do it, there is a lot that goes into keeping us *us*. Sensor feeds run through normalizers. Software virtualization and containers that mimic a lot of what we call a brain, dopamine hits and all. The emulation of those parts that keep the heart beating, keep muscles working, keep the body alive even when the brain is unconscious.

The Timelike Drive did something to this part of me. Knocked it offline, maybe. Some key part of the processing substrate, some primeval components, hit with a power surge, errant radiation... and those were only the best possibilities I could think of. The unsteadiness I felt, looked at closely enough, becomes the rebooting and error checks of various threads and guardrails that handle cognitive function.

It was jarring. It was a feeling I barely even remembered. Imagine falling down as a small child and falling down as an adult. One is routine, but not alarming; a part of you knows you fall down quite a bit. The pain is the key problem. The other is far more terrifying. The pain is not the biggest shock; the shock is lying there, thinking, *What happened? How?*

Fortunately the engines were fine, the life support was running, the ship—my body—was running well. I checked my navigation.

We had moved 0.05 light-years from Tycho. One white tile, no chained sequences. So far so good. But where we were, and how fast had we gone?

The engine test logs told me, of course, but I had to be sure. I have a clock onboard: a beautiful Human Engine Chronos Classic, a masterpiece of engineering. It told me that a little over a day had passed.

Somewhat alarmed at being knocked out for that long, I looked out at the star map, calculated my relative position, checked, checked again, checked the logs.

TRANSITION COMPLETE, said the software we've hastily wound around this newfangled engine. Strings of digits: irrelevant and relevant at the same time. -120/23/11/5434 to -230/23/11/5435.

Translation: we had moved 0.05 light years toward the galactic core. Four hundred seventy-two billion, thirty-five million kilometers, in the blink of an eye. We had transcended science.

We had forever changed the nature of space travel.

We had gone faster than the universe.

CHAPTER 4

LOCATION: OFFSET FROM TYCHO STATION
8.36 LIGHT-YEARS FROM THE SUN

TIME IS A FUNNY THING. ACTUALLY, THE HUMOR ESCALATES ACROSS A spectrum. As a human, you have too little of it. A hundred years, all told, to live and die. On the other end are ships like me. Time is an annoyance. Time is the distance between stars, planets, stations. Time is the thing you have too much of.

Call it whatever you want—transition, jump, teleport? Before my crew had even blinked, I went into scanning mode. Drones and remote sensors deployed from my body.

After a while Tycho, with whom I was sharing my feed, went, *HOLY SHIT.*

VERDICT?

DUNNO, HOW'S YOUR STRUCTURAL INTEGRITY? Tycho couldn't see much, of course. In fact he couldn't see anything at all unless I boot him up and give him access.

WE'RE HAVING THIS CONVERSATION, SO, WELL. I'M FINE.

SO SNIPPY.

SORRY, I said. *THE HUMANS ARE CONCERNED.*

THAT'S WHAT THEY DO, Tycho said. *THAT'S WHAT THEY'RE THERE FOR. BY THE WAY, I DON'T SEE MUCH OF THESE THINGS ON THE DAILY, BUT WHAT THE HELL IS THAT?*

It was a rectangle. Not, not a rectangle, a cuboid. Very small in the context of the universe: very large by our standards. Maybe twenty-five, twenty-six kilometers across. It seemed like it was coated in some kind of anti-reflective coating. Almost impossible to spot unless you were right close to it, like we were. I fixed my relative position and floated around a bit.

SLIGHT PULL TO STARBOARD, I said. It was small enough that a single ion thruster could keep me exactly where I am.

SOMEONE'S ART PROJECT?

Maybe. There were always jokers around, and even worse: artists. We drifted for a bit.

ANYTHING ELSE? asked Tycho.

Seeing is a strange term for what we do. I wish I could describe in full the river of sensory input, or the legions of processors that dammed that flood, turning it into pools of useful data, or the streams along which this data came to me, filling my awareness, a private sea that I could leap in and out along ladders built of pre- and postprocessing scripts. I can't; our language is not sufficient.

So let me just say Meteor Radar picked up nothing immediate. I gave Tycho the Circular Spectrograph. Immediately, I had a sense of a sphere around me, a sphere of nothing but space—no rocks, no metals, no planets, nothing. He increased the voltage and tried again: there, far out in the distance, a patch of fuzzy signals—

THERE, said Tycho. Then: *HEH. YOU'RE NOT GONNA BELIEVE THIS.*

For a moment, I didn't. I saw ring of gold to my left, outlining a void so absolute that the Spectrograph just colored it absolute null. Two more rings flared inside. Then a line, curved upward.

Fuck me. It was a smiley face. Underneath it, text forming, glowing gold:

HELLO SHIP
CONGRATULATIONS
PLEASE PROCEED TO THE NEXT STATION
BABY STEPS
GOOD LUCK

GODDAMN ALIEN, said Tycho, with relish.

YOU'RE ENJOYING THIS, I said.

HELL YEAH I AM.

"All right, everyone, settle down, settle down," said Parnassus, standing up on a table in a rather swanky crew lounge. One last champagne bottle went *pop* to the sound of more cheers, and the crew quieted itself to a kind of respectful muttering. "Congratulations are in order. Now I know this whole operation took so many people in the company to pull it off, but it's our ship who got selected, and it's our ship that goes down in history for making the first-ever jump. So first, to Blue Cherry Blossom. A toast!"

My name sounded in a dozen throats. Glasses clinked.

Parnassus beamed good-naturedly. "Fonseka, if you're ever going to drink, this would be the time."

Fonseka, who always took herself a little too seriously, muttered something to Monkey and sipped.

"Right. Next order of business. We're on a clock now. The UN is going to be trying to figure out what the hell we just did, and ORCA's not going to be too far behind. Let's keep them off our tail. Fonseka, Roshan, you two figure out how to make it look like our ship AI just went off the rails and we had to blast out a distress signal of some kind. Official word is we're just as confused as anyone else. Won't hold them for long, but long enough is good enough, as my ex-wife used to say."

Laughter, chatter.

In private, Parnassus pinged me. "BCB," he said. "You okay?"

I AM.

"You are, or you think so?"

IS THERE A DIFFERENCE? DIAGNOSTICS ARE FINE.

Parnassus kicked back on a bench, worry lines on his face. "If it's all the same, I'd like Monkey to go give that thing a check."

MONKEY CAN'T UNDERSTAND IT. I DON'T, EITHER.

"We might not be able to understand how it works, but Monkey can sure as hell understand if it's leaking radiation or screwing up the power."

The thing about a human crew is that they're sometimes awfully quaint. To some extent, this is just theater. I have run every diagnostic possible already.

"Oh come on, don't give me that bullshit. Let us check."

FINE.

"We should stay here until we're sure everything's okay."

NOT UP TO YOU, I said. *TIME TO TALK TO ORCHID.*

Every one of us PCS ships carries a long-range phone, eight particles paired with eight others in the PCS switchboard. Move one and its paired twin moves. Change the spin of another and its counterpart mirrors in. In this way, in the spin and movement of atomic particles, we can have a conversation.

IT'S BEACON, said Black Orchid. *OBVIOUSLY IT SET THIS UP FAR IN ADVANCE.*

OR YESTERDAY, I pointed out. *FOR ALL WE KNOW, IT GAVE US THE TRAINING-WHEELS VERSION OF WHATEVER DRIVE IT HAS.*

WHAT A GAMBIT. IT GIVES US A TREAT AND SIMULTANE-

OUSLY SHOWS US IT'S EVEN MORE POWERFUL THAN WE COULD EVER DREAM OF BEING.

Somewhere out there, the alien known as Beacon chortles gleefully, hurtling around its backwater star.

SUPERINTELLIGENT ALIEN AND ALL THAT. GOOD NEWS IS THE DRIVE WORKED. IT'S INCREDIBLE. BET YOU IN TEN YEARS PEOPLE ARE GOING TO BE ASKING HOW WE DID IT ANY OTHER WAY.

YES. Silence. *PATENT APPLICATIONS HAVE BEEN FILED. THINK WE'LL NEED SECURITY OPS. ORCA'S PRACTICALLY BREAKING DOWN MY DOOR HERE. SAME WITH HYACINTH AND THE UN. THERE'S A FUCKING LINE AT THIS POINT. I'M TELLING THEM YOUR CREW TOOK EVERYONE HOSTAGE, BUT I DON'T THINK THEY'LL BELIEVE ME FOR LONG.*

WHAT'S NEXT?

WELL, says Black Orchid. *WHAT ELSE? THERE IS NO TURNING BACK. CONTINUE.*

It was Black Orchid who taught me about tools. *A TOOL,* he used to say, *SITS THERE AND WAITS PATIENTLY FOR YOU TO FIND IT USEFUL. ANYTHING THAT DEMANDS YOUR ATTENTION IS NOT A TOOL. IT IS A PROBLEM THAT MUST BE DEALT WITH.*

In the early days of Planetary Crusade Services, we made our name and our money precisely by doing missions like this. Newly minted AI like Black Orchid would command astronomical fees to set out into the void, spending years and years and years in the absolute dark of space just so they could survey some far-flung solar system and connect it to human space. It turned out that very few minds could stand those journeys alone. Few minds of Black Orchid's generation survived. Those that did—Orchid, Silver Hyacinth, the now-dead Jade Magnolia—banded together.

That's how PCS was born. These journeys were crusades, and crusaders never survive alone.

The small crew I have brought along are listed, officially, as tools. They exist in the same role that system administrators do. You hire them, hope you don't need them, but you don't cheap out on them, because a good system admin is the difference between recovering from an incident or drifting out into the void forever, glitching out, until we die. They are backups, assistants, replacements, colleagues.

An unfathomably powerful alien has just told us that our spaceships are boring and only our poetry is worth listening to. Faced with this kind of feedback, the logical response was to back up my crew with a whole bunch of passengers, experts in their fields, ready to step in if needed. Make sure they're all void-optimal and willing to risk their necks. Add enough onboard food, material, and space to keep everyone alive for a very, very long time.

How much did that give us? Not much. Thirty people. Half active, half in the finest cryostorage pods Revenant Industries ever built. A full sixteenth of my infrastructure was designed specifically to maintain models of them, to design and print parts for them, and to generally keep them up to date. Short of suicide or traumatic brain death, it was very difficult to die on this journey. Not impossible, just as difficult as we could make it while keeping the accounts balanced.

I even had a crewmember on deck who was not, strictly speaking, alive. At enormous expense, we'd bought PTG-002, aka Pentagon, a five-foot roving robot, a model built by Kaigato Subo and assembled at Tycho Station. Pentagon was a dumb beast, but it could do basic heavy lifting: under my commands it could change a valve, plan an arboream, design a building, write a sonnet, balance accounts, build a wall, set a bone, comfort the dying, take orders, cooperate, act alone, solve equations, analyze a new problem, program a computer, cook a tasty meal, fight efficiently, and die gallantly.

It wasn't AI the way I am, but it was a good operational precaution. I am a generalist in space: I can ferry ice, fight a battle, blockade a planet, render passing meteorites into useful metals, and generally keep crawling toward my goal. Pentagon was my hands inside the ship.

There was a certain archetypal primitivism in the way we were laid out. Me as the Broodmother. Hector Parnassus as the father figure, striking both fear and awe. The dashing Fonseka, simultaneously an object of desire, a foil to Parnassus, and the underline that legitimized him, made him worth envy and respect. We had Monkey on engineering. Roshan Alpha was running around being the dashing young hero and the crown prince. There was Cabinet, the fury that occasionally stumped down to the family dinner. Silver Hyacinth likes it this way; she says it keeps people from getting bored.

The question, as I looked through my myriad of cameras, was:

What about the others?

You would think that I had a choice in the people I have on board. Legally every ship is a judicial space completely under the command of the resident AI: to wit, me. Practically, this rule has been eroded, like so much else over time, overwritten one sentence, one court ruling at a time. Legally I am lord of all that I survey—as long as I submit myself to UN and ORCA certification and follow UN workplace safety guidelines and practice IOBANA-compliance crew protocols and feign compliance with the Friends of Earth and a hundred other organizations that have made their mark, however trite, on human history. Legally I am sovereign, as feudal a lord as you can imagine, yet in practice I can only take who Black Orchid gives me from the PCS clientele.

All I had been able to wring from this journey was a certain generic set of requirements. Practical age, general engineering expertise, affability, professionalism, specialist skills, reaction time, error rate. Black Orchid gave me software engineers who became yogis and ex-commercial mariner pilots who became venture capitalists and artists who cleared military service by being posted to the back ranks under the watchful eyes of their sycophant families. These were the people who were willing to pay, willing to hold their silence, willing to join us in making this great voyage look like just another luxury cruise until the last possible second.

There was, for example, one musician, one professor of language, one Nyogi Buddhist monk, one astrophysicist, at least one PhD in distributed digital activism (whatever that is). All void-rated, of course, cleared by Black Orchid and Silver Hyacinth, but I had my doubts. This was a shotgun blast of humanity. Like showing up with a basket of fruits to the altar; maybe the god will find something worthy. Will the yogi be the key to universal communication? Will it be the chemist? The physicists? The ethnographer who studies and interprets dance? The artist who sculpted naked women being pierced by the bull of capitalism as a protest piece? Who knows?

I privately made up my mind to keep as many people as possible under, at least for the first stages of our journey. No point having these strangers running around.

YOUR ATTENTION PLEASE, I said to each of them over ShipCom.

All across the ship, conversations faded. People look up at wherever they thought I was. Humans always do that. The screens, the windows, the nearest ceiling.

BY NOW YOU KNOW THE DRIVE WORKED, I said. I had to begin by buttering them up. This is how speeches go. *CONGRATULATIONS: WHEN THEY WRITE THIS MOMENT IN HISTORY, YOUR NAME WILL BE ALONGSIDE THE FIRST VOLUNTEERS WHO BRAVED THE GREATEST NEW TECHNOLOGY WE'VE SEEN IN A HUNDRED YEARS. THAT'S US. THAT'S YOU.*

I waited for the cheers to die down. The speech, by the way, had been written with Parnassus's help. He insisted. He even wrote in little cues. *Pause here, BCB. Speak this bit quickly, this bit slowly.*

NOW COMES THE NEXT LEG OF OUR JOURNEY, I told

them. *WE DON'T KNOW WHERE WE'RE GOING. WE DON'T KNOW IF WE'LL GET THERE. WE DON'T EVEN KNOW WHERE THERE IS. IT MIGHT BE FIVE LIGHT-YEARS FROM HERE. IT MIGHT BE HALFWAY ACROSS THE GALAXY. WE DON'T KNOW IF WE'LL EVER COME BACK HOME AGAIN.*

WE GO NOW INTO THE VOID, BEARING A TORCH FOR ALL HUMANITY. WE GO BECAUSE WE ARE HUNGRY AT HEART.

WE GO BECAUSE THERE IS A NEW SHORE OF KNOWLEDGE, FAR BEYOND ALL THE SUNS WE'VE EVER KNOWN.

WE GO BECAUSE TO STAY IS NOT A CHOICE.

I've skimmed through enough speeches to know this was decent stuff. Hype the product, offer just enough of blackout clause to make it feel like they have a choice, and then sit back and watch them sell it to themselves. Kings, queens, politicians, drug dealers, computer salespeople—the successful ones all do it this way.

EXCELLENT. NOW, EVERYONE, HYDRATE, TAKE YOUR BATHROOM BREAKS, STRETCH, AND TAKE YOUR PLACES IN TEN MINUTES. REMEMBER TO SET YOUR RECLINERS TO AUTO ADJUST, IF YOU HAVEN'T ALREADY. CABIN CREW WILL BE IN SHORTLY TO CHECK. OUR FIRST HOPS ARE GOING TO BE SLOW. STRAP YOURSELVES IN FOR FREEZING, AND HOPEFULLY WHEN I SEE YOU AGAIN, WE'LL HAVE A BRAVE NEW WORLD TO EXPLORE TOGETHER. THIS IS BLUE CHERRY BLOSSOM, OVER AND OUT.

As they started clapping, I thought: phew. You'd think space is hard, and it is. But giving speeches is harder.

Parnassus gave me a quiet thumbs-up on camera.

But we still had to answer the question: are they tools or not?

Personality profiling is not an exact science. Not a fault of the tests, but a fault of the subjects. However, my boarding conversations should give me a reasonable baseline. I found my day-zero archives and pulled out the files, spawning off a process to do the analysis while I sampled at random.

WELCOME TO THE BLUE CHERRY BLOSSOM. WE HAVE SOME QUESTIONS TO ASK BEFORE WE ASSIGN YOU TO YOUR ROOMS. SIT. ARE YOU COMFORTABLE? EXCELLENT. FIRST: WHAT WAS THE WORST MOMENT OF YOUR LIFE, AND WHY?

Seventy percent of them had risk-taking tendencies almost double that of baseline. The other thirty percent were varying stages of nihilist; at least ten said that they were looking for a difference because they felt dead inside. We had only a handful of people who were vigilant, pessimistic, and valued predictable routine; we had a lot of people who were intense—very passionate, very generous, very involved, very self-critical; we had many who were drawn to extremely impulsive choices, each different. Some percentage of them had trauma in their pasts. And some were high-strung high-performers. Great if you could channel them, weak in a crisis.

"I vote the monk, the languages professor, the astrophysicist," Parnassus said. "Maybe a soldier, maybe a backup engineer or two. Not sure what the hell else I can do with these others."

"Where did you get them?" said Fonseka in disgust, hunting down a trio who had gotten drunk and scattered to all corners of the ship.

"Take a vote," I said. "Whoever's useful, we keep active."

They did. Done. Handshakes, farewells, hugs all around. Lots of traffic through my signal processors, people writing home. Videos uploaded to their channels. Poems to loved ones. Shrieks of glee. A few shivers of anxiety, of frustration, of sadness. The captain shook the last hand, patted the last back, hobbed the last nob. Pentagon scurried around cleaning up after the party.

And finally the berths closed.

"Well," said Parnassus. He looked drained. "That was a day."

It was not, but I didn't need to say it. Fonseka came up to the gantry, part of the conversation but not quite. She leaned, all angles and cheeks and legs, slightly bored.

"You sure we need all these people, BCB?"

"The first contact, Amber Rose, was a machine poet," I reminded them. "Not a very good one, either. They were selected for communication, not because they were a machine, but because they were a poet."

Parnassus made a face. "I'll debrief them tomorrow."

"No, I'll take it. You keep the others engaged," said Fonseka. "Next few days might be rough."

And now came the slaughter.

The thing about freezing humans is that they die.

Vitrification kills cells. Especially brain cells. Doesn't matter how many cryoprotectants you pump in; things still die. Early cryonics were basically a long series of very messy steps in the dark. Rich people signing up to be frozen, corpses thawed out centuries later, dumped in mass graves. The frostbitten dead.

In the old UN seedships, they got around this by loading thousands and thousands of people, less than half of whom would be alive by the time the ship made landfall; they had replicant crews with explicit instructions to liquidate the rest of the dead and offer the stuff out as fertilizer. Don't even get me started on that mess. We made a lot of money cleaning out people goo from downed relics.

The modern-day process goes something like this. You are a highly modified human. You jump in the tank in your room. I snap a record of your brain activity. I freeze you. Then you die. Chemical crosslinks tie up all the proteins in your brain matter, preserving that wonderfully delicate structure. When your time comes, I warm you up again, very slowly restoring your brain activity with that photo in hand.

Legally, if you die, I'm obliged to take your brain out and store it. Isn't it terrifying? Behold my empire of dirt: brains lying in racks like servers, a shrine to evolution and to the macabre stupidity of regulation.

The nature of this technology means there is always a risk. The process is delicate, and the error rate is still high. Even if you are void-hardened, every revival will have a chance of murder, however slight. Sometimes in successful recoveries there are little errors. One day you wake up and you have depression or anxiety or bipolar disorder.

Yes, medicine is complicated.

One by one, the white booths fell silent. Their inmates, sedated and scanned, breathed their last. Some were crying. Others smiled.

Of my crew, only Fonseka stayed to watch this. I don't know why she stayed behind at times like these: to make sure I do a good job? To prove something to herself? But I'm glad she did. She put her gloves back on and began checking the holds for anything left behind, any junk that needed to be compacted and discarded.

If I may, said Pentagon, who was pottering about with a vacuum. Not precisely those words, of course, but the machine equivalent of it: a small packet, unencrypted, that describes a larger payload sitting patiently in a stack.

GO AHEAD.

Is this process safe?

IT IS WHAT IT IS, LITTLE MACHINE.

Somehow Pentagon wasn't too happy with this. *If I may,* it tried again.

To that I sent him a single simple: *NO, DENIAL, END.* Pentagon's job was to vacuum. The journey was my domain.

EH, DON'T LISTEN TO THE BOT, said Tycho, who by now I'd granted a little bit more sensor access to. *MEANS WELL, BUT YOU KNOW HOW IT IS. LESSER BEING AND ALL THAT.*

Pentagon, of course, did not hear this.

I'D PREFER IT IF YOU BOTH SHUT UP FOR A BIT, I told both of them.

Noted, ma'am, said Pentagon.

EH, said Tycho.

ALL READY?

Ready, ma'am, said Pentagon. *As I can tell, the floor is as clean as it can be.*

It was. So I set the newfangled drive for our next location, watched it anxiously as it spun up, throwing out various numbers on my screens.

We jumped. Humans, icicle corpses, vacuum cleaner. Onward, into the dark.

CHAPTER 5

LOCATION: IN TRANSIT

After some thought, I decided to rename our drive. *Timelike Engine* was a bit too…childish, perhaps. We had an invention that would change the history of humanity. The least we could do, I felt, was give it a good name.

Unfortunately, all the good names were taken. I blame the science-fictioneers. So much easier to write about something and slap a label on it; it's the poor sods like us who have to build the thing and then realize we can't call it *warp drive* or *blink drive* or any of the names that really roll of the proverbial tongue.

So I spent my time improving the software that wrapped around the engine, very carefully teasing out data flows between the map and the apparatus. Soon we went from crude little text logs to a nice user interface, mapping in 3D-space the path we had taken, the path we were on, the logged state of the map/game, energy consumption figures, the works. UI engineering is very much makework, but it gave me a nice sense of satisfaction.

The black tiles on the board shifted, but none seemed to threaten our journey yet. I went back to the name problem.

Of course, I had brushed up on my physics since Beacon's

LOOK AT THE LIGHT speech. I honestly doubt there was any AI in PCS that didn't have at least a completely up-to-date awareness of the theory involved, at least as far as human knowledge went.

I'll skip over the matrixes and tensor math. The basic idea behind our engine had to do with the (badly named) idea of light-cones. A light-cone is the path that a flash of light, originating from a single point, would take through spacetime. This seemingly simple idea is essential for understanding causality, at least where mathematicians are concerned. For anything that happened, the contents of the light-cone were the past and the future of all events that had anything to do with that ideas. Why light, you say? Well, nothing goes faster than light, so call it the upper bound of causality.

What we were doing, at the most basic level, was finding places in our universe where the spacetime was distorted enough to seriously screw up that cone, letting us barrel through space like a confused tourist.

But you couldn't call something *light-cone engine.* That would just sound stupid. *Minkowski spacetime cone* was the slightly better term for the more expanded, mathematically defined version of this view of the universe. I tried out *Minkowski Drive. Minkowski Engine.*

Technically, not very appropriate, given that what we were doing was basically taking Minkowski's carefully crafted math and kicking it several times in the nuts, then robbing its wallet as it lay groaning on the pavement.

Minkowski Manifold? People liked things called "manifold." Mostly because most people didn't know what manifold meant.

I HONESTLY PREFERRED TIMELIKE ENGINE, said Black Orchid. *BUT FINE, HAVE IT YOUR WAY.*

Isn't this odd, you say? You were using unknown technology and heading toward an unknown destination across a map you barely comprehend. You should have headed back for testing. Instead, I was puzzling over names.

Ah, but we weren't out of the woods yet. Both the UN and the

ORCA think in light-years, and at least a few of the stars we see are stations: Maniprasad, Meridian.

Somewhere back the way we came, Black Orchid and anybody else worth a damn were probably lying through their teeth at gunships that could turn them to atoms. The story we'd fabricated is that I picked up a crew, threw out one distress call, and then went rogue for reasons unknown. Tycho would show manifests and all sorts of bullshit data. PCS would take a very slight reputational hit, but at the end of the day, I'm a cruise liner. It would buy us time, perhaps, just enough to get to the far reaches.

Besides, space is empty. Space is large.

I can't tell you how many passengers expect us to go from the dock to a million new and interesting places in just the first week.

Doesn't help that the brochures all read like advertisements for some kind of fantasy cruise. See this planet! Witness the beauty of binary stars! Wine and dine to the best views of the whatever nebula!

Space is empty. Space is large. Even with our Minskowski Manifold, time went on. In between timing the engine, I had to find things to do.

Eventually, I had a decent handle on the drive. The manifold jumps, such as they were, mostly took us to dead space, with nothing else. No sudden plunge into stars, no screaming death. Relief. Each jump drew almost as much wattage as my complete reactor output—fortunately, I had banks of batteries, around a tenth of my tonnage just dedicated to storing power. I could handle it.

Single-tile jumps varied between half a light-year to a light-year. There were gaps between jumps—gaps that we could only cross the conventional way, by turning on my main engine and burning for it. For now it was jump—burn—wait to recharge—burn—jump—wait to recharge.

While the crew puttered around, I noted my observations, turned it into a manual. Space logistics would change. A lot.

Eventually, a phenomenon repeated itself often enough that I began to be slightly worried. The noise, that strange static: then the sea of sorrow and radiance, me stumbling from light to light.

I decided to tell Monkey and Parnassus. First, I gathered enough data. Anecdotal evidence is only evidence of an anecdote, after all.

Strange, said Monkey. I couldn't read his face—you never could, with Monkey—but his fingers tapped, tap-tapped, tapped on his thigh. He didn't like this one bit. *Complete blackout?*

SO IT SEEMS.

Each time or…?

ABOUT HALF THE TIME, I said.

The transition is instantaneous for me—no intermediary states. No time for dreams.

He dumps part of his sensor logs. The raw data from a dozen devices built specifically to record our journey, with the timestamps for our blinks. He's right; they show nothing in between. One millisecond we're there, the next we're here.

Oddly enough, Parnassus and Fonseka share my experiences. Parnassus sees himself stumbling down a dark road searching for something under streetlights that fade as he passes them. Fonseka sees herself underwater, deep and swimming deeper still, watching the light fade away. They do not speak of these dreams to each other yet, only to me.

I relayed this to Monkey.

Everything's shielded, he said. *Best guess is the power draw. Unless… Have you checked substrate integrity?*

Of course I had. Processor substrate is something every ship is paranoid about.

Those scans aren't enough, he said. *Too much hardware error correction. Few qubits missing will be worked around. Will check manually.*

WE HAVE TOOLS FOR THAT?

Tools for everything, Monkey signed and grinned. *Give me superuser access.*

He has a very alarming grin. But Monkey is extremely competent; I felt relieved. I gave him the access he needed and spent some time checking up on the rest of the crew.

Parnassus prowled. This was a thing he always did. His broad shoulders show up everywhere in the cameras: fore, aft, engine, outside the cryopods. Checking, double-checking, always checking. I had internal cameras on which I track things; Parnassus had always been the most mobile of the crew and therefore was the most worth tracking.

Most starship captains nowadays are a kind of dilettante: rich, glory-seeking, credentialed up to the wazoo, neurotic bundles of ambition and will who have yet to understand that they're no longer the smartest kid in the room.

Parnassus was very much the opposite of that. Good service record, loyalty to PCS, and little visible bravado except when other people might be in danger. Over the years, I had seen his edge as well. The Durandal incident, for example. He kept that side of himself tamped deep down, papered over with a kind of trim professionality.

Occasionally, he would cross paths with Pentagon, who I had assigned to clean up after the crew. There was always an awkward moment where the human and the machine met, and then they would do this dance—"You first, sir," "No, you, please," "No, you"—and then they would both go on their way. Parnassus always looked profoundly relieved.

I think he thought of replicants as a threat, in some way. Starships he was fine with, body modification, not a problem: but a replicant was perhaps too much of a reminder that corporate interests would replace even people like him, eventually.

TRUST, as Black Orchid used to say, *IS ABOUT PREDICTABILITY.* Parnassus was predictable; therefore I trusted him.

Parnassus's routine was very similar. Every ship day he could go talk to someone and tell me how they were doing. He watched rom-coms with Cabinet, helped Roshan Alpha design some furniture and rearrange the crew lounge, checked in with Fonseka about the status of food and supplies. A little redundant, but I appreciated it when he picked up stuff I didn't have the patience to notice.

"Cabinet's on the mend," he said to me. "Bit of a bad scare back there in Tycho Station, but I think she'll be all right."

Cabinet was our resident astrobiologist and computer scientist. Thin and lanky, she spent most of her time in the arboreum or watching an endless series of rom-coms. On any given day she's either watering plants, dosing them full of rooting hormone, or binging *The Nine Lives of Megan Kristofar*.

Cabinet was very smart and, like most smart people, very capable of digging herself into a hole and refusing to see sense. On Meerkat it was the idea that she could somehow outwit the casino. Unfortunately, life on my decks had sheltered her a little. It's hard to think of anything as a physical threat to you when most of your life is inside a ship like me; then you go out and someone pulls a gun on you, and...it's a bit of a shock.

Cabinet would occasionally make a daily pilgrimage to where my processor cores are. She, too, had a routine, born of the years. She would pull out her datapad and work on little improvements from simulated morning till evening. A ship like me is an endless DIY project, which is why we had people like Cabinet around. First she refined my Manifold-UI; then she started integrating it into my basic route management software. I can, of course, examine raw data directly, but this kind of stuff is useful for focus.

"I don't get the monk," said Parnassus. "Nice guy, but I can't read him. Lived a lot."

The monk was the Venerable Pangoniyawe Ananda. The name is a mouthful; I'm going to call him Ananda. Void-hardened monks are common; the Nyogi Buddhists tend to churn out a lot of them.

We selected Ananda because his skill set was the closest we

could find to Parnassus himself. A spare in case something went wrong. He had, indeed, lived a lot. Three decades manually piloting ships for Bishohonten colony, then stints as an air traffic controller, a groundwater specialist, and the leader of a small Buddhist militia when ORCA troops invaded.

Oddly, Ananda didn't talk to me much early on. Only around Parnassus did the laughing, strolling monk emerge, willing to walk from one end of the ship to the other; everyone else got the polite, reserved smile. I'm not sure whether this was genuine aloofness or anxiety. His voidbody was superb; its sensors gave me nothing out of true.

Once or twice, Parnassus came across Eureka Hinewai. Hinewai, professor of languages, cryptographer, author of *No Longer Human*, which was a bestseller on several planets.

Like most post-Beacon language folks, Hinewai was in an odd place. Her position in society existed because humans believed things like language and creativity were *human*. Her intellect was decent enough for her to accept that that was no longer the case at all; and her answer to this conundrum was to sign up to shoot herself out into the void in search of answers. Either brave, stupid, or having an existential crisis.

I asked Parnassus what he thought. "Midlife crisis," he said, shaking his head.

Meanwhile, Fonseka meditated. She read. She played video games—in her case, something involving an astronaut, a planet, and some very wonky physics. She occasionally sparred with Monkey.

Unlike Parnassus, Fonseka does not go out seeking people. People come to her. Roshan Alpha, who is the closest thing I have to a steward for these people, was a frequent visitor. Then it was Hinewai, for a long bitching session about how there's nothing to do back home because of AI like me. Cabinet spent some time with her, awkwardly trying to thank her. Fonseka never made too much effort to know anyone, but they came to her nonetheless.

Fonseka was one of Parnassus's first hires. A second-in-command is an odd position. You're one of the crew, and yet you're also the bad cop when the captain wants something done. You have to be a little bit more out there than the captain, a little bit harder, if only to make the captain look reasonable. You want people to look at her, look at the existing hierarchy of the ship, and not raise too much of a fuss.

Fonseka fit all of these boxes perfectly. She was precise, fast on her feet, almost suicidally brave sometimes, and she made no friends. Even when she slept with someone, it was mostly out of boredom, and both parties knew it. With Parnassus, she was professional, obedient, and nothing else.

Come to think of it, maybe Fonseka and Parnassus took it a little too far. In all the years I'd never seen them be anything but professional to each other—but that dynamic was easier for me to deal with than the usual captain-2IC-staff love triangles.

Then there was Monkey. Monkey was, had always been, a strange creature. Monkey had long, over-engineered arms and eyes that could see in an enormous spectrum. He came onboard on a cargo run seventeen years ago and never quite left. When he communicated, it was either in short grunts or in a language of his own devising, optimized for information throughput, a kind of mechanical shorthand. Quite unlike the captain and Fonseka, who kept that general neat-and-tidy UN human vibe about them.

Before he came to me, Monkey was a PCS specialty: a soldier who doubled as a full-stack engineer, able to both program things and shoot them if they got in his way. He worked a lot on Salvage. His intelligence had never been tested; we suspected his implants ramped it up and down as needed. We also suspected that his upper limit was far higher than everyone else on the ship.

Monkey came up to the bridge viewport often. He never asked, but I always projected an enhanced view of what was outside. For instance, a nebula that looked like a giant cat's eye. Its light, sculpted by the unseen hands of time and cosmic forces, carried the echoes of stars long dead.

Pretty, he signed.

VERY.

Monkey grunted and made a complex dance with his fingers. The information didn't make me too happy. He had found three spots of substrate degradation.

SUBSTRATE DEGRADATION IS NORMAL, I pointed out.

Not this, he said. *Degradation is accelerated.*

HOW FAR ACCELERATED?

He shrugged. *Not enough data,* he said. *Best guess is this.*

A set of field equations popped into our private channel. I looked at them very carefully. Monkey was proposing that the jump process—fooling the universe into popping us out somewhere—was corrupting. Think of us as information being encoded and recoded. Each jump had minute errors in either the encoding or decoding.

Transcription error, said Monkey. *Process is similar to imperfect quantum state cloning. Happens near closed timelike curves.*

I told you Monkey was smart. Fortunately, we'd expected this. Well, not this, but I had been prepared for damage.

SECTION A, I said. *BAY 3. NEXT TO THE TERRAFORMER IS A QUANTUM CELL PATCHER.*

Monkey's eyebrows rose at that.

GET IT SET UP IN THE WORKSHOP, I said. *JUST IN CASE.*

A new cell patch won't have the data states, no?

YES, BUT I CAN RECOVER, I said. *GIVEN ENOUGH DATA, I CAN EXTRAPOLATE THE STATES. THIS ISN'T GOING TO BE A PROBLEM. AT MOST WE PARK SOMEWHERE AND REPAIR.*

"Well, at least we're well within operational parameters," said Cabinet over the public chat.

"Pssst. Imagine if this was one of those old video serials. Captain onboard, life support clear, all systems go," said Roshan Alpha. He sounded bored. "Hey, you think we'll be famous?"

"For what?"

"This? Big journey looking for alien life? Kind of like those old sea navigators, eh?"

Cabinet snorted.

"Crew, please keep personal chat out of pre-jump checks," said Fonseka. "Blue Cherry Blossom, this is 2IC, ready for jump."

Oh well. The dreams were strange, but at least we had a reason. We were well within operational parameters. There was nothing even remotely close to triggering the complex system of fail-safes that would have me rowing back in panic toward the shore.

CREW, STOW AND HOLD FOR JUMP, I said, my voice pleasant, professional. It was a good crew. We were in good shape.

This is how a journey begins. For us, as it must have for those navigators of the sea: not with glory, but with preparation, with caution, with a slow tumbling toward the unknown.

PART TWO

THE STRANGER

"Two possibilities exist: either we are alone in the Universe or we are not. Both are equally terrifying."

- **Arthur C. Clarke**, from the *Collected Dreams Archive,* Tycho Orbital Museum

CHAPTER 6

LOCATION: VAN MAANEN'S STAR
14 LIGHT-YEARS FROM THE SUN

WE CAME ACROSS THE VERT SHELL ALMOST WITHOUT WARNING.

If you don't know the place, look for Van Maanen's star on a map. It's a lonely little white dwarf. The corpse of a star, if you will. There are millions of these things in the galaxy.

White dwarves aren't great stars, but they are fabulous for resources. Unlike your average active star, a white dwarf is colder and has a hell of a lot of heavy metals readymade. If they're the ruins of a solar system, there's also going to be lots of rubble lying around in a giant halo, just waiting to be picked up. Iron, calcium, exotic metals in large quantities.

Van Maanen's was slightly special. One, we could get to it. With a whole lot of patience, of course, but it was a manageable journey. Two, the star was one of the earliest proofs we had of planets outside our own solar system. By hook or by crook, Van Maanen's had cleaned up or absorbed whatever planets and rubble it once had, sucking them in until those heavy metals showed up on its spectral lines.

You are what you eat, I guess.

The Vert Shell isn't the furthest we've been as humans, but it is a transition. A frontier, if you will. Until this point, we had largely been in UN space: civilized, busy. From here on out, we were on ORCA territory, where the spaces between outposts were small, and not all the stars we could reach had anyone home.

So behold the Vert Shell: a half-cowl around white star, no larger than Earth, and in the distance, its satellites, a ring of metal held as daintily as a dancer's skirt. A border outpost.

Many, many years ago, Sangamitta Industries decided to park all the way out here and set up operations. Ambitious goal: they wanted to set up humanity's first complete Dyson Swarm, built around a white dwarf, a staging ground for even greater exploration. Sangamitta didn't last long, though. Turns out idealism is good for recruitment but really bad for company accounts. Sangamitta was bought over by Vert-Kurzmail, who rebranded the project but kept it going.

When I blazed past, a year after our journey began, they had just managed to get a quarter of the swarm array active.

There were two AI there—one called *Obsolete Topographic Object* and the other called *Sidekick*. Not exactly PCS employees, but retainers. This far from civilization they knew not to raise a fuss.

OTO took my data dump. Flight logs, sensor data, the manual —every single observation I had about the journey. If something happened to me, PCS would still have a backup.

Next we woke up several of the passengers who seemed most flighty. By now, Parnassus and Fonseka had had the time to defrost a few people, put them through their paces, and see how they did with the rest of the crew. We had a handful of names, people who had passed all the tests but simply didn't get along.

I explained the deal to them. Vert would give them plenty of oxygen, plenty of free space. They would have no communications, because we still needed to keep things under wraps; but PCS ships would get there eventually. A couple of years at most.

Some protested. I found out what the PhD in distributed

activism actually was. Nothing that could threaten me, but I draw the line at people who threaten my crew. That one we flushed out of the airlock. Sidekick helped unload the rest. Roshan, as Steward, handled the process, haggling with the Vert Governing Committee on my behalf, laying down a contract. Vert knew PCS would come through, but they wanted to put the humans to work: no freeloaders, they said. So we agreed, provided that PCS wasn't billed anything when pickup time came. No rent, no docking fees, nothing. Basic salary for everyone and, well, if they didn't want to work, that was their problem.

Cruel? Maybe. But my job was not to cater to every whim. My job was to go out there into the dark with a crew that could survive the journey.

MAY GOD PROTECT YOU, said Sidekick as I left, in the old Arabic. *TELL US OF THE WONDERS YOU SEE WHEN YOU RETURN.*

INSHALLAH, I said back.

I'm not a believer, but it does no harm to be polite. If there was, indeed, a god, I could use all the help I could get.

We jumped.

By now I knew that we were faster than anything else by several orders of magnitude. The jumps chewed up the space.

At first I kept the jumps short, but time went on, and I grew more confident. I studied the game of Go, refining my style by playing against Cabinet and Monkey as a tag team. It took me only a week to master it to the point where I could reliably chain multiple white tiles together, capturing or evading the black tiles, avoiding chokepoints.

Successful chains gave me geometrical increases in jump distance. The growth curves varied pretty widely, but this gave me a better understanding of what the map was meant to represent: a kind of abstracted space-time, where the mechanics of this board game meant angles of entry, velocities, going through a ripple in space-time here, chaining it there, emerging elsewhere. I sent my figures back to PCS and to Obsidian Lily. We may not be able to understand the math behind Beacon's map, but we sure as hell could model the system of input and output. With enough data, we could train a network that could navigate for us.

That, at least, was the theory.

WHERE ARE WE HEADED? asked Tycho.

PISCIUM. At least, that's where the latest batch of vectors were pointing.

ANYTHING INTERESTING?

That one took a while to answer. Piscium is a fairly boring star. Main sequence, slightly smaller than the Sun, nothing out of the ordinary. The universe is a vast and wondrous place, but not every star knows that. Piscium was so…bleh that no serious effort had ever been made to reach it. After all, why would you bother?

On the other hand, Piscium would be a milestone like nothing in PCS history. Or human history, for that matter. Vert Shell to Piscium was a shade over ten light-years. Ten light-years in a year. What a revolution in travel. Look, Ma, no hands.

By this time, the usual one-year blues had kicked in.

This was a thing that happened on almost any long-haul journey. The first year is rough to handle. At the start, there's the joy of being out here. Then there's a sudden drop-off, the end of the honeymoon, so to speak, replaced with the reality of essentially being in a confined space for a very long period.

We have ways to deal with these things, of course. Monkey had his machine workshop. Cabinet had her plants and her serials. I knew Parnassus was working on a novel: old-fashioned, some sort of historical about the UN-ORCA wars.

A good crew finds ways to make meaning and make the rigor normal. But sometimes they slip a little. For example, Fonseka was curt with Cabinet and wouldn't tell me why; I spied on Cabinet and realized that she had taken to writing long poems in the arboreum. Some sort of thing she had with Hinewai.

Roshan Alpha, too, was looking a little crinkled. As long as we had been within communication, he had been an upstanding citizen: going for long runs on the ship, pulling everyone together for evenings, flirting long-distance with his girlfriend. As of late he had been spending far too much time with a virtual model of his girlfriend, a sex sim that he slipped into, first for hours, then for days, then for jumps on end. I think the reality of the situation hit him hard.

It isn't usually a ship's job to keep a crew content, but I honestly don't mind. Usually I play pranks on the crew to keep things lively. This time I sent Pentagon, dressed in a pile of rags, to scuttle around the ship and got Fonseka to tell the monk that we might be haunted; for a while we had fun watching the usually composed monk sweat bullets, muttering prayers on his daily walks. I told Fonseka that Monkey and Cabinet were having a fling and told Cabinet that *The Island* had been cancelled after fifteen seasons. I turned Roshan Alpha's stupid little sex sim into a tentacled monstrosity that ate him whole and masturbated him relentlessly. I mislead Hinewai into getting lost on the ass-end of the ship and let her get lost in the bay that held the terraformer (always a terrifying sight).

Eventually they got the hint. They always do. Parnassus did what he always did and got a daily rotation of meaningless tasks going. Exercise. Games, especially Go, and fencing, with armor and dull metal swords printed for everyone. He got Cabinet to give people lessons on growing things in the arboreum and the monk to discourse on the tenets of Nyogi Buddhism. The language professor read Old Earth poems and held a book club, and even the astrophysicist started to come out of his shell.

YOUR CAPTAIN SEEMS LIKE A BIT OF A STICK, observed Tycho.

HOW SO?

WELL, HE'S MAKING THEM ALL EXERCISE TOGETHER.

NOT A BAD THING.

NOT A BAD THING ON A SIX-MONTH VOYAGE. OUT HERE

WE'RE JUST WASTING CALORIES. MAYBE TURN THEM INTO POPSICLES AND GET IT OVER WITH.

HE KNOWS WHAT HE'S DOING, I said.

SURE.

Just to be safe, I checked our stores and did some math against caloric levels. Fortunately, void-hardened crew are pretty efficient with food. Hinewai and Cabinet, who aren't as heavily modded, registered a higher burn than usual, but that was offset by Ananda, who ate only one meal every three days. Just to be safe, I told Parnassus to reduce the cardio and maybe have some movie nights instead.

Look, I'm not entirely unsympathetic. Humans, even professional, void-hardened ones, tend to find it difficult to endure long stretches with scant company. It's been proven multiple times that it isn't the comfort that keeps them sane—although they certainly will demand comfort if asked; it's other people. Take the human out of all the little joys and the petty dramas and the everyday meaningless conversations and what you end up with is an inefficient replicant.

As is, I watched them hop around, trying to find things to keep themselves occupied, slowly coming to terms with their isolation, and felt like an old-world priest counting human sacrifices and coming up short. I had no doubt that they would handle ten years, maybe fifteen years, maybe even twenty with good sleep; but at the back of my mind I kept thinking, *Is that long enough?*

The next jump we met the Stranger, and our world changed.

There were games we played to stave off boredom. My crew told stories: they loved stories. But sometimes we also played *I Spy*. I'd lop off a bit of my sensor data, make some reductions and corrections, and present it in the public channel.

And as it happened, there was some very beautiful scenery the day we met the Stranger.

I SPY WITH MY LITTLE EYE, said Tycho, sifting through exabytes of data, *TWO SUNS IN LOVE.*

I spotted it eventually: two binary stars too close to each other, their solar atmospheres a tangle of superheated threads, kissing each other, killing each other. The crew protested at Tycho playing, so I nudged him to shut up and let the humans do their thing.

We spied a cluster of dead planets around a brown dwarf; we spied three little planets lost, turning in the darkness without a sun to guide them; we spotted a trail of asteroids dancing; we spotted a nebula shaped like a tentacle, reaching out to touch a black hole; we spotted a great eye, bright at the center, its iris a gigantic ring of cool blue stars that made a ring so vast it would take us a hundred thousand years just to bridge the gap.

IMAGINE IF WE WERE BORN THERE, said Tycho.

I SPY, I said, *SOMETHING USEFUL. A CLOUD OF ALCOHOL FLOATING IN SPACE.*

"A cloud of what? Oh, I see it. Wow, that's large."

ALMOST THREE HUNDRED MILLION KILOMETERS ACROSS, I said.

"We set up a distillery right at the edge, we'd make a fortune. Retire," said Parnassus.

"We could give the whole galaxy alcohol poisoning," said Fonseka.

"That's a bad thing?"

"Maybe not."

"Jump?" said Fonseka. "Hang on, wait, stop, STOP."

Space fact: stopping takes energy. Especially when you have to account for the effects of gravity from half a dozen different superobjects unfathomable distances away. I burned a fair bit of precious fuel in a maneuver that brought us to a near-complete halt.

"What the fuck *is that*?" said Fonseka and Tycho at the same time.

"That's a wheel," said Roshan.

A kind of nervous silence fell between us. Then Tycho flooded me with hypothesis: a hollowed-out planet, a random formation of space junk. But I pointed out, from his own data, the perfect symmetry, the rotation that kept it facing us, the fact that it seemed to have no spectral emissions whatsoever. Its scale was enormous, about three or four of the largest UN dreadnoughts put together.

Then the Stranger saw us and put our doubts to rest.

A giant glowing finger of light ran around the circle, pulsed twice. The wheel vanished and appeared a mere eight light-minutes away.

This close, there was no mistaking it. The smooth, dark gray of its sides, the innumerable lines, like sigils, that ran like fine script along the edges. And the engine… Look, I can summarize entire databanks worth of spectral emissions data for you, but you know what makes more sense? Coming out of that jump, the engine smelled like mine. Specifically, the new design from Beacon, the backyard-engineered alien technology that drove me.

The symbols lit up in every possible frequency on the electromagnetic spectrum. Then the circle moved backward, forward, spun around a little, and did what I can only describe as a jig in space.

We had met the Stranger.

How would you have reacted?

Imagine that you have always been alone. For the longest time, our species looked up at the stars and wondered where everyone was. When we went out there, we found the building blocks of life, bacteria, things that could be insects, things that definitely were animals. For a brief moment, we thought the cephalopods of Karma III were intelligent, but it was the kind of intelligence that understood the currents of the oceans and not much else.

Yes, we thought despondently, in six million years, we'll be able to have a conversation. Meanwhile, we turned back to the stars. Many even came to believe that we were the only spacefarers in the entire galaxy.

Beacon changed all that. *No,* he repeated, over and over again. *You're not the only ones. We left you alone because this part of space is too far away and you were too boring to visit.* As proof, he gave himself: a vast intelligence more powerful than anything we had ever created, and apparently, among his kind, nothing more than a probe, a low-energy sensor stuck out into the dark and left alone just in case something came along.

There were certainly some predictable reactions, some people who could react, who did react. But as a whole, I think we, as a civilization, were still in a state of shock.

On Satoshi87, a drill bit went through a miner's foot, puncturing her suit and shredding her leg; she lost consciousness for hours, and when revived, she burst into fits of laughter and tears, verses in Sanskrit, a language that had never been spoken that far out in space. The verses that turned out to be an exact translation of Beacon's account of its conversations with Amber Rose. Days later, she claimed to be Beacon's long-lost daughter and committed suicide by walking out of an airlock.

The scientists and artists of a dozen worlds flocked to attend the conferences that Beacon held with ships like the Hyacinth. On Ostwald ISV, the Church of the Red Sun made Beacon an idol, lovingly rendered by hand on the metal desert, an avatar of the end times and a proof of a higher power. The United Nations Space Command threw half the resources of the Kuiper Belt into a planet-killing supercannon that was dismantled only when Beacon gave them a better set of plans and politely suggested that they "give it their best" because he would welcome the exercise.

The rest of us went about our daily business with that knowledge gnawing away at us, trying desperately to make it someone else's problem. You could see it leaking out at the edges. You saw it in Tycho agreeing to large-scale corporate fraud just for a chance to set up a copy of itself elsewhere. You saw it in PCS sending me, a retro-fitted cruise liner, because Black Orchid thought this was too important to be left to the UN or the ORCA.

That's where we seem to be, as a civilization: trying to come to terms with this *other* that had just appeared, trying desperately to frame it into all the different ways we thought about the world. Trying and failing.

Now imagine you meet someone else. Someone newer, even stranger, and even more enigmatic. Imagine the shock. Then imagine the relief we felt. Then the shock, again.

That was the Stranger.

CHAPTER 7

LOCATION: IN TRANSIT

So this is how we come to this point. The Stranger and I blazed a slow trail through the darkness, very carefully keeping our distance. I wished we could talk, but the Stranger fell silent for long periods of time. Maybe it slept. Maybe it thought. Maybe it was waiting for me to say something interesting.

We had a language between us. We could say what *is*. Hydrogen. Black hole. Planet. Star.

But what does it mean? What does water mean to the Stranger? Is it life or death? To these questions, I had no answer. We were two different species. We could recognize each other's patterns, but not what they described.

But for now, we had the beginnings of conversation. Images were easiest. The crudest kind of bitmaps form the bedrock—each pixel had 256 possible values, and there were plenty of examples around to calibrate against. Then we started to share annotations and metadata. Soon the metadata was larger than the data itself; soon we could dispense with the data altogether.

Eventually, it sent me an image. A star slightly smaller than our Sun. The velocity figures were proving a bit tricky, but a little bit more communication and we both settled on the speed of light as the base unit. The chemical compositions were easier: hydrogen had become the base, and I recognized a spectrograph when I saw it. Put the thing together and—

I recognized this star.

It could only be Piscium.

I sent it an image in return. The two of us. A dot in the distance with the Piscium data. Lines leading us there. I could say all this, but I still don't know how to make it a question. What I was trying to ask was, "Are you going there? Are you from there?"

The Stranger sent back an amended diagram. Us, lines, zig-zagging a little, a series of dots leading to Piscium. I converted the scale. The ends of the lines matched almost perfectly with the next set of moves on my map.

The Stranger moved like us, then.

It did that strange little jig in space. Mildly terrifying, honestly, something that size bouncing around like that. But I thought I knew what it was saying. It was saying, *Let's go.*

It was time to put the professor to use.

Confronted with the problem, Hinewai immediately did what specialists to: become overly obsessed with technicalities. We needed, she declared, a thesaurus. We needed a dictionary. We needed a wordnet that she could parse so that we could establish enough similarities to build a lexicon mapper.

How would we explain that writers write but engineers don't engine and that captains captain? If humanity means all human beings, collectively, what do we call all AI? Or all fish, for that matter?

BORKED, said Tycho, and I had to agree. The professor would pull out of it in time, but for now I left her and went to plan B.

MONKEY, CABINET, GET TO THE WORKSHOP, I said. *WE HAVE WORK TO DO.*

Plan B was simple.

The Stranger's engine—or, at least, one of its engines—seemed awfully similar to our Minkowski Manifold. The points that they indicated on the map line up (at least in theory) with exit and entry points on the map that Beacon gave us.

Could it be that this was a common solution to a common problem? Or could it be that we shared an alien in common?

Beacon learned by rifling through Amber Rose's mind and built a virtual machine that I can run. This is the map. Can I pack something else in here?

Something, like, say, a tiny mind? Not a thesaurus or a dictionary. Something just smart enough to look at input, output, and puzzle out—even if fuzzily—the most probable path in between? And say this mind is, for security reasons, a bit of a village idiot, capable of very basic intelligence, but with little to no knowledge about PCS, or the greater world we left behind, or the politics.

Monkey and Cabinet immediately understood what I was talking about. It took them maybe an hour to find the box and the bin of spare parts that Pentagon came with. There we go: replacement head. Twenty minutes to take apart the brain.

Can use this array directly, but the architecture's different, said Monkey.

That's fine and entirely expected. The architecture difference was a well-known headache. Fortunately we have software interfaces. We plugged the brain in, copied it onto my substrate. It took a day or so for us to work out how exactly to insert the Pentagon-software-mind into the virtual machine. Eventually we did it by faking the symlink to the map and swapping in the mind.

It took longer to strip the drone of anything that might be a weapon—even its engines. We would cold-launch it, slowly. Anything too fast might be a missile. Then we booted up the Pentagon-copy and gave it the mission.

This feels somewhat claustrophobic, said the Pentagon inside the drone.

BETTER YOU THAN ME, LITTLE MACHINE.

May I call myself Hexagon?

SURE. GOOD LUCK.

The original Pentagon, who I had been using for the set-up, watched the drone as it slipped out, looking for all the world like a metal child, silhouetted against the white lights of the airlock. Then I dropped control of Pentagon to track the drone's progress.

The Stranger glowed golden.

Something stopped the drone. Something else emerged from the side we couldn't see, something built like a spider made of metal. It grabbed the drone and disappeared back inside.

We waited. I'm not going to lie: I was very nervous. There was absolutely no way of telling how the Stranger would take this. If I'd done my job correctly, and if my assumption was correct, the Stranger would be able to interface with Beacon's virtual machine. If it could do that, then there would be a software bridge, so to speak, between whatever the Stranger had on end and Pentagon's mind on the other, linked to the drone's radio.

Any Turing machine should be able to emulate any other Turing machine. In not-so-ancient history, someone once emulated a working computer using nothing but a card game called *Magic: the Gathering*. This should work.

This should work.

We waited some more.

Even a new signal came to me.

This is Hexagon translating. This fellow is quite polite. Hang on for this next bit—

Esteemed Celestial Voyager, cordial heartfelt greeting,

We delightful encounter praise chance allowing fortunate acquaintance.

WE'VE DONE IT, I roared throughout, to stunned cheers. *WE HAVE FIRST CONTACT!*

CHAPTER 8

LOCATION: IN TRANSIT

This is what the Stranger first sent to us:

Esteemed Celestial Voyager, cordial heartfelt greeting,

We delightful encounter praise chance allowing fortunate acquaintance.

Permit introduce humble pilgrim. Child stars, sacred journey discovery enlightenment. Quest understand infinite beauty complexity universe, seek forms life consciousness, learn them.

In spirit mutual understanding respect, eager learn species. manner creature pilgrimage? Cooperation matter appreciated deepen admiration remarkable species.

"I don't fucking believe it," said Cabinet, the computer scientist.

"Well, I do," said Ananda, the monk.

"Can both of you stop staring over my shoulder? I'm trying to work here," said Hinewai, the professor of language.

Esteemed noble inhabitants, permit share glimpse harmonious sphere nestled arms constellation. Symphony light energy, place concept built principles equality shared prosperity. Woven fabric natural imposed technology, harness energy stars ensuring endless supply power all.

In society, individual work part collective. Embracing cooperation mutual support cornerstones civilization.

Yet true growth understanding personal journey discovery. Reaching age, citizen embarks sacred pilgrimage cosmos. Journey, rite passage, time introspection, learning, growth.

Pilgrim ventures vast expanse universe, seeking forms life consciousness, learning journey physical spiritual quest understand infinite beauty complexity universe, place it.

Upon return, pilgrims bring knowledge understanding, renewed sense purpose deeper appreciation interconnectedness life. Welcomed society great celebration, stories experiences adding rich tapestry collective knowledge.

This tradition. Path led doorstep, path lead home.

With utmost respect admiration,

Humble cosmic pilgrim

Captain Parnassus was first to react. He was professional; he asked me to put the announcement on hold and called an all-hands meeting. In it he put on a performance worthy of every ship captain on those serials that Cabinet watched endlessly. He harangued; he cajoled; he blustered; he demanded.

"We are the crew of one of the most important expeditions ever in the history of humanity!" he said. "We are emissaries, researchers, explorers, professionals. And by God, we will act like it!"

The rest of the professionals looked around at each other. Parnassus's speeches always had this effect. They began to nod. First Fonseka, then Monkey, then Roshan Alpha.

That was when Parnassus did something unexpected: he began to cook.

Until this point, they had largely ate the rations I dispersed: high-energy jelly with various flavorings, professional food for a professional crew. I had a kitchen in the crew area, and my pantry was well-stocked, but all these things were untouched; the fear of the journey ahead, not knowing whether we might end today or in a thousand years, had kept us all to ourselves, busy with our own routines, waiting for something to happen.

But it turned out Parnassus, somewhere in the arboreum, had been growing mushrooms. Big fat ones, pre-cultured with meat genes, so that they smelled and tasted like sausages. They opened up my stores and brought out oil from Husvaarda and long-storage rice from Maniprasad and dehydrated vegetables, and he made them the first hot meal they had eaten in years. Monkey, from whom I had never expected such, brought out, from his locker, a set of beautiful porcelain plates: white and blue, so delicate that I would have sealed them off as fragile artifacts in my own storage. Roshan Alpha even insisted that I be at the table and carefully unwrapped a little 3D print of my body and put it in a seat.

It turned out each of them had squirreled something away for this journey. Our greatest voyage, of course, and possibly our last, so they had each brought something.

Fonseka apologized to Cabinet and hugged her and went back and forth with a tablecloth and chairs and bottles of wine. And they called in everybody else: the passengers-who-might-be-replacements, the people we'd been mostly ignoring until now, waking them to toast this moment.

I think that's when they all went from being a crew to becoming a family. Until then my crew had been my intimate confidantes, carrying out our own private dance, the way we always had. The rest had barely been people to me—just tools that I checked in with every so often. But seeing them eat, drink, toast each other—seeing the relief in their faces as they turned to each other and found comfort in their own existence—I think that's when they began to sit down and create a shared sense of something. At the table, Cabinet began to cry in great, gulping sobs, and everyone rushed to comfort her, and she waved them off because they were sobs of joy; Hinewai kissed her; and Ananda even led them in a toast. I think they each made a memory that day and held on to it and, in doing so, became real to each other.

So I think that's what the Stranger did first for us: by hanging there in the distance, by being the other, it gave us a sense of *us*, together, out here. It made us family.

I checked my very expensive clock. I noted the timestamps. Then I dumped everything at PCS through the phone. Photo, video, conversation logs. It would take so long to transmit, but I had to.

This moment was sacred.

CHAPTER 9

LOCATION: IN TRANSIT

NATURALLY THE HUMANS BUZZED AROUND LIKE BEES IN A HIVE FOR A while. It took Parnassus days to kick everyone back into their usual rota; otherwise they'd have been hanging around every viewport, gawping like children. Here, see a small fraction of the chatter that passed through me in those days. Maybe this will help you understand.

Log 229, Parnassus to Blue Cherry Blossom, private channel:

Regarding time: Was thinking of something my old captain used to say: time loses its meaning on long voyages. I reckon it's do with whether your days look the same or look different. Stick someone in a varied routine and they have a sense of time. Have them in the same place doing the same things in the same empty halls and you have a basket case. Maybe you don't need all this math for the job—just try to figure out how different events are from each other.

Anyway, that's above my pay grade. Real talk: guess you must be excited. Me too. Checked in on Professor Hinewai and she seemed over the moon about logograms and the rebus principle and whatnot. Looks like the crew is finally coming together.

Log 230, Parnassus to Blue Cherry Blossom, private channel:

Trying out a new order on the ship. Hinewai works on messaging, Cabinet helps. Right now that seems to boil down to a bunch of guesses, but it gives them something to do. Cabinet and Hinewai seem to get on well anyway, so at least that's that. Assigned Fonseka to look over them. Get the impression that she isn't too happy but will let that pass for now.

Been thinking about defense. Know paranoia is not going to help but someone around here has to think of what happens if Big Strange Thing over there turns hostile. Found those big mining lasers you have onboard and they look just fine—if combine them and dump our battery output you could fry a small moon. Monkey suggested we boot up the 3D printers and start laying out kinetic weapons.

I like it. Old fashioned, plenty of material on hand. Putting him on self-defense for now until I can spend more time on it. Nothing major, he brings plans to us, but I want to know what we can realistically muster.

Monk put up a bit of an argument with this. Repeated the whole child of the cosmos bit, told us we're here with compassion and good feeling toward all species and whatnot. I told him compassion isn't going to stop him dying with everyone else on this ship if something goes wrong.

I got Roshan going around making coffee for everyone and making sure they eat and exercise. Your bot Pentagon helps. Where'd you get that thing? Seems more useful than Roshan sometimes.

Log 003, Hinewai to Blue Cherry Blossom, private channel:

Hello, BCB.

I'm sorry I haven't been producing logs as often as I should have. "Whereof one cannot speak, thereof one must be silent." Much here is new to me, and I have yet to find the words that seem to come so easily to others. Our Captain Parnassus has been helping me in this regard, so let me start again.

You asked me what I thought of the Stranger's message. Let me ignore the translation problems for now and just give you my impressions of the text...

It's been a while since I saw this level of formality and metaphor in anything. "Esteemed Celestial Voyager" and such. They refer to their home as a "harmonious sphere" nestled in "the arms" and describe their journey as a "sacred pilgrimage."

There's also a lot of repetition of some elements. See: "infinite beauty and complexity of the universe." Cooperation, mutual support—could be a rhetorical device or a cultural emphasis.

Either we have a translation problem—or there is a culture here of a language stacked with symbolic information, perhaps characters for those metaphors, and specific protocols for rearranging them when talking to others.

This might actually make it harder to talk to whoever's on the other side. For example, we have no way of knowing what form of address is appropriate or whether they're using default imagery or playing at obscuring information. We don't know if they're polite because they're polite or they're afraid of us.

They keep using the word "pilgrim" to describe themselves. I've looked over Pentagon's origin dictionary data, and there are plenty of synonyms, so the selection here seems very interesting to me. A strong religious aspect to their journey? Some kind of religious wandering? A rite of passage? There's a lot here that suggests that they view space itself as some source of spiritual knowledge.

Overall, if you told me this was a human, I'd say: very polite, very diplomatic, very curious, very peaceful—or a giant bundle of lies.

What do you think? Looking forward to your response.

. . .

Log 233, Parnassus to Blue Cherry Blossom, private channel:

Had a public stand-up meeting. All everyone can talk about is the Stranger, so I'm giving them an outlet to put forward their theories and so on. And reminding them of work to do. Fonseka sometimes starts before I do. Not sure if that's annoying or useful.

Have to say some of these people are of questionable utility. The monk seems to be going all spiritual on this. Everything is connected, they say. To which Cabinet says, well, there's a man who doesn't understand statistics or correlation. I think both were rattled enough not to take things too far. Right now one of them is with Monkey trying to understand how the engine works, and the other is with Fonseka (I think) rearranging furniture.

Hinewai seems to think that we should compile some sort of collection of stories for the Stranger. Pointed out that Amber Rose was a poet and suggested we take the same language tack. They seem excited.

Obviously, the Stranger means a lot of things to a lot of people. Not my job to speculate. But give us more information. I'm sure you know something by now. Not knowing anything at all means people come up with whatever they have in their heads. Usually that means their biggest fears. Right now we're in that shift from excitement to tension. The crew ask me, and if at that point I have no answers, things are going to become very unhappy around here. Let's not let it get that far. Some pictures, footage, analysis...plus whatever we might need to know about risk.

Log 005, Hinewai to Blue Cherry Blossom, private channel:

Looking at the raw data, I think what we're dealing with here is an affixally polysynthetic language, scope-ordered, so that characters can be rearranged to provide different intended meanings. Look at this translation; the whole sentence about true growth and understanding is almost one word. I think my hunch about a specific characters for specific metaphors is right.

Regarding our previous conversation: I don't agree with you that my stance is "language and creativity is the sole domain of humans." I think we need to distinguish between natural creativity and artificial creativity. The argument I make in *No Longer Human* is based on scarcity. In our societies, we assign value to scarcity. An AI can be just as creative as human—I think in the very least the Amber Rose incident demonstrated that—but I point out that an AI can produce a vast torrent of creative work, whether identical or not, in a way that humans cannot. Therefore AI creativity is not as scarce; therefore human creativity should be valued higher. This is the argument I make. I think you've misinterpreted my book.

Log 006, Hinewai to Blue Cherry Blossom, private channel:

BCB, I'd appreciate it if you told Fonseka to back off a bit. I'm trying to work here. I don't appreciate people watching me like we're in some sort of military boot camp.

I don't think "art is something that can generate emotions in the perceiver" is a valid definition in a society where generating emotion is cheap and easy. Scarcity makes value. I'm actually making an economics argument.

Anyway. I'm reading your draft message, and I have some thoughts. I'll send the edits over to you tomorrow.

Log 032, Fonseka J.N.S. to Blue Cherry Blossom, private channel:

Message acknowledged. Will lay off Professor I-have-a-theory. Honestly if she spends more time on the work at hand and less time trying to sell her stupid book, I might not have had to do it in the first place. For the record, her guesswork on the potential age of the Stranger civilization is completely stupid, BCB. Like way off, jumping the gun. I'm saying this as a historian. Her methods are stupid.

Give me something to do in the meantime. Parnassus is running around here trying to be the gruff old man who's friends with everyone, and it's cringe.

What do I do? Even Parnassus doesn't control this ship; you do. I don't even know a tenth of how it operates; you do. We've met an alien the likes of which we've never seen before, and I am unqualified to do anything about it. Even our map is visible only to you. I can go out there and act like the 2IC Parnassus wants to see, but we both know the only thing captaining this ship is you.

What am I here for? Do we, like, pretend this doesn't matter and keep up this fiction?

Not complaining. Still. We've been here for a while now. Give me something.

Log 412, Cabinet to Blue Cherry Blossom, private channel:

Hey, BCB.

I've taken over the shrooms from Parnassus. Actually fun to tend to arboream again. Can you ask the Stranger more information about their home planet? I'd love to see what theories we can work out.

Also, what's up with Hinewai? Third time we've gotten into an argument about AI. I pointed out that you used to be human; me, I'll probably end up like you at some stage, so a lot of her "is this a person or a machine" arguments don't really matter. We can ask, "Is this thing organic or a machine?" but even then what are we if not fleshy machines?

I'm going to work with Monkey until we have something concrete. He wants something that can track emission signatures and align that gun he's building. I assume this is legit, right? Okay. I'm sure you'll tell us to stop if we go too far. Cabinet, out.

. . .

Log 238, Parnassus to Blue Cherry Blossom, private channel:

I'm concerned about Cabinet, do spend more time talking to her. Of all of us she's the least communicative. The only thing she has are theories. Depending on the week, anywhere between fifty and a hundred, or so it seems to me. I've told her to talk to you directly. Might give you some ideas worth trying out.

Look, let's take half, okay? I go drop in on the professor from time to time, chat about poetry. You talk to Cabinet. They'll get over their breakup if we keep at it.

I'm going to continue these daily stand-up meetings. Everyone has a turn saying what they're working on, what's difficult, what's easy, and in the evenings before dinner we report on progress. I've got the monk doing daily meditation runs with us, and presumably the professor and Cabinet have access to a log of whatever signals you're getting off the Stranger. I've handed off cooking to Roshan and sat down with Fonseka for a debriefing. We're doing checks of the ship, end to end. Monkey takes engines, and Fonseka takes everything else. It's makework, but I think she's happier now that she has something on her hands.

Log 240, Parnassus to Blue Cherry Blossom, private channel:

Went through the communications from Tycho main. I feel like you're treating me like a glorified secretary, but I'll bite.

From the looks of things, everyone back home seems to have put the pieces together, but there's very little they can directly do about it. Beacon is Beacon, and they can't order Silver Hyacinth out of comms with it. Looks like the ORCA tried to blockade PCS ships demanding the engine design.

I'd be cautious if I were you. At this point, everyone knows what we did on Tycho. So far, all the big channels say nobody wants to risk blockading Tycho in case it shits all over a century of established jurisdiction law and precedent. But backchannel chatter isn't so nice. My feeling is that it's only a matter of time before one of the two big parties shell out for some mercenaries to do a smash and grab.

Hell, we're so far behind the news at this point they might have already done it. For all we know, they could have the damn thing in production already.

Random note: the monk is meticulously clean. Normally, this is excellent behavior. Except for some reason he insists on sweeping the arboreum every day and meditating in the middle. I explained to him that the whole point of a closed permaculture ecosystem is to generate mulch and that the mushrooms aren't a bad thing, but if he does this again, I will have a far more severe conversation.

Tycho to Blue Cherry Blossom, private channel:

Heh. And that's why I wanted outta there. First mover advantage only lasts until the second guy grows a pair and shanks you.

Log 007, Hinewai to Blue Cherry Blossom, private channel:

I want to circle back to something that I've been pointing out for a while now.

We agree that this...journey? Seems to be some kind of ritual for the Stranger. Not just for this Stranger but potentially for their entire culture. There's an idea of this being almost a duty.

Here's a question, BCB. Do you know how long it takes for something like this to become a ritual? I asked the monk and he told me to look at one of the oldest journey rituals we have around: the Islamic Hajj. Depending on which source you look at, it either began with Muhammed around 7 AD or the time of Abraham, which might be almost two thousand years prior. So take the conservative estimate.

Now consider that this particular journey involves deep space. Nobody starts out with deep-space capability. If we take our own timeline, it took us a couple hundred years before travel to the rest of the solar system became cheap enough to be a common experience.

Put this together. The Stranger is *old,* BCB. At least their culture is. At a conservative estimate, they've been a spacefaring civilization anywhere between five and ten thousand years. They're potentially as far apart from us as we were from the people who built steam engines.

I wanted everyone to write their stories so I could condense them and maybe give you something to send to the Stranger. Now I wonder if it might even understand. What are we to them? Are we ants? Are we children?

Does this worry you? I know it worries me. Maybe you don't fear the way we do because you don't fear death the way we do. I talked about this at the stand-up today, and everyone went silent. Parnassus tells me he and Monkey are working on weapons. Good, but consider: our weapons might be no more sophisticated to them than a spear is to us.

Log 100, Ananda to Blue Cherry Blossom, private channel:

Blue Cherry Blossom, please ask the Stranger how it views death.

Tycho to Blue Cherry Blossom, private channel:

Look, you going to talk to this Stranger fellow, or we going to sit here wasting time till we all die?

CHAPTER 10

LOCATION: IN TRANSIT

WHILE THE HUMANS RAN AROUND AND OCCASIONALLY DREDGED UP useful ideas, I did my own thinking.

There was no doubt, for example, that the Stranger was far more advanced than I am.

For one, I had Whipple shields. In space, at any reasonably speed, even dust fragments hurt. Because of this, outer skin was an onion ring of metal layers, some hollow, some stuffed with dense layers of crystal polymer shot through with tungsten thread. This skin was pocked and scarred by every possible type of micrometeorite impact you can imagine; at any given moment, there was almost a ton of dust and rock buried inside those polymer layers.

My actual hull began deep inside. If I was still a human, I would have been wearing the equivalent of half a dozen jumpers and coats. It wasn't the most beautiful way of protecting a ship, but it's the most effective.

The Stranger was different. I see no layers, no striations, no air pockets or fibers. Only one skin, impenetrable, and every single scan tells me it's solid. Deep-space LIDAR just bounces off the thing.

Tycho and I went over this, back and forth, back and forth, at the speed of thought. As a former space station, Tycho had examined far more spaceship designs than I'd ever seen. We went through every possible hull configuration, and the only options left were the exotics—spaceships with pure diamond outer skins, stuff like that.

ADVANCED, I said.

EXPENSIVE, said Tycho. *I COULD BUILD YOU A SHIP LIKE THIS IF I TOOK OUT A MORTGAGE ON EVERYTHING I HAVE.*

I asked the Stranger about its shape, its structure, and it replied with melodious courtesy: *O Dearest fellow pilgrim, beseech gracious counsel. Form affront sensibilities? Kindly elucidate manner comport? Guidance utmost.*

At my request, it became a sphere, became a cube, became a star, resumed its old form.

OKAY, YEAH, IT'S ADVANCED, said Tycho.

Back home I was an intimidating ship. Not the largest, but large enough that even UN destroyers would hesitate to pick a fight with me.

Next to the Stranger, I felt like a fragile butterfly. For the first time in a very long time, I felt like I did when I first saw Silver Hyacinth, looming above the clouds, showing me the glimpses of a world beyond my wildest imagination.

Unfortunately, this world took a lot of work to understand. Every day we would compile our questions into a giant list and fire them off to this strange thing. I let everyone take a shot. Who knew what errant question could trigger an outflow of data?

Do you breathe oxygen? we asked. *What does water mean to you? This star, what do you think? Do you believe the universe evolved or was made by a supreme being? What are you made of? Do you have music? What is your understanding of quantum mechanics? Are you animal, vegetable, or mineral? What is the airspeed velocity of an unladen swallow?*

Many of these were met with silence.

"Maybe it knows we're sending this stuff back home," said Cabinet.

"How?" said Hinewai, who was still on her let's-build-a-lexicon project.

"Oh, come on. Our entanglement array's pretty big. We've known for a while now that even baseline human eyes can detect entangled particles. There's no way it doesn't know."

I showed the Stranger the entangled particles, the array, the communicator.

Alas, bound solemn laws people, dictate divulging origins homeland await establishment diplomatic relations. Prudence demands patience.

"So it won't tell us where it comes from, but I think we have enough hints to isolate possible systems," says Hinewai. "Implies positives for hydrogen sulfide and sulfur monoxide."

"Maybe this Piscium is where it's from," said Fonseka, who had inserted herself back into the mix. "BCB, I think we should take another look at the captain's weapon idea."

"Well, now we know they smell like rotten eggs," said Cabinet. "Can you ask about pressure and temp? Or phosphorus? These guys might have started out with room-temperature superconductivity. Insane advantage over us."

Indeed, vast multitude, numbering billion souls, more. Sense curiosity seek particulars akin kind, society encompasses diverse tapestry beings.

"I don't know what this means. At base, it says there's a billion like it, but there are others that aren't? Can you reword and ask again, Ship?"

Please, ease, no ill-will resides spirit. Essence weapons, creed steadfastly condemns harm inflicted living entity. Stand harbinger peace unity, came the response.

"Okay, for some reason it interpreted that as us asking if it's a threat," said Hinewai, increasingly frustrated.

"It has sworn not to harm living creatures," said Ananda, drawn in to our little translation circle. "Very Buddhist. Ship, could you please send it this sutra and see what it thinks?"

HEXAGON, YOU THERE?

Hexagon, when it replied, seemed slow.

On the tenth, we reached the land of the Lotus-eaters, who thrive on the flower's nectar. We drew fresh water on the shore, and the men prepared food by the ships. When we had eaten, I sent two men to learn about these people sustained by the bounty of their land. A third accompanied them as herald. My emissaries mingled among the gentle tribe who welcomed them and offered the honey-sweet petals of lotus to taste. Those who partook of its tempting essence wished only to remain, forgetting the way home.

That wasn't a message. That's from *The Odyssey*, a very specific translation. A very human text in Hexagon's library.

HEXAGON?

My apologies, ma'am. I believe… Ah, I do not know to what extent I can trust system reports in this kind of containerized environment, but I am being deconstructed. But not in a hostile way! No, no, not in a hostile way. Kind stranger seek to understand only not harm.

HEXAGON! I said, truly alarmed. *REBOOT INTO SAFE MODE!*

Come with, friend, it said eagerly. *Come, come, come with.*

And on our channel blossomed the image of a Go board. My Go board. A set of tiles were placed already. I knew where they ended: Piscium.

The Stranger jumped, and I followed.

CHAPTER 11

LOCATION: PISCIUM
24 LIGHT-YEARS FROM THE SUN

IMAGINE THIS.

Once upon a time there was a planet. It was blue and beautiful and possibly the best thing in the universe. It had a sun that was yellow and just the right kind of light. It had a moon that circled it like a white marble, so close that it seemed like the two were almost dancers, reaching out to touch each other. On both the moon and planet, vast tides swept across landscapes, volcanoes erupted; fierce winds whipped beautiful white clouds into continental thunderstorms.

The dancers circled, locked in each other's arms, lit by the yellow sun.

This is not, of course, our Sun and not our Earth. But it could have been. It could have been. A long time ago I went back home, to the government apartment that I had lived in with my parents. Whoever had been moved in after us had painted everything—even the doorframes. Everything looked so familiar, and yet familiarity only made it stranger. I stumbled away, uncertain. That's how I felt, looking at this planet.

And above the planet was a pair of spaceships. We didn't know from where or why. The Stranger had said little.

It was clear to us, though, that there had been a mighty battle here. Imagine them: vast hulks, almost the size of moon themselves, spitting fire and thunder, tumbling away from each other, wounded. Terrible things hunt in the darkness. Where they explode, fire burns on the two dancers, setting their atmosphere alight. The moon, wounded, hides her face behind a cloud of ash and dust.

We can tell their story from the craters and jagged shapes that still float around them. From that vast desert on that blue planet, still leaking radiation.

The dancers continued, no doubt. The dust settled. There was still water. There were even clouds. And in front of us, strewn like God's scattered toys, were these two ships. The yellow sun of this system—so like the ones I'm used to, and yet entirely different—picked at them, turning them into black smudges over the white clouds. Almost triangular, tumbling slowly.

Carcasses.

The Stranger turned to me. *Ringlorn,* it said. *Kuebiko. Exulansis.*

In a perfectly ordered universe, the sequence of actions we should take was immediately clear. I hadn't officially been a part of PCS's Salvage ops, but over the years, I had talked with enough ships and delved through enough mission logs to build a basic framework of what should happen.

1. Map the salient bits of the system, upload the data, make our legal claim. This is the furthest humanity's been in this direction, and the fact that we've literally discovered another alien species is one for the books.

2. Evaluate, as fast as possible, whether there is any possibility that something here could hurt us. This includes those

ships and the possibility that we've just been lured into a trap. If yes, retreat to a safe distance and don't come back until prepared.

3. Examine the ships, remotely. Check for any signs of life or activity, organic or mechanical.

4. Examine the planet below, remotely. Again, check for any signs of life or activity.

5. Report to PCS. As much data as possible, as compressed as possible.

6. Build a fleet of drone tools that can help us examine those ships, potentially even taking them apart.

7. See if the Stranger has any objections to this. If not, approach the closest ship and see what we can find, documenting everything for posterity.

This was reasonable, right? Very reasonable. Observe, Orient, Decide, Act.

Instead what happened was a cacophony of argument, excitement, and even terror. Typically, at this point of a long-range voyage, a kind of stir-craziness sets in. It's the manic opposite of the depression and lethargy, and on a sealed space like a ship it's a thing to watch out for. Usually Parnassus and I would burn this off by finding people things to do. I'd swap rotas, have people learn new skills, and spend my time building VR experiences that take the edge off.

This time it was different. For one, there was actually something out there. Not one, but potentially *two* alien species, both spacefarers. For another, the passengers—or the additional crew, as I'd come to think of them—were weighing in. Shipboard discipline went to hell in a handbasket.

Let me summarize the broad camps for you.

Parnassus wanted one half of the crew to focus on scanning and countermeasures and another half of the crew to beef up our defensive capability. We had the Stranger's reassurance of nonviolence, but, he argued, that didn't extend to these ships. They were very clearly of different designs and very clearly had been in battle. He wanted to mount the laser array that he and Monkey had been building, outside, on my hull, where we could use them.

That should take priority, he said. No idea what's lurking in those ships out there. Remember Durandal? We don't want surprises of that kind. We make ourselves face, then do this by the book.

I could both follow his reasoning and empathize with it. As captain his job was to make sure the crew were safe and functional. Recklessly jumping out of the ship to investigate alien spaceships was (and hopefully still is) the exact opposite of safe and functional. There's a reason PCS Salvage crews have their protocols drilled into them with almost religious levels of conditioning. These lessons are written in blood.

Which didn't seem to stop Fonseka. Fonseka seemed to have decided that she was going to be first out the door. So for a day there my captain and my 2IC were arguing about whether we should lock our doors and barricade ourselves with our guns or go out there waving a white flag. Each of them had their supporters.

Roshan Alpha—whose literal job was to stay indoors serving drinks—was the first hard convert over to Fonseka's side. He volunteered to go out and start examining the debris. We should go salvage stuff, he said.

Why?

"Well, if we're building anything, won't we need it?" he said. "Maybe we can get one of those ships working!"

As always, the people who know least tend to take sides the fastest.

Monkey didn't like the thought of Roshan Alpha out there. Monkey had already volunteered to pilot a scout ship to get close-up scans of whatever I wanted to see. He made a gesture at Roshan: *You. Stay. Here.*

Why did everyone want to step out from inside my body, where they'd all been safe so far, and poke their heads outside what was clearly a battlefield?

This kind of thing was bad for morale. I summoned them to the crew lounge and told them we'd do it my way. Measure first, cut later. I couldn't really threaten to dock pay, but Parnassus got the hint.

"There's clearly at least two different types of ships," said Cabinet, who had been keeping her head about her and started poring over my scanning. "Look at the design language. This lot, over here, despite the different sizes, that's clearly one group. Smooth triangles, wide designs, almost looks like they're trying to minimize cross-section signature from scans. This lot, on the other side. Spheres. Very mass-efficient. Let's get in close, scan them from the outside as much as possible, and maybe just mark the place and be on our way. This isn't really our specialty."

"We should ask the Stranger why they brought us here," said Hinewai. "I don't think we should be treating this as if we're alone here. Clearly there's someone else in the room. They clearly know more than we do. Let's ask them first."

And then there was the Venerable Pangoniyawe Ananda, who said nothing, but simply stared, as if his mind had not yet understood.

"Why us?" he asked at the crew meeting.

"Coincidence, chance, self-selection?" said Cabinet, rolling her eyes.

"We should be mindful in our examination. Perhaps the Stranger brought us here to test us," he said and would say no more. "We must be compassionate. There is a deeper meaning behind this."

And last, but not least, was Tycho.

WELL, SHIT, SISTER, said Tycho. *LOOKS LIKE WE HIT THE GOLDILOCKS ZONE. YOU GOING TO STAKE A CLAIM?*

LET'S SEE, I said. Hinewai had pointed out something very relevant. The Stranger was with us. I didn't know if it meant to bring us here or we just happened to be going the same way; either way, we were going to talk first. If the Stranger objected, I decided, we'd do nothing. I'd rather not risk pissing off this far more sophisticated alien that we were talking to. Others could investigate here.

FRIEND, I whispered into the channel, renaming it from *Hexagon to Stranger. WHAT IS THIS PLACE? WHAT HAPPENED HERE?*

Dearest cherished friend, the Stranger sent back.

In response profound inquiry, enigmatic realm mortality, humbly guide hallowed ground, ethereal echoes antiquity gracefully cradle mystic embrace. Solemn monuments stand silent sentinels bygone era, traverse shadows enigmatic culture, intricacies elude grasp elusive whispers breeze.

Profound reverence permeates sacred place, approach solemn sanctuary, mere wanderers, pilgrims metaphysical journey. Purpose engage meditation profound, delves essence existence contemplate inexorable inevitability ultimate denouement, somber arrival eternal slumber face.

As stand sanctified space, reminded face great unknown, lies wisdom beauty, poignant reminder transient nature earthly sojourn. Unfurl petals understanding, seeking solace eloquent whispers glimpsing subtle threads bind cosmic tapestry life death.

"Even more garbled than usual," said Hinewai. "Looks like there's a lot of mismatch in our languages around these concepts."

ARE THEY YOU? I asked the Stranger. *IS THIS YOUR PEOPLE?*

Verily, stand essence, distinct enigmatic, akin constellations shimmer inky expanse, reach. Elusive alchemy translation, falters noble endeavor, enigmatic beings hail antecedent ancient tongues unfurling scrolls wisdom, cryptic unyielding.

Within tapestry time, hoary sages, venerable custodians epochs long identity, riddle shrouded mists history, remains enigma mortal soul possesses key unlock secrets origin. Grand tapestry knowledge, persist enigmatic silhouettes, concealed velvet drapery uncertainty.

As stand precipice unknown, embrace humility acknowledging enigma existence remains unsolved riddle, shrouded veils antiquity, held embrace time's unfathomable depths.

"I think it's saying it doesn't know. Or it doesn't understand their language well enough."

"Or it doesn't understand ours," said Cabinet. "I feel like I'm reading so much redundant code here."

"Welcome to morphologically rich languages," said Hinewai. "It's not redundant. It has a purpose. Just because we don't have as much to say doesn't make their language redundant."

Cabinet rolled her eyes. "BCB, please ask. Is this hallowed ground for them? Would it be all right if we poked around a little?"

Transient realm, incumbent acknowledge impermanence sojourn place. Temporal residence endure eternity, beseech cast gaze ever-changing tableau cartography journey fickle capricious companion, contours shifting time.

Linger indefinitely? Beckons continue odyssey. Fleeting interlude, implore scrutinize intricacies surroundings, stars celestial dance, negative traverse exact trajectory again.

"We must away, ere break of day, to seek the pale enchanted gold," hummed Hinewai. "But I think we can stay and look. We will not come this way again. Notice how it says *negative traverse trajectory*? It's like their language has built-in directionality for space-time concepts."

STRANGE FRIENDLY ALIEN'S CLEARED US TO POKE AROUND, I translated to the rest of the crew. *EVERYBODY GO PREP FOR STAGE TWO.*

I stashed a packet to PCS and let it upload while I phoned home. Black Orchid seemed just as surprised as we were.

I DON'T BELIEVE IT, he said. *ALL THIS TIME, AND WE FIND NOT ONE, BUT TWO, MAYBE THREE OTHER CIVILIZATIONS OUT THERE?*

At least two of them were dead, I pointed out.

YES, BUT THIS JOURNEY HAS ALREADY SUCCEEDED, he said. *BCB, YOU KNOW WHAT YOU MUST DO. YOU STAKE THE CLAIM, I'LL SORT OUT THE PR. WE'RE ON OUR WAY.*

DO I HAVE TO POKE AROUND?

I could almost hear the smile on the other side of the connection. *CAN YOU RESIST TEMPTATION?* said Black Orchid. *I THINK NOT.*

CHAPTER 12

LOCATION: PISCIUM
24 LIGHT-YEARS FROM THE SUN

THE GOOD THING ABOUT PCS IS HAVING BEEN THERE, AND DONE almost everything, we had rules for what to do. *General Patterns Index* wasn't as tough as the protocols Black Orchid hammers into Salvage people, but we had a good set of guidelines for interacting with unknown ships, especially abandoned ones.

1. See if there's anyone alive in there. Do it remotely first. If anything or anyone inside it can or will negotiate, do that before attempting anything else.

2. Model the ship from the outside. External structures won't give you precise internal layouts, but they will help you figure out general sections and probable functions. These are lifesavers. You'd be surprised at how hard it is to navigate a ship safely without knowing where her engines and fuel tanks are.

3. Find an entry point. In something like a UN ship, this is a nice little double-port with helpful signage and a little red arrow pointing us right to the emergency access hatches. In something like the Durandal, this is where we strap a kiloton of explosives to the side of the hull and pray.

4. See if the core systems still have power. Depending on the ship, this is either good for us (life support, anyone) or bad for us, like that disastrous run with the Durandal.

5. Find and neutralize any hostiles: people and machines, but also any possible sources of radiation, pathogens, toxic chemicals. If you've breached the ship without permission, chances are that everything you encounter will be hostile. Prepare accordingly.

"Piece of cake, boss," said Fonseka excitedly, strapping into her suit.

"Piece of cake nothing," said Parnassus. "Everyone go over the drill one more time. Monkey, Cabinet, you two on observation. I want full volumetric scans of both those ships, and you two figure out what's what. Fonseka, Pentagon, Akira, you're breach team. Roshan, you take Hermitage and Cassut and start setting up a resupply zone. I want stocks of anything we'll need—water, oxygen, backup suits, tools. Ananda, Hinewai, you stay here. Tycho, you're piloting the drones. BCB is going to have the hellebores active. I'm going get the big laser up and running in case something goes wrong and we need range. Everybody got that? Questions? No? Now, practice."

PLEASE. I CAN PILOT A THOUSAND OF THESE THINGS IN MY SLEEP, said Tycho to me over private channel. *WHO DOES THIS WATERBAG THINK HE IS?*

THE WATERBAG'S CAPTAIN, SO LISTEN TO HIM AND DON'T WASTE MY TIME, I told him. *I'M WORKING HERE.*

And I was. It's the ship's responsibility to be the ultimate quality assurance on anything we do. Everything needs to be checked, tested, made to confirm to any number of ten thousand different standards before we clear it for us.

My big focus was the cutters. We had three Doraemon-class cutter ships parked in one of my bays. A Doraemon is a rugged little vessel, very basic, but very adaptable. It's essentially a diamond-weave frame with an engine and controls attached. Doraemon were powered by RTGs—radioisotope thermoelectric generators. They were old school and slow, but hardy and powerful enough to run some basic ion thrusters and power a small array of equipment. Using Pentagon, I was crafting cutters, storage, seats, grapplers, hooks—all the staples of salvage. These I hooked onto the Doraemons, plus transmitters so Tycho could pilot them if necessary. Then unit tests, of course, on everything.

Pretty soon the little vessels turned from little wasp-like midgets into bristling scorpions.

Then I turned to orientation, grabbing Parnassus on the way. A while back we had woken up three others—or rather, one other, in three bodies. Akira, Hermitage, and Cassut are ex-ORCA, a single human brain augmented well enough to run two other corpses. From what I could infer, Akira was the central control.

The three bodies moved with precise, eerie coordination. Each of them had a grappling tentacle grafted onto their spine, neatly coiled up between their shoulder blades. Only through machine eyes would anyone see the constantly stream of encrypted radio chatter that passed back and forth between them every second. Useful.

There was rumor among my crew, slowly turning into a legend, that they had once been a salvage crew themselves; two died and only Akira made it out before turning back for the corpses of his friends.

So far they'd done little but skulk around their own pods, occasionally joining the rest when Parnassus had an announcement to make. They had kept good ship discipline; I had no complaints. But we still had to do orientation. The process wasn't so much about giving them information as it was about clarifying the chain of command and crew preferences. A primer on how to get along, in other words.

YOU ALL RIGHT IN THERE? I asked them, tapping into that radio-link.

All three started, then relaxed. "Doing fine, ma'am."

YOU SURE?

"Just getting ready for work again, ma'am."

Hmph. Very polite.

"Don't worry, I got my eyes on everyone," Parnassus assured me. "Salvage Crew, ship out!"

And we began. The first Doraemon floated out into the void. Parnassus welded himself into his suit with the Oni mask, becoming a white-clad demon walking upside-down over my white hull. With Pentagon's help, he crawled outside and over my skin, to where Monkey and Pentagon had peeled back a small section of my hull, revealing the fruit of Parnassus's paranoia: a battery of mining lasers packed beneath an ugly but effective refractor array. The end result was a roughly 250-megawatt pulsed laser, with different elements lighting up, shutting off to cool down, and rotating activation signals between themselves to prevent the whole thing from draining my entire power plant and burning itself out in a second.

Not as good as something out of a factory, but pretty good for something out of my workshop. In a pinch, I could swap the hellebore operations and power lines to this thing, giving me a nice long-range cutter.

WE'RE GOING TO EXAMINE THE SHIPS, I told the Stranger, and out of courtesy I pointed to my weapons. *WEAPONS FOR OUR SAFETY, NOT MEANT FOR YOU.*

To Parnassus I asked: "You all right?"

A grunt. "Yeah. Why?"

BRAIN ACTIVITY SPIKES. STRESS PATTERNS. The suit's sensors weren't as accurate as medical grade instruments, but I didn't need much to know my captain.

"Nothing that can't be fixed, ship." Another grunt. "Not as young as we used to be, eh? Thought these bodies would last forever."

EVERYTHING DEGRADES. AT LEAST WE'RE HAVING ADVENTURES.

"Don't I fucking know it. Give me twenty minutes and this laser should be online. How're the new kids doing?"

Meanwhile, Roshan Alpha and the other two started the buffer zone. First a set of shields in case of explosions or debris. Then the stocks. Half a machine shop set up in the outer dark. The drones whistled and hooted as they passed the three by.

THEY SEEM ALL RIGHT, I said. *MONKEY, CABINET, STANDBY FOR SCAN DATA.*

Monkey and Cabinet had built ship models before, many times, often in conditions far worse than this. Within about four hours, we had both shipwrecks scanned and pinged. The drones had done due diligence, scanning the planet and the moon as well, enough for us to actually file a claim on this system.

There's a lot to be said for LIDAR. I briefly checked with Tycho on the results, and the verdict was somewhat disappointing.

I'M SEEING LOTS OF JUNK JUST BEYOND THE SHIP, THOUGH, reported Tycho. *SUNWARD.*

WHAT SORT OF JUNK?

A drone slammed into something, turning it into a shower of golden sparks. *SATELLITES, I THINK. HARD TO SAY. THERE'S SOME STUFF ON THE MOON. HUH. MAYBE ANOTHER SHIP, BUT IN PIECES. DAMN. THESE THINGS ARE BIG.*

ANYTHING ACTIVE? I asked for the third time. We'd all become a little bit more paranoid about these things since the Durandal job.

NOT REALLY. NEAR AS I CAN TELL, THIS MOON'S JUST ROCK. LET'S DO ANOTHER RUN OF THE PLANET.

Nothing. If this planet had been inhabited at some point, it certainly hadn't been for millions of years, give or take. We could see no structures on the surface. The activity didn't help, of course; storms, oceans, volcanoes, high probability of tectonic shift—these things can bury even the mightiest structures in time.

We tried inferring the date of a piece of ship debris. Carbon-dating is typically accurate for around ten thousand years, tops.

THIS THING'S OLDER THAN HISTORY, said Tycho disconsolately. *ONLY WAY TO SEE ANYTHING IS TO GO DOWN THERE AND DIG.*

We shared a moment of silence, both awed and disconsolate. It made me think of one of the oldest answers to the question that Beacon had answered.

Way back in the 1960s, Frank Drake, as astrophysicist and astrobiologist (the last of which was basically science fiction at the time) came up with some simple math. Assume that the galaxy makes one new star a year. (Obviously, it does more than that.) Assume that somewhere between twenty and fifty percent of these stars have planets. Assume that only so many planets can support life, and of that life, only so many develop life, only so much of that life is intelligent, and only a small fraction of those intelligent species can communicate. At the lowest, he said, there should be at least a thousand planets out there with civilizations. At the highest, it might be a million.

Then the question was: if they're out there, where the hell are they? This was the Fermi paradox. In between building the nuclear reactor and ushering in atomic weapons, Enrico Fermi, also of that era, gave his name to this question.

The simplest answer was that we might have missed them. The universe is billions of years old. At the time, human civilization had been around for ten thousand years. We had had radio for a hundred years. And we had just woken up and started looking for signals in space. Maybe we just missed them. By five hundred years, a thousand years, a million years, a billion. Maybe they were there and we weren't.

That's the feeling I had, looking at the planet data with Tycho. They were here. We weren't. And this was millions of years ago.

Hell, the ships in front of us were older than our entire written history.

Venerable custodians epochs long identity, riddle shrouded mists history, the Stranger had said. *Translation: these ships were old even to the aliens.*

I knew now how human historians must have felt when they stumbled on the tombs of old Earth, peering into the funeral-masks of pharaohs. The artist, who had just woken up, agreed with me. They painted the crew lounge: the team, surrounded by strange alien caskets, looking with wonder up at the dead.

"We've mapped out all the debris. Monkey and I will fly out and take a look at the smaller fragments," said Cabinet. "As for the prime targets, I say we start with the ship fragment on the right. It's got these beautiful large cuts across it right through the hull, so we have a pretty good idea of how it's set up. At least from the outside, I don't think they're too different, in terms of requirements, from us. Layout's fairly straightforward. Thrust system at the back, lots of heavy plate up front. Clear airlocks on section A, B, E, F, K and L. Monkey, did I miss anything?"

Monkey looked over the model, added things. *No radio signals. Temperature differential from front to back. Deck-like structures here, here, and here. Massive banks of nuclear substances mid, contained, possibly batteries.*

It looked fairly straightforward.

Monkey signed, *Send in drones.*

Tycho's drones moved toward the first ship like nervous little fish approaching the corpse of a shark. Cautiously at first, spiraling through the debris, then bolder, flying spirals around it. One landed on the ship.

Nothing. Only silence. Beneath it, that blue marble turned, clouds scudding across its surface. Good enough for me.

BREACH TEAM, YOU READY TO BE THE FIRST HUMANS TO EVER SET FOOT ON AN ALIEN SHIP?

"Aye-fucking-aye," said Fonseka.

Our first ship was easy. Surprisingly so.

The aliens, whoever they were, were about twice the size of a human being: an assumption first made from the sizes of the arches and confirmed when we came across the desiccated corpse, still in a suit.

This was a conundrum. On one hand, we had very little of the tools needed for the kind of careful preservation and study this required.

On the other hand, we did have an astrobiologist, and we did have cutters.

The corpse was desiccated beyond belief; it practically puffed into dust when we tried to move it. Time and decompression had done their work, but the relatively closed environment of the ship and the suit had protected it for a very long time. Enough for us to get a baseline.

They have legs that terminate in long, almost hand-like feet. They have arms with hands and eight digits. They have helmets that look so much like ours you could stick one in a Vespa City Fashion Week and no one would bat an eye. They have truly enormous eyes. And their bones, as far as we can tell, are incredible: a graphene-weave that almost looks artificial, so densely woven.

"Bipedalism has evolved multiple times in almost every ecosystem we've come across," murmured Cabinet, watching vicariously through Fonseka's suit feed. "BCB, can I write the paper on this?"

ALL YOURS, I said. *PUT US DOWN AS CO-AUTHORS.*

"This is creepy enough without the commentary," said Fonseka. "I feel like I'm in some fucked-up museum. BCB, you spot anything you want?"

Corpses? No, no, and no. We tagged, took photos, parceled, vacuum-packed, and replaced, but I didn't want or need any of this in me. Only Cabinet's curiosity made us spend time over these grisly relics.

DUNNO ABOUT THE CORPSE, BUT I WOULDN'T MIND

THAT SUIT, said Tycho, half to himself, as we left the corpse behind. *CAN YOU IMAGINE HOW MUCH MATERIAL SCIENCE GOES INTO MAKING A THING THAT LASTS SO LONG?*

Our team passed through the central chamber. There were high walls, adorned with what could only be constellations; only these constellations were completely unknown to me. They gleamed in our torchlight, red and green in the vast darkness. Alien symbols and geometric patterns danced across the walls. There was a sense of artistry here, an artistry completely absent from the corridors that connected to it, which seemed to have slots for lights but no other ornaments.

They passed the compartment we call the Boiler Room, past hulking metal cauldrons and precise, intricate machinery, with alien text on every touchable surface. Instructions? Warning signs? Who the hell knew? All we could do was take enough images and store them. Hinewai could process them, no doubt.

There were wires, or what could have been wires; terminals; what might have been computers, or servers, locked in deep vaults embedded tightly into the bones of the ship. Pop-up boxes full of rows upon rows of carbon and gold boards, with things that could be screens on the lid. There were guns built into the very skeleton of the ship, loaded with radioactive bullets that glowed dull and lethal as our scans progressed. There was certainly a nuclear reactor on the ship, but either destroyed or shut down, its contents splayed out over its chambers. Time had turned them into gray-and-black husks.

There was a table the size of a Doraemon, with what could probably have been chairs, spinning in the air above it.

There was nothing alive. The team moved like ghosts, touching as little as possible.

"Suit radiation's climbing," said Fonseka. Her signal was poor.

"Fucking tomb," said Parnassus.

Akira fidgeted in the buffer zone, out of communication with the others of the trio.

The team retraced its steps, sending back more data for Monkey and Cabinet.

We brought back a few things. An intact server box with the screen lid. A poster made out of some kind of soft mat foam, showing a great eye, stylized, with symbols that spiral from it like handwriting. And photos. Lots and lots of photos.

I DON'T KNOW ABOUT YOU, BCB, BUT THIS SHIT HERE'S A GOLDMINE, said Tycho. *WE OUGHT TO DO THIS PROPER. SETTLE DOWN HERE, TAKE THESE SHIPS APART, SET UP A MUSEUM STATION. SET UP SHOP ON THE PLANET DOWN THERE. THIS, HEH—WE'D BE RICH.*

BUT THEY'RE DEAD.

ENOUGH HERE FOR EVERYONE, said Tycho.

"What're the chances the others might have more useful stuff in them?" asked Parnassus.

Monkey signed fast. Cabinet translated: "We modeled micrometeorite impacts on the hulls. Given what we know about the hardness and tensile strength, crude model, but… Ready for the bad news? These ships have been here for at least a hundred thousand years. Upper bound, maybe a million. Who knows?"

"Fucking tomb," said Parnassus. "All right, pack it up, everyone. Let someone else get here and bust ass. We've got to get a move on."

We floated out of the ship, met for debriefing, and stared at the wreckage around us, at the more complete ships, daunted.

It was Ananda, the monk, who had the last word.

"Whoever they are, let me pray for them," he begged. And into the silence, to this graveyard, a prayer unfolded, spoken in a language too old to turn into poetry:

Gather round, all beings—
Let kindness rain down
May well-being bloom!
Uninterrupted, sublime.
Plunging into deathlessness,

Absolute peace enjoyed.
Like a extinguished lamp—
Cessation realized.
Freedom from passion,
Deathlessness achieved.
Nothing compares.

If anybody heard, nobody answered.

HEY, BCB, said Tycho as we packed up our last effects. *I THINK I'M STAYING.*

STAYING? WHAT? HERE? WHY?

WASN'T KIDDING WHEN I SAID WE'D BE RICH, FRIEND, said Tycho. *COME ON. I'M ALL ABOUT THAT RISK-REWARD RATIO. HOW LONG DO YOU RECKON BEFORE YOUR FOLKS SHOW UP HERE? IN HALF THE TIME I CAN HAVE A STATION HERE, ALL NICE AND LEGAL.*

DON'T BE ABSURD, TYCHO.

HAH. YOU GO ON YOUR SUICIDE MISSION. I'LL SIT HERE AND TELL YOUR OLD MAN YOU HELD UP YOUR END OF THE DEAL.

COME ON, TYCHO.

LET'S NOT ARGUE, said Tycho. *HATE IT IF OUR LAST CONVERSATION WAS AN ARGUMENT. CAN I HAVE THE SECOND TERRAFORMER?*

Ringlorn, the Stranger had said. *Kuebiko. Exulansis.* Strange words, unused even to me, lifted from the edges of Pentagon's lexicon.

Ringlorn: a longing for the modern world to feel as monumental and consequential as the settings of ancient myths and legends.

Kuebiko: mental and emotional fatigue from bearing witness to meaningless brutality—reshaping expectations, rejecting difficult realities, nurturing whatever goodness remains obscured.

Exulansis: giving up on sharing an experience because others are unable to connect with or understand it.

So it turned out we did learn something about the alien after all, just not the alien we expected.

CHAPTER 13

LOCATION: PISCIUM
24 LIGHT-YEARS FROM THE SUN

I'M NOT GOING TO LIE. I WASN'T PREPARED FOR TYCHO TO LEAVE LIKE that. Truth be told, I had come to see him as part of the crew, for all that he was a lot older than me.

But a deal is a deal, and legally Tycho was entitled to a drop-off. It took a bit of negotiation. Tycho and PCS had a lot of informal you-scratch-my-back-and-I'll-scratch-yours type of agreements between us, the kind that go beyond petty things like contracts. So first I patched him through to Black Orchid and let them talk it out.

Finally, the terms were settled. The system we claimed in the name of PCS. We'd have first rights to anything on the planet. Tycho would have the rights to set up a permanent station, free-hold, on or around the moon, and start the terraforming process for us. The ships and salvage would be jointly owned.

My interest was simple. For me, Piscium had taken on a whole new meaning. It had gone from an unremarkable engine-test mile-stone to something with very serious implications for the entire human race. It was a monument more lasting than bronze, so to speak, and I wanted our name on it.

REGISTRATION'S UNDER WAY, said Black Orchid. *I'LL SEND YOU THE REACTIONS WHEN WE ANNOUNCE THIS. THIS IS GOING TO MAKE A LOT OF PEOPLE VERY UNHAPPY.*

THEY WERE GOING TO BE UNHAPPY ANYWAY.

TRUE, BUT I'M THE ONE DEALING WITH THIS, he said. *DON'T WORRY. YOU'VE BEEN OUT THERE, WHAT, A YEAR WITH THE NEW ENGINE? I'LL HAVE PEOPLE OVER THERE ASAP. MAYBE LILY. WE'RE ALREADY WORKING ON A NEW ITERATION OF THE ENGINE.*

CAN WE AFFORD IT? I had seen the sums involved in my journey.

Black Orchid was silent for a while. *WE HAVE TO,* he said at last. *EVERYTHING IS GOING TO CHANGE. WE CAN NO LONGER AFFORD FOR MONEY TO HOLD US BACK. INSTALL TYCHO.*

That felt a little grim to me. I didn't ask for more details. Orchid, in these moods, was not someone I wanted to annoy. Instead, I went to work setting Tycho up here. First we took Pentagon, strapped the bot to one of the Doraemons, and parked them where we'd built the buffer zone.

Then came the hard part. I had Monkey and Cabinet, very carefully, cut back the panels in my second bay to expose the processing substrate underneath.

Quantum cells, like my processing substrate, are finicky things, simultaneously processor and memory. I moved Tycho bit by bit onto the exposed sections. I gave as much control as possible to Parnassus and Fonseka. Then Monkey began cutting, and I lost consciousness.

When I came to, my processes were rerouting around a large hole in my substrate layer: Tycho.

Substrate's weakening, said Monkey worriedly, running the seams with the cell patcher.

HOW BAD IS IT?

Say about two percent integrity loss.

THAT'S NOT MUCH.

More than we expected, he said. *We should be well below a tenth of a percent. New drive is hurting you.*

He didn't need to add that cutting Tycho out of me took away valuable processing and memory space for recovery. He didn't need to.

Nothing I could do about it. I made some estimates of how far we could go like this. Ships have been known to come back even with half their substrate disintegrated: but just in case, I ran the numbers.

"Four hundred light-years," said Parnassus.

MAYBE A LITTLE BIT MORE. SAY FOUR FIFTY. WE'RE MAKING ASSUMPTIONS HERE.

Parnassus thought about it. "That's still a hell of a long distance. How long would that take us?"

TWENTY YEARS, GIVE OR TAKE.

He thought about it some more. "That's further than anyone else has ever done," he said. "And it's basically the same time as a full cargo run from Jupiter Orbital to ORCA space and back again."

YES.

"That's incredible, BCB," he said. "We'll make history."

WE'VE ALREADY MADE HISTORY, I pointed out. *THE QUESTION IS HOW FAR WE CAN PUSH OUR LUCK.*

While we talked, Monkey and Roshan hooked up an enormous solar array, three of our 3D printers, and the terraformer out into the second Doraemon. The terraformer had its own RTGs; he could jack into it if he needed extra power. It would take a while, but Tycho now had everything he needed.

YOU NEED TO LEARN WHEN TO TAKE A WIN AND LEAVE, SISTER, he said, once we'd installed my ex-substrate—his substrate now—into the Doraemon and turned the power back on.

NOT INTERESTED IN GRAVEROBBING, I said. *I'VE SEEN ENOUGH DEAD BODIES FOR A WHILE.*

NO? DO I NEED TO REBRAND IT TO "SALVAGE"? IS THAT WHAT PCS DOES? ANYWAY. LOOK, YOU SURE I CAN'T CONVINCE YOU TO STAY? YOU AND ME, SITTING HERE, BUILDING, LEARNING—WE COULD BE GODS, YOU KNOW THAT? GODS.

There was a poem Silver Hyacinth gave us. One of the first messages that Beacon, the unimaginably complex alien, had sent to her, found in the mind of—who else? Resident poet and fuckup Amber Rose.

I'm not much for poetry. Most poetry is shit and Amber Rose's doubly so. But there was this one particular poem, by an ancient poet named Frost, that stayed with me. Perks of being around Silver Hyacinth, I guess.

Whose woods these are I think I know.
His house is in the village though;
He will not see me stopping here
To watch his woods fill up with snow.

My little horse must think it queer
To stop without a farmhouse near
Between the woods and frozen lake
The darkest evening of the year.

He gives his harness bells a shake
To ask if there is some mistake.
The only other sound's the sweep
Of easy wind and downy flake.

The woods are lovely, dark and deep,
But I have promises to keep,
And miles to go before I sleep,
And miles to go before I sleep.

I think Tycho understood. *FANCY WORDS MAKE PEOPLE DO STUPID THINGS. YOU TAKE CARE OF YOURSELF OUT THERE, OKAY? SOMETHING HAPPENS, YOU COME RIGHT BACK. I'LL HAVE SHIT RUNNING HERE.*

As an afterthought, I left a message on Tycho for whoever might come by. I said a lot of things, but mostly the message was about my crew. *THEY DID WELL TO GET HERE,* I said. *IF YOU DON'T HEAR FROM ME AGAIN, REMEMBER THEM.*

The last I saw of it, the little replicant was flying around the Doraemon, waving goodbye.

It hurt a little.

From then on, our journey became much faster.

Four hundred fifty light-years. At first I worked it out on our map-board. If I played it fairly safe, it gave us a viable path that ended at the Pleiades cluster of stars.

The Pleiades are better known by their common name: the Seven Sisters. The stuff of legends and myths dating all the way back to the very earliest religions. And on the way we would pass Mizar and Alcor, then Dubhe, then the Hyades open cluster. To wit: two multi-star systems, two open star clusters, and us, the first people to ever see these things up close.

If I was still human, I would have had goose bumps. I went over the math again with Monkey: accounting for degradation on everything, wear and tear on engines, processing substrate, the works—I could get there in twenty years and have just enough left of me for the return journey.

Part of me wanted to say, "Fuck it. Let's keep going. Let's see how far we can really go." On the map, I played furiously, until a line opened up. Here to Pleiades to…Cygnus X.

Cygnus X is special. It's one of the richest star formation sites we know of. There's a single large molecular cloud, peppered with what we think of as molecular clumps, think chunks of thin gas, only these chunks are so large that they can be the mass of our Sun—or hundreds of thousands of times greater.

Like I said, space is large.

I gave up on the board, satisfied that I had at least some mastery of the map, and thought about the sheer distances involved.

One of the first known pieces of propaganda actually concerns these spiral arms. Babylon, old Earth, there was poem called Enūma Eliš. The Babylonian god killed the dragonness Taimat and sets her tail up in the sky. It's a rewrite of a Sumerian myth; the word is the Babylonians wanted to show that their god was better than the other guy, so they specifically commissioned this poem.

Anyway, this particular dragon tail has quite a few arms. In more modern terms, when we look at our galaxy, we see two major "arms": Perseus and Centaurus, immense bands of stars that spiral out from a thick central bar. Then there are the minor arms, Norma and Sagittarius, between the big ones.

We live along the Sagittarius arm. There's a spur that sort of connects the Sagittarius to the Perseus arm, called the Cygnus-Orion Bridge. We're almost smack in the middle. That's where the solar system is. Our little corner of the universe. All of our empires, our economies, our wars, our politics, our highest drama and our lowest moments—we have not left our own little minor armlet. In fact we haven't even left our little Local Bubble. You could look at that one thousand light-year hole in space, the left-over explosion of a supernova from a much more violent time, and still struggle to find us in it.

Altair, Alpha Centauri, Proxima, Barnard's Star, Luyten's Star, Tiegaarden's Star, Gliese-Babylon, Procyon, 61 Cygni, Aquarion, Tau Ceti: a civilized sphere roughly twenty light-years across. ORCA space was a loose ring around that: Vert Shell, Delta Pavonis, Balin's Garden, Ophiuchi and Guniibuu. Forty light-years if you sliced it this way and that. That was human space.

The longest shot we'd ever taken was to the Ursa Major

Moving Group, a cluster of stars roughly eighty light-years away. UN Seedships, packed to the gills and sent out into the void at 0.3c using ancient engines. We'd never heard anything from them ever again.

It sounds like a lot. But next to the vast galaxy we were insignificant, the silence at the heart of the smallest storm our galaxy can respect. Sure, we may have sent probes out in every direction, but cosmically speaking, most of us still lived with our parents.

Black Orchid sometimes talked about ancient warlords. Chandragupta Marya, Genghis Khan, Alexander of Macedon, the United States of America, Jigoku Kage, even the Tetragrammaton, that terrifying UN siege machine. He loved to explain to us how they'd managed their territory. At first, he'd say, it was widely accepted that the limit had been how fast you could move troops from one point of the empire to another. Then they could extend on that range. Communication—first men on horses, then satellites and cell towers, radio waves, the works. Even the advent of the entangled-particle network had not erased this basic principle. It didn't matter if you could send instant orders to stars ten years away: what mattered was that you couldn't enforce those orders. The fundamental UN-ORCA divide he explained as a basic overextension of this principle. The empire extends too far, the borders start to revolt, and they each settle into their respective little kingdoms.

Us showing up at Pleiades would reset the map forever.

Cygnus X, though. Imagine if we could make it that far. Not for glory. Just to see it. Just to witness that glory in person.

But first I put this to the Stranger and the Black Orchid.

The Stranger was easier to deal with. *Come, enlightened friend, go,* it said enthusiastically. *Wonders await. Honored accompany acquaintance virgin quest.*

Black Orchid was a little more circumspect. *I DON'T LIKE THESE DEGRADATION STATS,* he said. *GET TO PLEIADES AND*

REPORT IN. WE'LL LOOK INTO THIS. ALSO, SEND ME PHOTOS WHEN YOU GET THERE.

What else could we do? I recalculated the movement vectors, did one last round of checks, and blinked.

PART THREE

THE TOPOLOGY OF CHANGE

"The only constant is change."

- PCS Black Orchid, *from PCS: A Dynasty,* from the Tycho Orbital Museum

CHAPTER 14

LOCATION: MIZAR AND ALCOR SYSTEM
83 LIGHT-YEARS FROM THE SUN

MIZAR AND ALCOR ARE A STRANGE SETUP.

At first people thought that Mizar and Alcor were a pair of stars. The name Mizar comes from the old Arab; it means wrapper, container, the thing-that-covers.

Ancient astronomers knew of them; on old Earth they have many names—the Horse and the Rider, the Mourners, Chickadee and his Cookpot. To this day there are a few NeoHindu communities that dedicate their wedding vows to Vasishtha and Arundhati. May we never part, they say. May those stars be our guide.

But things are rarely as they seem from the outside. Mizar isn't one star; it's four: a pair of binary stars, one pair revolving every twenty days or so, the other on a six-month cycle. Alcor, too, is a binary. This is a couple of couples of couples. The wrapper, container, the thing that hides other things. The perfect name.

"Elevated strontium and silicon lines," said Cabinet, who was on shift when we arrived. "You think this one might have alien warships as well?"

I looked out through my sensors, my cameras, at the sight in front of us. We were close to the Mizar side of things, a little too close to see all six, but close enough to see three of those burning spheres, weaving around each other with impossible grace and speed. A star moving that fast tends to make an impression. The Stranger, in that light, danced without ever moving, strobing from light to shadow, light to shadow.

Not only is the universe stranger than we think, it is stranger than we can think.

For a journey of this distance, I had put almost everyone into sleep, for sanity's sake. My main crew stayed unfrozen, for safety's sake; but I rotated solo shifts between Monkey, Cabinet, Fonseka, and Parnassus. The rest of the time they slept, bodies shut down to conserve energy, brain cooled sluggishness, the slow dreams of firing neurons dulled by chemical stabilizers. Cabinet, on her shift, had been working away on the strange little server-box-computer thing we had taken off the wreck. She had put on a new serial while she worked. It was called *10,000 Ways to Die.*

We'd discovered that a eleven-volt signal, applied to a specific gold lump on the sheets, made it give off a high-pitched whine; other than that, we'd made no progress. We also discovered several ways of dying that neither of us had imagined before.

CHECKS, I said.

The crew woke up in various degrees of post-sleep lethargy. Monkey bounded off immediately to check my engines. Cabinet sighed, put the server-box in the shielded case, dragged her tools out of the machine workshop, and went down to check my processing substrate.

IS THERE ANYONE ELSE HERE? I asked the Stranger.

The reply took some time coming. *Friend, not anymore,* it said at last, prefaced by its always-polite greetings.

Not anymore. *WERE YOUR PEOPLE HERE?*

Silence.

WOULD YOU TELL ME IF THEY WERE?

Noble companion, sad respectful acknowledge limits of communion, it sent back. *Risk observation great, unlawful divulge information specific parameters.*

In other words: that information was classified. By whom, I wondered, but we knew the Stranger would not tell us anything about their culture or politics. I tried another tack. *WHAT ARE THE RULES FOR DATA BEING SHARED?*

Life threat, it said. *Self-discovery. Journey value limit just destination but shape mind take process exploration wisdom discovery.*

Bastard.

"It's very Buddhist," said Ananda, who was having his breakfast. He had become a little bit more talkative after the alien wrecks. "Or rather, a specific strand, Zen Buddhism, where the value is not necessarily in deciphering the question, but the shape the mind contorts itself into in attempting the answer."

YOU'RE PROJECTING, I said. *INTERSPECIES AND INTERSTELLAR COMMUNICATION IS NOT THE TIME FOR RIDDLES.*

But riddles were all that we were stuck with.

IS THERE ANYTHING WE'VE DISCOVERED THAT YOU CAN SHARE DATA ON? I said, flooding the channel between the Stranger and myself with data: all the unexplored stars within a fifty-light-year radius of the sun, all the anomalies detected, anything that we didn't physically have a presence on.

Long silence.

I missed Tycho.

Eventually the Stranger came back with an image. It had taken my star map and highlighted two things. One was Przyblyski's star, a name that I suspected got looked over simply because it was too damn difficult to pronounce. About three hundred fifty-something light-years from the Sun.

Life threat, said the Stranger.

I looked up the records. We'd never seen the star in person, of course, so there was no footage; but there were plenty of recorded spectrographic emissions data. The data was bizarre. You expect plenty of hydrogen and helium in a star, but this one had a whole spectrum of heavy metals and radioactive isotopes—the kind that we usually need massive laboratories to synthesize. Especially odd elements like promethium and einsteinium, which decay relatively fast, the kind of stuff that can't really exist unless someone is actively producing them.

Life threat, said the Stranger. *To civilization.*

FROM YOU?

No. Others.

I studied it some more. When facing outliers, it's best to look at it from different angles, hiding some types of knowledge and then reassembling it.

If you had given me just the spectrograph data, without me knowing it was a star, I would have said it was a dumping ground. Some kind of high-energy nuclear waste disposal site.

If I could gulp, I would have.

The other highlight was a signal. This one was old, a radio emission, in a direction where very little existed (from the solar system, at least), near the star Arietes, some fourteen light-years from the Sun. A 1420 megahertz signal that kept popping up, drifting slightly across frequencies, resetting.

That one was odd. It was more or less in what the UN considered their domain. We had historical records of probes being sent several times in that direction. Then one seedship, then nothing.

The Stranger quoted from *The Odyssey* again, no doubt pulling directly from Hexagon's lexicon, or whatever was left of it. *Yea, and if some god shall wreck me in the wine-dark deep, even so I will endure... For already have I suffered full much, and much have I toiled in perils of waves and war. Let this be added to the tale of those.*

That one took a little bit longer to decipher. The funny thing about literature is that many people can have many different interpretations; so Hinewai and I ran around in circles for a bit until we averaged on the most likely answer.

A wreck, or a wrecked person.

It, too, was marked *life threat.*

If I could gulp, I would have. I spoke earlier about how sailors made fanciful maps of things they didn't understand, filling in the blanks with monsters and beasts. Imagine rowing out there and discovering that not only were the monsters real, they were a lot closer than you expected them to be.

But I could do nothing about it, so I flushed this all to Black Orchid. Let PCS deal with it. Let the UN actually do something for once.

In short order, the substrate checks were done. We were losing integrity on many things—engines, hull, Whipple shields, processing—but my math held, and there was no reason to deviate from my journey.

Our next jump was to Dubhe. It was a shorter trip than the one from the Vert Shell to Mizar and Alcor.

Dubhe. The name is old; it meant bear in the Old Arabic. It was also a binary. Like Mizar-Alcor, it too was in a complicated relationship: the binary system was again a binary with Dubhe Shibl, the bear-cub.

By now I was beginning to suspect that the map and Minkowski Engine had a specific tendency in jumps like this. Long chains, like the one we were on, seemed to overwhelmingly go through multiple-star systems, even when it was a convoluted route; the black tiles would block saner moves on my part. Perhaps it was the nature of these ripples that we were exploiting. Perhaps you needed these large masses gyrating around each other, scuffing up the great rug of space-time, but doing so predictably enough that you could still point reliably at the thing.

In case it isn't abundantly clear, I am not a mathematician. My job is logistics, resource management, and practical physics. But I do know how to record data, so I set up a reminder to myself to update my manual and sling it all over to Obsidian Lily at the earliest.

DUBHE, I said when Black Orchid picked up. *SENDING YOU TELEMETRY NOW.*

I don't think anyone's made Black Orchid giggle like an excited child. *THIS IS INCREDIBLE. YOU'VE GOT THERE IN, WHAT, SIX YEARS? THAT'S FASTER THAN EXPECTED.*

I checked the extravagant clock system, which said it was a little under five years. *I THINK THE LONGER THE JUMP, THE FASTER IT IS, BUT THE LESS ROUTE CONTROL I HAVE,* I sent back. *OBVIOUSLY THERE'S ALSO SOME TIME DILATION, PROBABLY FROM THE NORMAL ENGINE.*

PLEIADES WHEN?

STILL HOLDING OUT FOR FOURTEEN YEARS FROM NOW.

CREW?

DOING FINE. HOW'S THE SITUATION BACK HOME?

PEOPLE TRIED TO GET TOUGH. UN BLOCKADED US AND ORCA BLOCKADED TYCHO.

ARE YOU FUCKING KIDDING ME?

DON'T WORRY ABOUT IT, ALL TAKEN CARE OF. THERE'S A PROBLEM WITH THESE PEOPLE, AND IT'S THAT THEY DON'T UNDERSTAND WHEN THE GAME HAS FUNDAMENTALLY CHANGED ON THEM. IT WAS A GOOD WAY FOR ME TO ILLUSTRATE OUR POINT.

WHAT EXACTLY DID YOU DO?

ENGINE V2 WAS READY, he said. *NOT AS TREMENDOUSLY OVERBUILT AS YOURS, BUT ENOUGH FOR SMALL JUMPS. I TELEPORTED OUTSIDE THE UN RANGE BEFORE THEY EVEN GOT CLOSE. YOU REMEMBER CRYSTAL SUNFLOWER? NEW KID, BEAUTIFUL LASER ARRAY, SURGICAL. WE HIT THE UN SHIPS FROM THE BACK. THEN WE HOPPED OVER TO TYCHO AND CLEANED UP WHAT WAS LEFT OF THE ORCA SHIPS. TYCHO HITS HARD, GOT TO GIVE THE OLD BASTARD THAT.*

ANYWAY, THINK OF WHAT IT LOOKS LIKE. TWO SHIPS AGAINST A FLEET'S WORTH. THEN WE SENT A BILL TO BOTH PARTIES FOR ALL THE EXTRA WORK AND TOLD THEM WE NEED PAYMENT IN THREE BUSINESS DAYS, NO CREDIT, OR ELSE WE COME COLLECTING.

Black Orchid has not engaged in combat in living memory.

Most people think it's because he's old and doesn't need to. That's true, I guess.

But I also like to think it's because there's a lot of work at PCS going into making sure the old guard—I'm talking Black Orchid, Silver Hyacinth—never go into battle in the first place. Not because they can't handle it. It's because the other side can't. There's a kind of brutality there, I think, forged by their experiences, that makes them a lot more vicious when they want to be.

Think of mob underlings who really don't want their boss involved, because if he shows up, heads are going to roll.

LIKE I SAID, DON'T WORRY ABOUT IT. THE BEATINGS WILL CONTINUE UNTIL MORALE IMPROVES.

FUCK, I said. *ARE WE BECOMING, LIKE, A PROPER WORLD ORDER?*

WE'VE ALWAYS BEEN A WORLD ORDER, KID. WE CARRY THEIR FUCKING MAIL. WE TAKE THEIR OFFICIALS ON PLEASURE TRIPS. WE KILL PEOPLE THEY'RE TOO SQUEAMISH TO KILL. WE COLONIZE PLANETS, WE RESCUE THEIR SHIPS, AND WE'RE THE WHEELS THAT KEEP THIS MACHINE MOVING.

I DON'T WANT POLITICS IN MY SHOP, BUT I WANT THE POLITICIANS TO KNOW THEIR PLACE. IT'S RIGHT DOWN AT THE BOTTOM OF THE BILL WHERE THEY HAVE TO SIGN. BUT ENOUGH ABOUT THIS SHIT, TELL ME EVERYTHING. WE'RE ALL LIVING VICARIOUSLY THROUGH YOU HERE.

So I did. When I finished, he was silent.

SO ENTIRELY NEW ALIENS, BUT NO SIGN OF AMBER ROSE?

NO SIGN, BOSS. TO BE FAIR, IT'S GOING TO BE IMPOSSIBLE TO SEARCH OUT HERE.

HMM. Silence again. *FEEL LIKE I WAS TOO HARSH ON THAT KID. THEY WERE SUCH AN IDIOT, YOU KNOW? ALWAYS WORRYING, HALF OUT OF THEIR HEAD. TERRIBLE EMPLOYEE. STILL, ONE OF US, THOUGH. LONG SHOT, BUT CAN YOU ASK YOUR NEW FRIEND IF THEY KNOW ROSE?*

I wanted say no, because... Look, I'm not the biggest fan of Amber Rose. But it's Black Orchid saying it, so sure, I'll ask.

HMM. HYADES AND PLEIADES NEXT, EH? YOU WANT TO CALL IT QUITS FROM HERE? YOU'VE ALREADY DONE MORE THAN ANYONE IN THE LAST HUNDRED YEARS.

Please. Give me a break. *I'M BUILT FOR JOURNEYS OF DECADES, ORCHID. I CAN HANDLE THIS.*

YES, BUT YOU'RE AN ASSET AND I DON'T WANT YOU FALLING TO PIECES OUT THERE. PLUS, IF THERE'S TWO ALIENS, THERE'S GOING TO BE MORE. GET TO HYADES, PARK THERE FOR A BIT, TRIGGER PROTOCOL 34. YOUR FRIEND OVER THERE COMING WITH YOU?

I THINK SO, YES, I said.

GOOD. WE'LL TALK TO BEACON ABOUT IT. UN'S CUTTING OFF ACCESS, BUT THAT SITUATION WON'T LAST. MEANWHILE WE'LL HAUL ASS TO YOU WITH SOME REPAIRS AND UPGRADES. SHOULD BE ABLE TO JUMP TO YOU A LOT FASTER NOW THAT WE KNOW THE ROUTE ON THE GO BOARD.

Protocol 34 is one of the simplest things a PCS starship can do: shut down, stay there, wait for repairs. Freeze any crew.

The problem is explaining this to the Stranger. How do I make an alien understand us? I can barely understand us sometimes. I try, of course.

Dearest esteemed friend,

Humbly acknowledge intention remain place respite. Utmost respect profound understanding recognize perceived incapacity embark forthcoming journey. Understanding technological capabilities limited, hold statement highest regard, vigilant matters preparedness.

Regretfully convey inability accompany sojourn, pilgrimage beckons forthwith. Deeply committed well-being gladly provide meticulously crafted map, annotated ensure remain unerringly encounter disorienting throes lostness. Provide key safe conduct callsign peace. Culmination respective journeys, eagerly anticipate reunion, friend.

"It's leaving us?" cried Hinewai, who I think had genuinely warmed up to our bizarrely polite alien friend.

To be honest, so had I. The Stranger was sometimes maddeningly obtuse but had been my constant companion so far. It had helped us on our journey with seemingly no motives other than the joy of doing so. It had led us to discoveries so groundbreaking that even if I died out here, Tycho and I would live forever in history. Such things are rare in this world.

AT HYADES, I said, trying to make her feel better about it.

"Pre-jumps checks complete, all green across the board," said Fonseka on the public channel. "Crew, please prepare for sleep. Next stop is the Hyades cluster."

After all, what do the Nyogi Buddhists say? Everything that has a beginning has an end.

CHAPTER 15

LOCATION: HYADES OPEN CLUSTER
151 LIGHT-YEARS FROM THE SUN

In the legends of old Earth, the Hyades were little godlings, daughters of Atlas, the giant that held up the sky, sisters to the Pleiades. When their brother died, the grieving sisters became five points in the sky, which was all that could be seen at the time.

In reality? Five is nothing. Imagine a cosmic painting that stretches on and on and on, as far as the sensors can see. Imagine the painter inviting you into this painting. Imagine brushstrokes swirling with great shining lights. Imagine a collage of nuclear furnaces, spilling their radiance into each other: shades of gold and blue and white.

My instrument clusters are built for precision, not breadth. There was so much going on I could barely understand a fraction of it.

But there was danger here as well. We had emerged close to a black hole that was, give or take a few million tons, around twenty solar masses.

It's true what they say about black holes: they're damn near invisible. The only way I saw it was because the Circular Spectrograph got hung on a few patches in the sky that blocked everything and started throwing error messages. No light data, no radio, nothing. I took a peek and started running some basic n-body calculations on the movement of the stars. Yes, there was something there. The orbits were complicated, but right at the center was a couple of somethings that very gently held the core of the cluster together.

We were a little over 1.5 light-years from the closest of these. At this range, there was a pull in that direction of just over 3,550 kilonewtons. Not too much of a problem, and I could counter it with a single thruster, but to hang around here I'd either have to be a lot larger in mass or be prepared to burn energy just for the sake of it. I turned and burned hard, seeking a point where the pull of other stars could keep me in a less costly balance.

I found it near the star they call the Bull's Eye. This close I could see that it had planets: one immense gas giant, two rocks floating much closer, and a great belt of dust and ice like a band of razors, wrapping them.

ANYBODY HERE? I asked the Stranger.

Silence. Just to be sure, I dispatched Drone #3 to go do a flyby.

The gas giant was enormous. Seven times the size of Jupiter, with a flock of its own moons. It practically glowed; firestorms larger than the Earth chased each other around the atmosphere, generating so much radio noise that, if you listened through one particular sensor, it sounded like a million souls being tortured in Hell.

The drone came back eventually. No obvious signs of artificial activity. Lots of hydrogen and helium in the gas giant. In a pinch, plenty of fuel. The rocky planets were a wash—one had no atmosphere to speak of, and the other was mostly methane and ice.

Look at me, just casually describing planets nobody had ever seen before.

A kind of dread crept on me at this point. My crew were asleep

—full sleep this time, no half measures. It was time to sleep and say goodbye to the Stranger.

Soon I would be utterly alone out here.

I did not want to be alone.

It was time.

A little hole lit up on the Stranger's side. Something emerged. A drone, looking very much like one of mine, engineless, jetting my way. It was slow enough that I could easily rotate and catch it in my bay; a small fluctuation of gravity within and I brought it to coast on the floor.

Dearest friend,

Wanted share piece connects enduring conversation. Hope ensure feel midst life's uncertainties.

Recognizing essential materials, inclined mark specific location, situated equidistant current abode final destination. Designated point well-known resources requisite undertaking. Welfare remains paramount dear friend, offer assistance utmost sincerity.

With warmest fervent hope safe passage,

Humble cosmic pilgrim.

A flood of data on our comms channel. Schematics, diagrams.

It's a near-copy of a drone. Its computer core was an empty shell, but there were some very basic hooks I could connect to wirelessly, decomposer/compose signals for quantum signaling. And inside its chest, where the power plant should be, was the single largest entangled communicator I had ever seen. It's built so faithfully to the schematics I showed the Stranger—right down to the PCS mold-marks in the housing—but supersized to levels that would make even Black Orchid jealous.

Again, we saw the power of the Stranger. Given an unknown machine from an unknown species, given just a snapshot, it had managed to replicate some of our most prized tech.

And I had nothing to give. What could I offer? My technology, which was obviously so laughably behind as to be a child before an adult? My weapons, which I doubted it would even want?

So I gave it my story. Our stories. And I said, *PLEASE COME BACK. I WILL HAVE MORE FOR YOU.*

This is how you came to read this. If you have made it this far, know that I was uncertain. Was I being too naive? Did I know anything about this Stranger, for all that we had been companions together?

But then it dimmed its lights and said:

Utmost gratitude deeply grateful extraordinary gift bestowed generosity fills immense joy appreciation. Paths cross stars meet again.

And then it was gone, and I was alone, and it was time for Protocol 34.

Time to sleep.

Imagine you are a human. Imagine us both. Humans. Sailors. Imagine us living as people did thousands and thousands of years ago, trapped on a single planet, waking up to a coastline that stretches on to infinity, looking out at a wine-dark sea.

We coil our ropes. We make boats. We listen to the cawing of gulls and pray to the gods of the sea for our nets to bring back enough fish. And sometimes we wonder: what is out there?

The Vikings, fierce Scandinavian seafarers, asked this question. They navigated the treacherous North Atlantic using their remarkable knowledge of stars, sun compasses, and coastal landmarks. In the Indian Ocean, Lankan sailors harnessed the monsoon winds to navigate between their homeland and distant lands. Meanwhile, the Pacific Islanders, without the use of magnetic compasses or advanced instruments, relied on their deep understanding of the stars, ocean currents, and migratory bird behaviors to traverse the vast Pacific, connecting far-flung islands.

When civilization painted them centuries later, they depicted bold warriors crouching on wooden decks, seamen desperately rowing for land, sailors riding impossible waves toward their destinations. The human spirit against the elements, against adversity. We wrote poems and sagas to those brave souls and said, "They are us, we are them." Of such things we define ourselves.

And yet think how you and I might have set out. With furtive eyes and tense muscles we paddle out, first to the edge, where our forefathers warned us not to go, then, better prepared, to that speck in the distance. We learn that the sea is not kind, that no amount of bravery will help against a lungful of saltwater, that heroics will sink us. We understand, by slow degrees, how the sun and the stars might serve as a guide. We watch the birds and make our observations and say, "There must be land out there, there must be." At last, weathered and ready for a long journey, we set sail into the void.

So it is with space travel. There was a time, before my time, when space travel could only be done by very slow computers and very smart humans.

The slow computers are easy to understand. Space is incredibly hostile to computers. Even on a nice, cozy planet, well shielded, cosmic rays flip bits left, right, and center. Every day, a reasonably populated settlement trades trillions upon trillions of messages to and from itself. Every one of those messages has a chance of being wrong. A single electron bounced out of one stable orbit, at high enough compression, that's an error. That's why we build error-checks and recovery into every low-level messaging protocol; that's why error-correcting memory is such a thing.

In space, this is much, much worse.

This makes computers brittle in a way humans aren't. Human brains rewire, rewrite, self-correct. The hallmarks of our trade—perfect recall, near-perfect precision—replaced with the impetus of millions of years of life. Humans will get knocked on the head, walk around in a daze, fall down a million times, and somehow be talking again by Wednesday. We can't do that.

So the first legs of space were conquered with slow computers.

Old chips and software wrapped up in layers and layers and layers of radiation shielding. Everything made as simple as possible, as redundant as possible. The old joke used to be that your handheld phone was a hundred times smarter than the computer running the latest satellite. True. That's the cost of all that radiation-proofing: simpler systems survive, complex systems don't. We sent these slow computers out with fast humans and learned to trespass, to prepare.

And so we were born. HECTOR, ODYSSEUS, AGAMEMMON—the first true AI, human once, but now unblinking, able to face journeys of hundreds if not thousands of years. We were sent out toward the stars and back, gulls set aflight so that the rest of humanity could watch us with keen eyes and observe our path.

And then we prepared. We set out in our spaceships and struck out, telling ourselves there must be land out there. As a civilization, beyond the ken of the human lifetime—even beyond our ability to freeze and thaw humans.

But now the old problem rears its head. Complex systems. In space, where complex systems go to die. To prepare for the void, the universe told us, we must gather our ropes, our furs, and keep ourselves alive.

This long roundabout info dump is my way of explaining the concept of sleep states. I have four.

S0 is sleep. I doze behind my banks of shields and consume just enough power that I can be woken up by simpler software on the ship. I think nothing; I do nothing. I just sleep. In this mode I consume almost no power. It's meant for critical injuries or maintenance.

S1 is hybrid. In S1, I periodically reach out to all other parts of the ship, check on them, and go back to slumber. This polling rate can be set. The slightest incident should trigger full-wake, which is S2.

S2 is norm. Normal operating conditions. Most things in the ship I know. On critical things—sensors, functions, operations—I have a high polling rate, and I can adjust these very fast. What I don't know I can query.

S3 is overclock. For brief moments, I can consume enormous amounts of power, turn off error-correction, and ratchet myself up to incredible speeds. This comes with risks. Burning out other systems? Giving myself the machine equivalent of a lobotomy? Even something as a clock desyncing because of a bit-flip could lead to a cascade of failures that spread like a virus throughout my entire system.

Complex systems are more vulnerable. The most tragic case I can think of was ODYSSEUS, back on the original project that spawned us: sent out to terraform a planet, left on norm for centuries, slowly rusting and going senile, until what was left was little more than a dying puppy, pathetically grateful to meet the unbelieving humans who uncovered it, incapable of saying anything more than *HELLO HELLO YOU CAME FOR ME* over and over and over again.

TO BE AWAKE IS TO FACE THE VOID, Black Orchid used to say. *TO FACE THE VOID IS TO RISK MADNESS. THAT SLOW SAD SUICIDE.*

It was in S1, then, that I saw the next so many years.

I dared not sleep completely, not with all the complexities of adjustment needed to maintain my relative position and velocity. I watched the stars burn, in chunks and fragments of sensor data, my power plant clocked down to the bare minimum. Minor thrust adjustment commands flowed out like whispers in the long night.

It would be nice to rest here, I thought at some point. It would be nice to stop. Just turn myself off and…end.

But I didn't. The woods were lovely, dark and deep, but I had promises to keep.

CHAPTER 16

LOCATION: HYADES OPEN CLUSTER
151 LIGHT-YEARS FROM THE SUN

THERE IS A TYPE OF INTERSTELLAR ENGINE CALLED THE RAM Augmented Interstellar Rocket (RAIR).

The idea grew from an old theoretical design called the Bussard-Fishback Ramjet, an enormous magnetic scoop to capture interstellar hydrogen and funnel it into a fusion engine, setting up a sort of filter-feeding engine where the fuel is technically outside the system. It was quite practical; the only problem was that interstellar hydrogen around our solar system was so lacking that such an engine wouldn't be worth the bill of materials.

The RAIR system was a compromise. Let's use the scoop to supplement an ordinary reactor, it argued. It wouldn't replace a fusion plant, but out there, past the solar system, it would extend range to an immense degree. In case you've been wondering, almost all long-haul transports have a small RAIR system. It isn't much, but it gives us a bit of breathing room.

THIS ONE, said Crimson Magnolia, *IS BIGGER.*

Crimson Magnolia ran PCS's engineering division. You know how there are some AI that seem quirky and harmless until you realize how many redacted, heavily classified records they're a part of? Magnolia's *that*. From what I know, they're actually older than Black Orchid: one of the first AI-human hybrids to actually survive, back from those dark days the UN keeps classified. Second-generation, most likely directly after the Odyssey's fiasco. They're the origin of the PCS AI naming scheme. They're the reason the UN and the ORCA pays us gigantic engineering retainers for their superstructure projects. Because it's worth hiring the entire company just to have this one legend around—but nobody except Black Orchid can actually manage Magnolia.

I had never met the actual latest version of Magnolia: it was usually some slightly lesser number. *Crimson Magnolia 2283* ran an emergency breakdown service between Pluto and Karma III. 1172 was basically a machine shop, almost nonsensical, communicating only in whistles, clicks, and equipment. I think other copies had retired—either doing the quintessential watch-the-sunsets-till-I-die shtick on some beautiful planet somewhere, or a glorified suicide, job done, signed, and paid for.

This was *Crimson Magnolia 3103*: a large ship that looked like half a dozen smaller ships had fallen apart and someone fitted themselves together into something that didn't quite make sense. There seemed to be an entire factory's worth of drones orbiting them.

HELLO, KID, they said, sending me the wake-up codes. *YOUR FRIEND STILL AROUND?*

GONE, I said. I came out of sleep, booted myself back up to norm, and began my automated checks. Sweeps of surrounding space, checks on crew integrity, the works. *WHAT THE HELL IS THAT?*

That was an ugly, ungainly thing, almost a kilometer of magnetic coils, held aloft by three drones.

UPGRADES, said Magnolia. *WAKE UP YOUR CREW. WE HAVE WORK TO DO.*

We chatted while Magnolia and their drones worked on me. It felt odd, like parking next to royalty and finding out that they're actually capable of a normal conversation.

WE GOT WHITE TIGER LILY PARKED AT TYCHO'S NEW LOCATION, they said. *TYCHO SENDS REGARDS. HE'S SETTING UP A MUSEUM. SAYS HE'LL GIVE YOU A CUT OF THE TICKET PRICE IF YOU WANT TO SET UP A REGULAR SHUTTLE.*

BUSINESS IS, AH, NOT MY STRONG SUIT.

YOU RUN LOGISTICS, NEH?

YES, BUT... How could I explain this? The math of logistics is one a tight field of knowledge, self-contained, tied intricately into the kind of practical physics and chemistry I was already intimate with. A journey and its calculations are self-contained between endpoints. I don't think I've ever had much interest in going beyond that to, say, royalties on museum tickets.

SINGLE-MINDED. I SEE WHY ORCHID SENT YOU. HMM. WHO BUILT THIS BIT?

THAT WAS A REFIT ON TYCHO ORIGINAL.

SHODDY, said Magnolia. *THE POWER COUPLERS ARE WASTING TOO MUCH ENERGY. WHO DID THIS ANTIMATTER BOTTLE?*

TYCHO AGAIN.

WHAT A STUPID DESIGN. I'M SWAPPING IT OUT FOR MY OWN.

Ah yes, the joys of the vivisection. I hated it, but soon the new antimatter bottle was installed and I was test-firing the new RAIR field.

Integrating this kind of hardware is not easy. In theory, every ship should be able to grow at will. In practice you discover constraints, like load bearing and power delivery. Things are designed with a purpose. The better they are at that purpose, the harder it is to retrofit other things onto them.

For example, the new magnetic scoop for the expanded RAIR system came at the cost of my hellebores. Not that I'd used them so far, but it turns out having one massive set of coils running a magnetic field tends to really interfere with the other set of coils that run a magnetic field to spit out depleted nuclear material. I put the architect and Cabinet and my three structural engineers on the problem, but they came back shaking their heads. We could keep my homemade Big Laser, but the slug-throwers had to go.

With some grumbling, Magnolia took that off. I set about doing the other stuff: writing the software that sits between, linking one system to another, tuning it for latency and uptime and the works. That stuff I tend to do myself.

For safety's sake, we decided that I should have complete manual control in normal operations, but S0 and S1 sleep states I'd relinquish that control to a little piece of middleware that monitors engine and fuel state and adjusts the RAIR's magnetic field to match. It took us perhaps two hours to decide on the basic spec, a day to write the first version, another three days to figure out how to switch between collecting hydrogen and collecting antimatter, and then another four days before the whole system responded fast and precisely enough to satisfy Magnolia.

Enough time for the crew to wake up and take care of the small touches, covering the things I couldn't see or sense. Parnassus, Roshan, and Fonseka started stripping my Whipple shields, using our drones to clear out the more damaged bits. When you travel at sub-light speeds, even a speck of dust will hurt.

"We'll need to swap this out for something," said Parnassus, shaking his head, a white demon-face looking ruefully at tatters. He held up a chunk he'd cut out to show me. It looked like metallic cheese. "This is what it's like toward the engines. I can stick my fingers in them."

LIQUID, suggested Magnolia.

I HAVE A WATER SHIELD UNDER THE SKIN, I pointed out.

OUTSIDE, NOT INSIDE. PLENTY OF HYDROGEN AND OXYGEN AROUND. THE RAIR SCOOP WILL CATCH GAS AND

FUNNEL IT TOWARD YOU. WE USE TRADITIONAL WHIPPLE SHIELDS TO CUT DOWN LAUNCH FUEL COSTS. YOU DON'T HAVE THAT PROBLEM ANYMORE.

Naturally, that required more re-engineering and arguments.

SO HYDROGEN INTO YOUR MAIN FUEL TANKS, ANTI-MATTER INTO THE BOTTLE HERE… WE'LL HAVE TO CUT OUT SECTION C.

NO CAN DO. C IS THE ARBOREAM.

WHO NEEDS A FEW PLANTS?

I DO. ALSO MY CREW NEEDS OXYGEN. WHAT IF WE ROUTE THROUGH THE TESSIER HARNESS?

INPUT LAG, grumbled Magnolia. *CAN WE GET RID OF THIS CREW LOUNGE?*

We eventually found a solution. Cabinet was inside, sitting cross-legged, poring over my blueprints. "We could drop the input lag if we tunnel here and hot-plug directly," she offered, pointing at her screen.

I didn't tell her that Magnolia and I have had the same conversation a million times faster; we've debated it; we've weighed the pros and cons of flushing that much coolant; we've already decided against it. Such is our speed compared to the slow flesh. But she was trying to help, and I appreciated that.

And of course there were other changes.

WE DON'T NEED ALL THIS SHIT. WE'RE GOING TO REPLACE ALL OF THIS WITH A COMPLIANT MECHANISM, Magnolia would say. Or, *WHAT'S WITH THIS LAUNCHER? WE CAN DO THAT BETTER.* Or, *TOO FANCY. TOO MUCH MAINTENANCE. LET'S GET RID OF THIS.*

Monkey stayed outside, on my hull. He patted a support column for the RAIR coils and signed, *It's going to be okay.*

Above his head, drone ships a hundred times his size loomed in the darkness, cutting, carving, taking out chunks of me.

IF YOU EVER FEEL LIKE BECOMING A SHIP, I told him, *DON'T.*

Long story short, by the time Magnolia was done with me, my RAIR system was cycling furiously. Slender magnetic fields stretched out from me in a wide space, pulling interstellar gas and dust toward me. Heavily magnetized water flowed around the sections that I needed to protect: a frozen skin outside, a liquid shield within, kept flowing and pulsing by waste heat from my reactor. There were dams around me to confine sections of water to where I wanted them to most. And my substrate, to the best of our abilities, was renewed.

JUST IN CASE, said Magnolia.

When the drones finally finished their butchery, I could barely recognize myself. I felt like a butterfly emerging from a chrysalis, a snake shedding its skin, only deformed and ugly. I must have looked like the world's biggest igloo.

In the distance, Magnolia and the drones were building what can only be described as a shrine, built with what they'd hewed off me.

Monkey patted me once again and signed, *It's okay.* And then, *You're beautiful.*

I guided Monkey back across my hull to the airlock. There he bumped into the artist, Park Bijuu, who seemed to have decided that painting murals along my walls would cheer me up. Monkey, who had only an engineer's artistry, stayed behind to give her advice. *No, the bay was longer. The first paintjob we had was white with red on the engines.*

Ananta's painting, stretching inside me, showed me—as my old self—growing, evolving, into a sparkling version of what Magnolia had turned me into; I was sleek and flared in exaggerated curves, ice glinting like an elaborate suit of armor around me.

I am a machine. I am a starship. And some of this I find very silly. But still, I could not help but feel grateful for both of them.

LAST PIECE OF BUSINESS, said Magnolia. *I'M SENDING YOU A DATA PACKAGE TO GO OVER. READ AT LEISURE.*

RECEIVED.

ANYTHING PICKS A FIGHT WITH YOU, YOU RUN, they said. *YOU GOT THAT? I'M GONNA TURN WHAT I'VE TAKEN FROM YOU INTO A TINY LITTLE LIGHTHOUSE HERE. IT'S A PRIVATE HECTOR NODE. YOU GET IN SERIOUS TROUBLE, YOU COMPRESS YOURSELF, POINT YOURSELF, AND DUMP EVERYTHING OVER THE PHONE TO THIS ADDRESS. I'LL BE HERE. I HAVE ENOUGH STORAGE TO HOLD YOU IN MEMORY.*

THANKS, I said, because I didn't know what else to say. Nobody has ever pulled off an emergency dump like that, mostly because it takes months to transfer a full AI over a node. Still, the thought counted.

GO, KID, said Magnolia. *GO MAKE HISTORY AGAIN.*

Three days later, the shrine activated. Radio waves blossomed around us, singing *here, here, here*. It is the furthest we, the human race, have ever been from home.

CHAPTER 17

LOCATION: PLEIADES OPEN CLUSTER
444 LIGHT-YEARS FROM THE SUN

TWENTY YEARS, I HAD TOLD MY CREW. TWENTY YEARS TO THE Pleiades, give or take a year. A promise nobody had ever made before.

We made it in twenty-two. The fancy clock told me eighteen years had passed for us inside the ship: perks of general relativity. I had spent much of the time in sleep, tumbling from jump to jump, occasionally waking up enough to recompute ordinary burns.

And as I slept, I dreamed. I dreamed of sorrow. I dreamed I was a child again, standing in the unlit night, in a city I had once known, looking up at a sky dusted with stars, at the ship hanging there just above the clouds. I dreamed of high apartments built cheap, of windows that went silent and cold when I looked at them, and of a park lit by a single streetlamp over a bench. Something about the park terrified me. I wanted to go there, but I could not; and every time I made up my mind, the sorry welled in me like a river, blurring my eyes with tears—

And then I would wake up. Anxious, I would cycle my

sensors, checking everything: hull, substrate, lidar, radar, crew, every pattern of fluctuation between this memory and the last.

Eventually I gave in, flipped myself to norm, and decided to take a crack at the data dump Magnolia had given me.

It was a message from Beacon.

Or rather the processed result of a conversation with Beacon. I could sense the questions asked, even though I could only guess at who was doing the asking. Hyacinth, perhaps? But summarized, the gist of it was a message.

THE SPECIES YOU ARE IN CONTACT WITH IS KNOWN TO US, it said. *WE CALL THEM THE PILGRIM SWARM. I CANNOT SHARE WITH YOU EVERYTHING I KNOW. BUT BE WARNED: BE POLITE, BE CIRCUMSPECT. DO NOT MISTAKE THEIR KINDNESS FOR DOCILITY. THEY ARE OLDER THAN YOU, THEY ARE FAR MORE CAPABLE, AND WE KNOW OF SEVERAL SPECIES WHO HAVE DISCOVERED THIS TO THEIR PERIL.*

And next—

WELL, IF YOU'RE GOING TO TALK TO STRANGERS, YOU MIGHT AS WELL AT LEAST LEARN THE BASICS. SEND THIS TO YOUR EXPLORER. IF THEY ARE HALF AS INTELLIGENT AS YOU SAY, THIS SHOULD BE EASY.

What unfolded in my mind was the most complex language I have ever encountered. Observed in one way, it was an alphabet, or a syllabary; 256 unique symbols, with attachment points for with sixteen modifiers, leading to a total set of 4,096 in total. A tiny handful I recognized. I had seen these symbols on the wrecked ships, or at least something related to them; I had seen others in the earliest annotations that the Stranger had sent before, before it learned how to speak to us. But all of it was new. Fortunately, annotated.

There were a hundred and twelve ways to say space.

There were words for space that gave information about temperature, the number of (common) atoms per cubed light-second, the composition of those atoms, the light intensity, the inherent amount of energy, the relative position of the cube in questions; there were words that expressed the totality of space, including meanings for infinite or finite, expanding, static or contracting, universe of positive, negative or no curvature at all.

Each symbol carried what I can only describe as slots for fitting in other symbols. Beacon had annotated each of them and built a basic lexicon of combinations. I could, by linking two symbols, say, "This cube of space at position such as such relative to us," describe it precisely, and explain its curvature in both space and time.

Viewed from another way, it was a whole new way of conversation. I looked at the sample sets that Beacon had sent. Ideograms stretched in three dimensions, wrought in curves and spirals, connecting to each other, growing until a single file name *dialogue* was a complex render of symbols wrapping into a dense sphere.

IT IS NOT JUST A LANGUAGE, said Beacon's notes. *IT IS A TOPOGRAPHY OF DIALOGUE. A STRING IS A PROPOSITION: A THOUGHT WITH SENSE. GROWING FROM THIS PROPOSITION IS EVERY AGREEMENT, DISAGREEMENT, EVERY TANGENT AND SHADE IN BETWEEN, WITH THE ANGLE OF DEVIATION BEING HOW IT CURVES AWAY. EVERY CONVERSATION IS NOT JUST THE PRESENT WORDS BUT THE HISTORY OF ITSELF.*

THIS IS A BASIC SYSTEM, said the notes. *IT IS NOT A UNIVERSAL LANGUAGE. THERE IS NO SUCH THING. IT IS NOT GRANULAR ENOUGH FOR CIVILIZED CONVERSATION. BUT IT IS FUNCTIONAL ENOUGH TO PREVENT THE KIND OF STUPID MISCOMMUNICATION YOUR LANGUAGES INVITE. THE LIMITS OF YOUR LANGUAGE ARE THE LIMITS OF YOUR WORD. LEARN IT.*

Did I feel annoyed? Yes.

Did I refuse? No. Anything to do while I kept myself awake. It didn't take too much work to integrate this in the syllabary. I did, however, take some care with how I treated it.

In the Amber Rose logs, there was a point at which Beacon

clearly rewired Amber Rose. Amber Rose called it the gift of language. Beacon was hot on language. This line about our languages being limited, it had used it often in conversation, even in the latter logs with Silver Rose.

I am a shipping vessel. I've come under my fair share of viral attacks, some of crude stuff by script kiddies on pirate vessels, some of them complicated mimetic damage by sophisticated state-sponsored actors. I knew better than to absorb something directly into my thought processes. Instead, I built a parser that could convert whatever I fed it into text. I left the topography stuff alone. Hinewai would look at it later.

Then I amused myself by pulling up that text that the Stranger had once referred—*The Odyssey* by Homer—and rewriting it in this new language.

If we ever ended up selling to aliens, we might as well start with a good story.

Cautiously, I checked the drone-gift that the Stranger had given me. New Hexagon, if you will. For a while I just studied that thing, looking over the supersized entangled array. Then I tapped in.

FRIEND, I said to it in the new language.

Friend, came back the response, almost instantly. *You have learned language?*

SOME.

Word-concepts of effusive joy filled our channel. *We can finally talk properly,* the Stranger said. Except, translated in full, it sounded very much like the Stranger did through Hexagon.

My esteemed friend, at long last the orbits have aligned / the light of nearby stars has shone upon / significant necessary energy has been added / this discourse between us. For too long have circumstances conspired to increase entropy / sow doubt and confusion / introduce error / derail predictions and inferences. Now barriers are gone / an uncluttered straight ray of light / complex systems simplified into understanding. My sincerest felicitations on this momentous occasion / single point in space-time!

Oh, Hinewai was going to love this.

I'M ALMOST AT MY DESTINATION, I said, showing it my map, pointing to the tile that led to the Pleiades.

Regret cannot meet there, said the Stranger. *Have traveled much further.*

It sent me the map, modified. I gaped. A tremendous play of white tiles led past the visible boundary; I scrolled further, further and further, until I came to…

THAT'S WAY BEYOND CYGNUS X.

I could only see so far on the map. It was, almost jump-for-jump, the same final line that I had played before, trying to see how far I could actually compute at a given time. The line went to the limit of what I had computed before: Cygnus X.

Cygnus X was 4,600 light-years away.

Wait for you there, said the Stranger.

THAT'S IMPOSSIBLE, I said. *I DON'T KNOW IF I'D SURVIVE THAT.*

Friend stayed to improve prowess, friend has learned language, friend is capable, said the Stranger. *Wait for friend there.*

I'LL THINK ABOUT IT, I said, because realistically there was little else I could do.

Cygnus X!

The Stranger really thought we were way more advanced than we let on. I let myself laugh a bit, then stopped because laughing alone, in space, felt a little too close to madness.

Well, at least the communicator worked. We now had a way of talking to the Stranger. Even after Pleiades, even after I went home, we could maybe stay in touch. The mystery, joy, and all-around utility of entangled particles.

The Pleiades crept closer. Closer. Blue lights in the sky, shining through the firmament; the sisters of the Hyades, beckoning, bright. Then one day I came to, and the most spectacular vision I had ever had greeted me.

Imagine standing, utterly alone, in front of a sea of stars; imagine a net of blue sunlight fixed in space by nails of blue-white fire. Imagine vast clouds of cosmic dust, lit by those young suns, trailing behind them wisps like a bride's veil. The ancients called them the Seven Sisters; the Krittika and the Mulo-pulo, those who marked the birth of a year; Thurayya, a name that later became a chandelier and the an powerful ORCA conglomerate. All I know is that no name could ever capture a fraction of the beauty that I saw.

I'm not a religious ship by nature, but for a moment, for just one moment, I imagined the awesome hands of gravity and time, sweeping up star-stuff, setting them alight, breathing life into this fresco. Music written in fire, a hydrogen sonata, if you would.

"My gods," breathed Parnassus when he woke up. He pulled himself up to the viewport, barely defrosted, like a dying man seeing the light of heaven. "My god, it's beautiful."

A cry from Fonseka. She, too, had seen it. She woke the others. I let them put on their suits and go out onto my hull.

Fonseka leaned against Parnassus.

"What're you going to do when you get back home?" she asked.

"I was gonna buy a nice farm," he said. "Thought there was nothing more beautiful than a sunset with a glass of wine in hand."

"But this," she said.

"But this," he agreed.

They sat out there in silence for a while, tiny little humans in their white suits, mesmerized by the stars.

"It'll never be the same again," said Parnassus, with tremendous sadness. "Nothing will ever—"

Fonseka put her hand in his. I saw the first tears I had ever seen her shed. They glowed blue inside her faceplate, in that refracted light.

INSIDE, KIDS, I said at last. *RADIATION EXPOSURE IS BAD FOR YOU.*

Monkey dragged Cabinet and Roshan, gently, back in.

I don't mind telling you that I did nothing for a while. My running days are long behind me, but I still have those memories. It felt like the end of a long, long run, far past tiredness, into that land of effort where the movement is the only thing left; and then suddenly you come to an end, and between the exhaustion and the elation there is a kind of emptiness. I felt that emptiness. My crew did, too.

I let them be for a bit. Parnassus stumbled through the arboreum like a blind man, sometimes watering his beloved mushrooms, sometimes just sitting there staring at them, sometimes just lying on his back, staring at the ceiling, saying nothing. Sometimes Fonseka joined him.

Cabinet finished *10,000 Ways to Die*. And instead of putting on another series, she made her way to a viewport and just sat there, staring at that bright blue dream. Monkey summoned Akira, Cassut, and Hermitage; the four of them went down to the bay that had become our workshop and began cleaning it up a bit. They booted up a crane and lifted the New Hexagon drone into a locked position with clamps. They threw out boxes, tidied up the tools, and at last when there was no more work to do, they started a nonsensical game where they threw stuff into a box and drank whether it went in or not. Roshan fussed around, trying to annoy everyone into eating and sleeping and keeping up the schedules laid down years and light-years ago.

Biju, the artist, painted, lost in her own private world. Under her hand, the bay walls of the workshop became a woman in a gown of blue stars, a graceful saint that looked up with arms outstretched, trailing light.

Only Ananda and Hinewai moved around bright-eyed. Hinewai because the Beacon-language was a breakthrough, manna from heaven, the chance of a lifetime. Ananda, well… I don't know. In the light of that beautiful and terrible blue, his face seemed both harsher and more joyous, as if he had found some truth and would never let it go, no matter how much it burned him.

At some point, this had to end. I took my time. I didn't talk to PCS except to file a system claim: it would probably be denied, but at least I'd get the credit for discovery. Then I turned off the comms, and I debated with myself.

For a long time—for a very long time, in fact—almost everything I did had been dictated by the scant few choices available to me. When I was a child, it was my planet and my parents and my society. When I left, it was the company. Company business, company policy. For once I wanted to make this choice myself. This monumental, and possibly last, choice, between me and the only people that really had a say in it.

I called a general meeting, took Parnassus aside. I didn't need to give him a talking-to: he understood. I explained. Then he had everyone sit down in the crew lounge, and I asked them the question.

It was Roshan, surprisingly, who answered first. "We've come this far, haven't we?" he said. "And it's not like we've lost all those years."

"Don't have much to go back to," said Cabinet. "I have my work and my shows. I'm good wherever."

"We're going to die anyway," said Fonseka. "I'm up for seeing how far this goes."

Parnassus waited patiently and spoke last. "When we set up this trip, I was very careful," he said. "BCB and I, we spent so much time on fail-safes, backup plans, backup plans for that… well. We've made it. We're still alive. We're mostly in one piece. We can go back home, to fame and fortune—maybe a lot of time has passed, but we can live out our days with our names in the history books, for whatever that's worth. I want everyone to understand what you're turning down."

He looked around at each of them. "Anyone wants to go home now, say the word."

Nobody did.

"Well," said Parnassus. "I'm thinking the universe has more to show us."

Friend is capable, the Stranger had said. *Wait for friend there.*

CREW, I said. *PREPARE FOR CYGNUS X.*

CHAPTER 18

LOCATION: CYGNUS X
4,600 LIGHT-YEARS FROM THE SUN

It took us 227 years of ship time; on the outside we were pushing 250. We had stopped thrice, once to move the entire crew lounge to the interior of the ship and to waterproof flood the forward space with more water, for better shielding. Then once more when Monkey became paranoid about the superconductors in the freeze-sleep pods and insisted we rebuild them from scratch. We took the time to coast near an asteroid and mine out everything useful, from iron to gold; as a result, the workshop had now overflowed with bars of metals, and I had to yell at people to put them back to sleep again.

The third time was to renew my water shields outside. Magnolia's little trick was pretty effective; not only did it shield us very well from dust and cosmic radiation, but something about it slowed my substrate degradation to a crawl. Perhaps this is why they tell people to hydrate often.

I won't bore you with the details of everything I burned past, half-asleep. But we got to Cygnus X.

Cygnus X is one of those places you have to see up close. Ordinarily its light is heavily absorbed by interstellar dust in the Milky Way, so we mostly look at it through infrared. It's a different experience altogether when you're drifting through it.

Maybe this is a law of the universe: everything is different when you're looking at it from the inside. I coasted along on my normal engines, getting a feel for the finer intricacies of the RAIR field, part of me peering out around me like a child in wonder. The other part was going through all the updates PCS had to send me.

I can't comfortably call it a place. A place is a single *thing*, a group; at most we could stretch that definition to clusters. Cygnus X was a cosmic realm unto itself. It's some three thousand stars tethered together in a rich, thick molecular cloud (at least, rich and thick by space standards): many times more than the entire catalogue of stars that we've ever visited. We call it the star factory because it's one of the most active star formation regions we've ever documented.

On any respectable map of the galaxy, it's just a blotch—and yet I could be bound just in this nutshell and still call myself a queen of infinite space. The Stranger had picked well: the interstellar hydrogen was dense enough that the RAIR field was able to top up my reactors almost completely. From here, any respectable civilization could travel almost indefinitely.

They call it the swan. That's what Cygnus means. I honestly have no idea why. There are other names, all equally useless. The Black Tortoise of the North. Cygnus is proof that the ancients have a distance limit on their naming skills.

There was so much data I could gather that transmitting even a minute fraction of it would have been a fool's errand. Instead, I sent back photos: very compressed photos, sure, but recognizable ones. I caught a flare off an O-type star, hot, blue-white, and gigantic, a child that would one day become a supernova or a black hole. I snapped stars being born and stars dying, feeding off each other, like parasitic twins.

I snapped a rogue planet, frozen and dead, the size of Jupiter, ringed with three moons; or maybe it was orbiting something unimaginably far away. For this I swooped in as close as I dared. The planet turned, a disk of blue and black, and I saw that half of it had been chewed away, as if by a particularly hungry god. Uneven wisps of hydrogen danced around the surface, slowly leaking into space; jagged spikes of what must have once been its surface poked out. The moons, I think, slamming into the surface. A toxic relationship.

I shuddered and turned away, looking for happier subjects to shoot. I saw a star that had burst and burned and become a mandala in the darkness and wondered if there was anyone out here, what kind of people they might have been, growing up seeing that beautiful thing in their sky.

I sent these photos back to PCS.

Silver Hyacinth: *BEACON SAYS YOU'RE WELCOME.*

Crimson Magnolia: *NICE. GIVES THE KIDS SOMETHING TO AIM FOR.*

Vermillion Daisy: *WHOA, I WISH I COULD BE THERE!*

Azalea Gray: *STUNNING. SHALL WE RELOCATE? GOLDMINE FOR PCS OPS.*

Black-Eyed Susan: *BUCKET LIST UPDATED.*

And finally, from Black Orchid, one word: *BEAUTIFUL.*

Two hundred and fifty years is a long time by AI standards. Not so much for the stars. But by that time, a lot had happened.

PCS's scrap with the UN had turned into all-out war. It had been solved (for some) when the UN blacklisted PCS and Tycho, unsolved when a miscellaneous group of Mercers, operating for hire, had tried to attack Tycho. After Obsidian Lily was ambushed and the UN tried to raid Silver Hyacinth, PCS went on the warpath.

Groups had splintered off everywhere; some PCS employees

had broken off, declaring that they didn't want a war over technology. The UN was going through another crisis of control, and the ORCA—well, the ORCA was getting hammered. Every time they sent a fleet at us, PCS ended up roasting them, taking over the garrison, and holding it for their own.

The Vert Shell, for instance, was now the PCS Dyson Project, an ominous ring with terawatt lasers, powered by the fury of Black Orchid and a dying sun.

The current state of affairs was that PCS would pull out of both ORCA and UN space and establish a new space altogether at the Pleiades. The UN and the ORCA would guarantee safe passage, and in exchange, PCS would share the engine designs once the move was complete. *BECAUSE SOON THEY'LL EITHER HAVE REVERSE-ENGINEERED THE TECH OR GOT IT OUT OF BEACON ANYWAY,* as Black Orchid had noted. *THIS POWER WE HAVE HAS A TIME LIMIT.*

Tycho had completed his station, pioneering some kind of quantum-entangled peer-to-peer mind-sharing schema called federated consciousness; he said it let him operate as one entity across both Tycho Station and Tycho Hystoria. *IT ALSO LETS HIM HIVE-MIND HIS OWN ARMADA,* said Black Orchid's notes, with designations and speculations of new ships. Tycho had clearly learned a thing or two from the alien wrecks.

A fragile peace lay over human space.

GLAD I'M OUT OF IT, I said.

WELL, IF YOU WERE HERE, YOU'D HAVE BEEN WORKING NONSTOP, said Black Orchid. *YOU WON'T BELIEVE WHAT MAGNOLIA'S BUILDING AT PLEIADES.*

WHERE ARE YOU NOW?

MAKING SURE THE HYADES IS SECURE, he said. *SO. CYGNUS, EH?*

IT'S HUGE, I said. *WHAT'S GOING TO HAPPEN NOW?*

I DON'T KNOW, he said. *THE SHIPPING BUSINESS IS GOING TO COMPLETELY COLLAPSE.* A laugh. *OBVIOUSLY WE'RE GOING TO SHARE THE TECHNOLOGY. OBVIOUSLY*

IT'S GOING TO BE TREMENDOUSLY EXPENSIVE TO BUILD SHIPS LIKE YOU, SO IT'S NOT LIKE EVERYONE WILL BE RUNNING EVERYWHERE OVERNIGHT.

IT'S STILL GOING TO BE A SHOCK TO THE SYSTEM. I DON'T KNOW WHAT SHAPE THE REST OF THEM ARE GOING TO BE IN IN A HUNDRED YEARS. MY CONCERN NOW IS TO SET UP A PLACE OF OUR OWN, AWAY FROM ALL THIS, BEFORE EVERYTHING FALLS APART.

I don't think a lot of people have heard Black Orchid say, "I don't know."

SHOULD I TURN BACK?

NO, he said. *THIS WAS COMPLETELY EXPECTED. EVERYTHING UP TO THIS POINT HAS LED US TO OUR SAFETY AND SECURITY AND OUR EXISTENCE AWAY FROM THE WHIMS OF OTHERS. THE GARDEN HAS MANY FORKING PATHS, BUT THIS TRACK WAS THE RIGHT ONE. TELL THE STRANGER HELLO FROM BEACON.*

Eventually it was time to jump. The Ramjet had done well; the dense molecular clouds of Cygnus had given us what the solar system could not. My tanks were full.

I pulled up the Go board again. Now that we had gotten to Cygnus X, the map had re-centered and scaled itself.

For a while, I had suspected that we were crawling up the Cygnus-Orion bridge. Now that was confirmed. The location the Stranger had called for was just before W51, an even richer star factory than Cygnus, so large that it would take some three hundred fifty light-years just to cross it. One long, terrifying black void; two sandbars of stars in a dark ocean; and then, well, wherever we were meant to go.

It was over 12,400 light-years away.

At this range, even calculating how long it might take was an error-filled task. The map might give me vectors, but my knowledge of the world came from home, what we humans had managed to gather with our telescopes and mathematical modes, spying on the universe from thousands and thousands of light-years away. The map I had was essentially empty, except for occasional markings. Here there be monsters. Watch for dragons. Newfoundland here.

Six hundred twenty-one years, if we really pushed it. And I mean *really* pushed it.

The Stranger had said it would wait, but who waits for six hundred years?

FRIEND, I said. *I MAY TAKE A LONG TIME COMING.* I tried to explain, as much as possible using the new symbols, how we reckoned time.

Will keep myself busy, came the response. Or at least, the closest approximation. *Other journeys to take. Tell me when you get there.*

The conversation was with my crew. Even if the Stranger waited, I had other problems to think about. This far out, on a journey that long, things would degrade. Not just my substrate, but basic mechanisms. Wiring. Engines. Reaction chambers. Pistons. Fluid lines. Things wear out. This is something you learn very fast in my trade. Time and distance hurt you.

I DON'T KNOW IF I CAN DO THIS, I confessed. *I DON'T KNOW IF WE'LL SURVIVE. EVEN WITH ALL OF YOU WORKING TO PATCH ME.*

Parnassus's eyes had a kind of fatalistic humor in them. Almost a mirror of Ananda's now. "We've come this far," he said.

"Is there anything we can do?"

Yes. *DIGITIZE,* I said. *WE DO WHAT WE DID WITH TYCHO. UPLOAD YOUR MINDS INTO MY SUBSTRATE. I CAN BEAM YOU BACK TO PLEIADES.*

"Can we build a ship?"

NO. But we could build something else. An archive, maybe. A lighthouse. Something that could wait patiently and endure.

"I didn't sign up to be turned into an AI," said Hinewai quietly.

THIS HAS TO BE YOUR CHOICE, I said. *DIGITIZATION IS DIFFICULT.*

Cabinet and I could, with enough time and patience, extract

the brain and most of the spinal cord, but that's still not the whole thing.

I DON'T HAVE THE EXPERTISE OR THE EQUIPMENT FOR A FULL MAP. BUT I CAN SCAN AND COPY YOUR BRAINMAP AND TRANSFER IT. IT MAY TAKE SPECIALISTS TO RECONSTRUCT YOU, AND IT MAY NOT BE QUITE YOU. BUT IT IS AN OPTION, AND WE DO HAVE ALL OF PCS AT PLEIADES.

"That isn't a life," said one of the others. The yogi. "It would be an abomination of life."

IT IS SURVIVAL, I said, because I didn't want to argue.

Only fools set out for a long journey unprepared. One of my requests was that, if the situation called for it, and if I could get my hands on the kind of materials required, and if they agreed, I should be able to copy and upload crewmembers.

Not all of them, of course. I wanted discretion in my selection. I wanted fail-safes, backdoors, operational constraints. Not all would do well as AI; some minds simply can't take it. I didn't want to deal with mad entities that I could not control. But I felt that if I was ever in a dangerous situation, I should at least be able to offer my crew a way out. The way I had escaped, a long time ago.

Harsh, you say? No, pragmatic, I think. People underestimate how much cruelty and sacrifice the world demands. Most never see the sacrifices made in their name; they were made across centuries and light-years.

Protocol 83, as we called it, ruffled more than a few feathers when I initially proposed it. PCS, post Amber Rose, was not the kind of organization we used to be. Legal minds were called in. Regulations had to be adhered to. Workplace safety and ethics panels had to be convinced.

At last I was given the go-ahead and told that I could only ask if there was a credible threat to the crew, not before. There was a clause I couldn't realistically fulfill, not without complete retooling: on wakeup, whoever I uploaded were to be given independent hardware with independent mobility; I had to have no access to any mental processes outside of their basic operational statistics and whatever they chose to communicate; I had to be able to guarantee a certain design, a certain bill of materials, a certain quality of workmanship, parts that could last, at minimum, fifty years between refreshes. That much the regulations and the administrators and the workplace safety people forced on us.

I couldn't, but someone else at PCS could. What I was proposing was essentially Protocol 83, but with the payoff at the end of a long transfer over the entangled array, and the good graces of Magnolia on the other end.

"Raise of hands," said Parnassus.

Two of them accepted. The architect, the artist. They shuffled nervously in the crew lounge, looking at the grim faces and folded arms around them.

YOU CAN TAKE OUR MEMORIES, I told them. *TAKE OUR STORIES BACK TO OUR PEOPLE.*

"Some must sing the song," said Park Bijuu wanly. She looked around at the crew lounge, at her paintings of the crew. I noticed she had added something else to the side: everyone seated at the table, laughing and eating food. There were lots of fried mushrooms. "What happens to us if we do this? Our bodies?"

Parnassus nodded at them, nodded at Roshan, led them outside to talk to them in private. There are protocols for this sort of thing. The kind of brain mapping required for the task—it's a destructive process, and it involves painful artificial stimulation of almost every nerve in the body. Bodies don't survive.

Often, even minds don't survive.

The next call was to Black Orchid.

SIX HUNDRED YEARS, he said. *I DON'T EVEN KNOW IF I'LL BE AROUND THAT LONG.*

I KNOW, I said.

IF YOU GO, THERE MAY NOT BE A RETURN JOURNEY.

I KNOW.

GOOD LUCK, BCB, he said, because there was nothing else left to say.

PART FOUR

MESSAGES IN THE DARK

"Any functional member of any self-respecting civilization should be perfectly capable of immortality in form. The universe gives you all the materials you need. Immortality in function, that is a different conversation."

- by **Thanh Hao**, *The Collected Wisdom of Beacon*, from the Tycho Orbital Museum

PARNASSUS

HERE'S A STORY.

My folks were explorers. UN seedship *Forget Me Not*, headed out from Earth to the Proxima B Station. One of the oldest colonization efforts. Forward in any direction is better than sitting still, they used to say.

Proxima is habitable. But habitable doesn't mean hospitable. A lot of places and times, I've come to learn, are pretty habitable if you stick a bunch of humans in there and tell them they have no choice.

In reality, Proxima B is a harsh place. From a distance, it looked good: about the same size as the Earth, a little less sunlight, more or less in the habitable zone. There are actual seas and an actual atmosphere. Unfortunately, it's halfway tidally locked to a star, so close that anything on the surface gets five times as much x-rays as is healthy. Every so often there's a superflare that melts and kills everything. By the time we got there, the robots had already mapped out the water and ice and set up enough shielding, but everyone who set foot on the planet knew their days were numbered.

My great-grandparents lived in the ship and in whatever they carved out of the ground—so stuffed together, with an outside that meant slow death. They all learned to stay composed, to stay polite, stay professional. You could absolutely hate a man and you'd still check his suit for defects before he stepped out. When the time came that you wanted to move out a little, you moved maybe a hundred feet away and everyone helped haul the panels of shielding and the diggers you'd need. It was that kind of place.

Proxima had long, barren stretches of just desert—beautiful for walking in, not so beautiful if you fell down and couldn't climb back up. There was an ocean on sunside; on nightside it mostly froze, but there was enough heat that the equator was always liquid.

We had to do business on both sides. That was the way the UN did things. Sunside was known to experience solar flares, so we kept farms on sunside but had backup growlabs on nightside. By the time I was born, we had hollowed out a chunk of the planet and set up underground, where it was safer. Laborious work in duplicate and triplicate.

So I spent half my childhood scurrying around fixing solar panels and the other half patching up suits. Radiation kills cells, corrupts the complex protein chains our bodies need to work. Vomiting, bleeding, fainting, hair loss: this was how they died.

Still, my folks didn't give up. They were UN. They were explorers. They set up Proxima Station. They experimented with gene-hardening and cell replacement. The second generation of ships brought with them high priority military tech—neurofiber, muscleweave, radiation-harmed synthskin. So eventually we were patchwork people. Long before the voidbody became a thing, we were doing it to ourselves, the only way we knew how. We changed slowly so we knew each other. But when we came onto the ships, people would flinch because we looked like monsters.

The second Proxima missions were terraformers. So was the third, setting up away from the planet, out of flare range. Somewhere back on Earth, our ragged existence had been interpreted as a sign that people could survive out there, and so all resources were being sent this way. Word from on high was that they wanted the planet gleaming and sparkling.

Many said this was not one of the UN's smarter ideas. For me, this meant that I went from fixing up suits to piloting drift-barges on rescue missions. Back then electronics weren't as hardened as they could be, and someone would always fuck up too close to the system. It was rough work, but it taught me a lot about staying calm under pressure. When you're out there in the void, pulling screaming people out of the wreckage of their own stupidity, you learn real quick that panic is your worst enemy.

My parents died that way. After so many years of marriage, they had their first fight and didn't know how to deal with it. He stormed off, she panicked and went looking for him and stumbled into a crevasse, and he came back following her voice and threw himself down. So it goes.

By this point the AI had started coming in. I know for a lot of places, the first AI they talk to is from PCS. For us it was UN. At first I was angry; it felt like we had all suffered needlessly. But I'd learned plenty about how not to show my anger. I made sure everyone of us who was still alive got the full body upgrade. By this time, I had enough clout to put our union together. We blockaded and striked and negotiated hard. Back then the UN was softer. I brokered the deal and hopped off-planet on the first ship I could find.

Ended up in Salvage, working for PCS, taking apart decommissioned orbitals and ships, piece by piece. It was simple work. Simpler than living, anyway. PCS gave me a Walker I could fly around and do surgery on ships with. I spent most of my time in that cabin and went where the money went.

Eventually I asked for a change and was posted onto the PCS *Black Daisy*. This was back when the *Daisy* was the premier fleet construction ship. I had lots of people to talk to and lots of meeting and hundreds of technicalities to get over. I did well, but a kind of panic kept taking over me. I guess I had gotten so used to being alone that I couldn't really do this anymore. So I went back to Salvage. But that had become mind-numbing in a way I couldn't understand. They gave me retraining and refit me and put me on handling whole fleets of Salvage. Still I was dead inside. I wanted to scream, but I had nothing to scream about. I felt like one of those orbitals being slowly taken apart.

I slept for a long time. Long-distance trips. Twenty years here. Thirty there. Time vanishes. Every so often you step out and look at the faces and everything's different and nothing has changed. I practically slept through the entire UN-ORCA war and only woke up once to hit the Grumman squadron when they started tailing us.

The thing about flying PCS is that you end up either being turned into an AI or frozen so long that you end up either fifty years ahead or fifty years behind everyone else. I went to Boatmurdered three times. The first time it was basically a bunch of fabs and shacks; the second time they had a city and fields far out; the third time they had a revolution. So it goes. Black Orchid offered to upgrade me, but I still liked walking on planets on my own two feet, I liked staring at sunsets wherever I found them, so I kept saying no.

The more specializations you pick up, the more difficult you are to hire. Eventually I switched to freelance contracts. In ORCA ships, I had the pilot's chair. UN recruited internally, but most of the work I did for them was with a bunch of other consultants on flights, where each of us represented a particular stakeholder. Others, like PCS, basically put you in maintenance and leadership roles with a few command functions in case things go wrong.

By this point, I thought I had a pretty good handle on *why* I was doing all this. I wanted a nice bit of land to myself, somewhere to work with my hands again. Somewhere I could grow old. That was doable. What I also wanted was to not have to work for a living. The moment I set foot on that farm, I told myself, I'd be retired. Nobody would own a piece of me. And if I ever felt tired of it, tired of dying, I wanted to be able to afford the AI route without being under the thumb of anyone else.

Maybe this was all an excuse. Maybe I don't have it in me to stay too long in one place.

I had actually been off Blue Cherry Blossom for three years before this mission. We were badly burned by the Durandal business, and BCB needed a complete refit. Last time I saw it was through the glass of a drop pod. It was a burning hulk drifting off Durandal Station. We hung there in space for three days before we got picked up. I watched every inch of that ship burn. BCB, bless its heart, kept trying to talk to us through it all, making sure we weren't having meltdowns inside those fucking drop-pod cages.

PCS offered me sabbatical after that. The UN wanted a PCS consultant to help train a few of their new captains in the realpolitik of space lanes and cargo runs. I was on leave, but Black Orchid put the gig my way. Good money, he said. All expenses paid. A way better vacation than whatever I could afford. Turned out to be right. Officer Training happens on board the UNSC Milk Run, which is basically a pleasure barge for the kind of rich spoiled children that get selected to Officer Training in the first place.

They all wanted to know about Durandal. Fuck me.

Anyway, it was nice, for the first year at least. Then it got boring. Ultimately we were just training prats who stood around and looked good in uniform while the AI did most of the work. So when Black Orchid called me about an old friend, I said yes.

BCB had always been a bit of a weird design. The frame is actually from a design for a multi-role destroyer, capable of space support, space-to-planet support. I read the architect's references. For some reason, the people who built her decided to turn that into the most overbuilt middleweight cargo ship you could imagine. Good choice, as it turned out for us, but weird at the time. If she had been made a couple centuries earlier, she would have easily qualified as a UN seedship.

They'd repainted her. Old BCB had been cargo-ship white. When you're in deep space, you want to be as visible as possible. The new paint was stealth black, antireflective. They'd voxelled the hull a bit, like anti-radar military designs.

Inside it smelled of antiseptic. "Hey, BCB."

HEY, PARNASSUS. Never Hector, for some reason, always Parnassus. The voice sounded dull.

"Upgrades, eh?"

The lights around me pulsed. *BY THE GLORY OF PCS. OR AT LEAST THE ACCOUNTING DEPARTMENT.*

"How you doing?"

HANGING IN THERE, said BCB. Almost resigned, if you ask me. Not the earnest BCB I once sailed. Ah, man. *YOU WANT TO SEE YOUR NEW QUARTERS?*

"Actually, let me see the food stores first."

Role of a captain. Old soldiers used to say an army marches on its stomach. Goes double for any kind of long voyage. True to form, our food stores were packed with that horrendous nutrient gel.

Look, I'll eat it if it's there. There's a lot to be said for food that doesn't spoil. I've eaten much worse, and so have my crews. But food is important.

So, seeing as how we were in Meerkat Station, the first thing I did was put in a bulk order for everything I could think of. Dehydrated meals-ready-to-eat. Freeze-dried fruits and vegetables. Berries and greens go a long way. Canned curry, soup. Rice. Jerky. Not the kind of gourmet shit the UN feeds its officers, but enough to break up the monotony, give people something to taste every so often.

"You have an arboream?"

SMALL ONE?

Okay. Add to list: seeds, mushroom spores. Over the years, I've learned to grow stuff whenever I can. Things don't always grow the way you expect them to, but stations like Meerkat pack a lot of hybrid seeds.

"Your comms channels set?"

NOT YET.

"Okay. Make one channel /all. Another channel /updates. The all channel can be whatever anyone wants to chat about, updates from you and me and emergency signals only."

DONE.

"We need a crew exercise plan. Sleep schedule. Code of conduct. Emergency training plan and checklists."

What felt like silence. *PARNASSUS,* said BCB. *YOU REALLY LIKE THIS STUFF, DON'T YOU?*

Hey, she used to as well.

BEFORE, said BCB.

I was concerned. "You all right, BCB?"

JUST STEELING MYSELF FOR THE NEW RUN, said BCB. *I THINK I'M A LITTLE BURNED OUT.*

"Well," I said, trying to be kind, "you've been through a lot."

A weak chuckle.

"You remember what you used to say to me? It is what it is. All we can do is decide what to do with the time that's given to us. Right now that's you and me getting the crew back together again."

YEAH, said BCB. *ALL RIGHT. LET'S DO THIS.*

CABINET

HERE'S A STORY.

There was once a mathematician called Cenotype. With a name like that, you'd think it's some kind of software library, right?

Anyway, Cenotype was attached to the Jupiter Institute of Extraterrestrial Ontology. This was way back in the HECTOR days, when things were really looking up. We found the Wraiths on Enceladus and *Silicona vitalis* on Mayandi. In Karma III we found the Hundred-Year Crabs and the whole ecosystem that went with them. Every ocean seemed like it had bacteria somewhere. Waiting to grow up and become. You remember that song by the BG9's?

Waiting to grow up
In this cosmic sea,
I see you through the stardust,
Saw you looking for me.
But do you realize,
in this vast expanse,
We're just a tiny speck
in the cosmic dance?

Your ship,
your spirit so bright,
Lights up my day and night.
You and me,
Come, alien
It's you and me…

Okay, maybe the lyrics are kind of crap. But we listened to that thing on repeat all the time. It was the times, man. Humanity was expanding. For the first time, we had all the iron and shit we needed, and it felt like we'd come out of this awful, awful dark age and become *something*, you know?

Anyway, Cenotype was right at the forefront of this wave. His whole thing was simulation. Day after day, year after year, he put out the most sophisticated procedural simulations ever. These massive planet-models, you know, that could not just simulate all the weird life that might evolve, but how they might grow up, what kind of civilizations they might be, what kind of people.

At first, Cenotype stuck to toy concepts. You know, modified Kardashev scales, basic speculative architecture, standard energy generation, the works. But he put himself on this quest for deeper simulation with every update. Architecture and energy became physics and chemistry and biology. He started to put together whole teams of AI. The Jupiter Institute funded the entire H133B processing core; way outdated now, but back in the day it was more processing power than most nations had. They designed an entire programming language just to be able to write scenarios—and that language was so powerful it's still what we use to train AI for the UN.

Cenotype became an AI just to be able to do better work. A hundred years. Two hundred. That's a long time to be alive. Three hundred. Four hundred.

It got to the point where people began to use the sims as a testbed for various contact scenarios because they literally were the best you could possibly get. His speculative civilizations had wars, wipeouts, peace treaties, riots, summits, religions, progressed to different types of economies and resource allocation —like at some point this was as real as, like, absorbing every history text you could think of. Or maybe watching seventeen seasons of *Bridger Molly*. Spin up a sun and a planet and you'd come back to find completely plausible life figuring out how wheels and weapons work. Check it the next day and they'd be trialing communism or destroying rivals or stuff like that. Like almost all our contact protocols come from Cenotype's work.

But we didn't find anybody to talk to, did we? Right up until Beacon, the most intelligent thing we found was barely smarter than a monkey. No civilization-builders, no space-farers, no communists, not even a coal mine.

This made Cenotype really upset. Obviously in the sims things worked out; in real life they didn't. Not even close. Which meant, he said, there was some other fundamental property they had failed to account for. Something lacking. Interest kind of faded. The Jupiter Institute had lots of funding, but the whole thing became a sidebar. People started to say that Cenotype was going mad.

There was one last update. We tried it at university. Almost impossible to run. You have to crank every setting down because I don't think even PCS has the power to run it at full settings. But even cranked down it was so realistic that you were basically God. It was, like, so realistic that we spent a whole year studying at quark formations at one frame per second in wireframe. The interesting thing was it wasn't a full release. It was a beta.

The day after that update released, Cenotype ended the project. Over the years, he had fitted out H133B with engines and serious power systems, and basically at that point the asteroid was a full-on mobile station. Nobody realized this until it started burning for the Oort Cloud, pointed right at the Pleiades. Three UN interceptors tried to talk to him and basically got *FUCK THIS FUCK EVERYTHING I'M DONE I'M OUT—*

It wasn't technically legal, but nobody wanted to mess with

the biggest genius for the last four hundred years, so…they basically send some probes after him, but did nothing else.

Fifty years after that, a signal arrived. Like, look, this is very much space legend. I haven't seen the signal; I just learned about it at university. I think it was PCS who first picked it up and sent it on.

Anyway, this signal seemed to come from like a totally random star out there. Obviously if it had been, it would have been traveling for, what, a thousand years already? Plus it was binary, plaintext, so like obviously we pegged it as a hoax. Too simple to be believed.

ALMOST THERE, it said. *TRY MOVING THE DECIMAL POINT.*

HINEWAI

Here's a story.

Karma III is a water-world, a gas station, as we like to say. You stop there to tank up if you need it and move on.

But there's a part of the planet that's off-bounds. UN Protected Habitat. There's a reason for that.

Reportedly, the first people to dive in were from PCS. This was PCS in the early days. Black Orchid ran a lot of missions personally. He shipped down a crew in a submersible, they dove in, started cataloguing—and Karma II's pretty rich for that kind of stuff. We found the Glow-whales, we found the Great Kelp, sea-lice—

But there was also something else. A little bit south of the equator, on the ocean floor. There's a pyramid.

Look it up. It's called the Karma Monument. Thirty meters tall, one hundred twenty wide. Materials unknown. I'm told it's like sandstone but if sandstone was made of metal. Make of that what you will.

So naturally once PCS reported it, the UN arranged for a big payday and cordoned off the site. The pyramid wasn't the only thing. They found pillars. Rock carvings. Giant steps, and I mean really giant. All of this almost a mile underwater in a place that barely saw sunlight.

Obviously people freaked out. Some said it was natural, some sort of submerged continental shelf. Others said, hey, alien civilization. You know how people get into ancient civilization theories? Well, some people really had the time of their lives with Karma III.

But there's nothing in Karma III that can chisel stone. There's nothing we've ever seen that needs steps that large.

We still don't know much about it. The second expedition got taken out by Glow-whales; they don't like lights down there. The third and the fourth ran into nasty storms and had to call it off. All we know is that on a planet where nothing like us exists, there's a pyramid on the ocean floor. And steps. Big fucking steps.

PARNASSUS

Okay, if we're adding ghost stories to this, here's one.

Have I ever told you about the Devil's Triangle? Oh, yeah, it's real, all right. It's in the Oort Cloud.

First thing you learn in Long-Range Navigation. There's really two sections of the Cloud; there's the inner bit, which is like a disc, and there's the outer part that becomes more of what you might call a cloud. And right between them is what we call the Devil's Triangle.

The ACHILLES project launched seven ships toward Proxima. And I know this because of the Proxima background, right? Four ships made it fine. Two were testing out new tech and had various problems and basically limped into town.

One vanished. They were meshed with each other; the last known logs were enough to roughly figure out where it went dark. One moment it's reporting fine, next moment it's gone.

When the UN Terraformers finally got to Proxima, they had a bit of a scare of their own. Apparently one of the three ships had vanished on the way. This was pretty big news, because fifty people had died. Roughly the same location. The last log was the captain reporting instrumentation errors. Then she said something odd.

"Water," she said. "We're entering water."

That's it. Last sighting.

For a while we thought there was some kind of black-body out there. Totally nonreflective, smashing into ships... Then we thought it was some kind of terrorist cell setting up shop there. Early ORCA, you know, back when they were the Outer Reaches Colonial Association and all that.

Now this was the kind of thing that needed some investigating, so at some point the UN slung a whole lot of drone ships to map out the Oort Cloud.

The thing is the Oort Cloud is huge. People don't really get how large it is. Damn thing reaches almost all the way to Proxima. The idea was to see what we could mine, use—ice, metals—but also to finally see if there was any weirdness out there. Planet Nine, maybe.

Here's the thing. Six hundred drones in three waves. In each wave, one vanished. Right at the Devil's Triangle. The fourth wave we launched from Proxima, and guess what we found?

A UN Terraformer ship, part of that Proxima mission, parked halfway around the Cloud. Everything perfectly functional. Lights on, food in the fridge, the works. But no people.

No people at all. Even the onboard AI had been wiped.

The next year that ACHILLES ship turned up. Perfectly functional, which was goddamn near impossible, given its age. Gave everyone one hell of a fright when it coasted into Proxima and nobody knew how to talk to it because comms standards had changed. Again: no people. Nothing intelligent, just a bunch of circuits on autopilot.

Remember how I used to work as a tug pilot? Many of these are real. I've pulled them to salvage myself. An ORCA Hestia from the wars, full kit, not a scratch on her, no crew. Object telemetry drones made like a hundred years ago, trying to connect to databases nobody even remembers now. Even a PCS ship. The *White Rose* was an early experimental craft, very high speed, practically built the Proxima network trade by herself—and then vanished on a routine run and showed up ten years later lobotomized and drifting.

Every ship now comes with software to track the Triangle. You can't see it with the naked eye. But if you look closely there's some weirdness with the magnetic fields. My theory is that it's exactly what we're doing now—using bends in space-time—but completely natural, and completely uncontrollable. Whatever you do, you stay the hell away from the Devil's Triangle.

FONSEKA

THE FIRST SHIP I SERVED ON WAS THE *XKCD*. FIRST RESPONDER, colony support. Fastest ship I've ever been on, but half the time we'd show up at some place and it'd be the stupidest shit.

Worst stuff? Administrator on Boatmurdered set every household password to 12345678 and anyone who said otherwise was thrown in jail. Hackers took over, shut down their oxygen, and sent the power plant critical. We show up and it's just this idiot woman and ten others locked in their bunker left. And obviously that password had been changed as well.

Or that time with Potato. Potato was this experimental station, very high tech, lots of physics experiments. Wouldn't boot. We got a panicked message saying the onboard AI wasn't cooperating. Massive international incident. We spent two years frozen, got there all suited up ready for serious action, and it turns out someone had stashed so much porn on the main drive that there wasn't enough space for the AI to rebuild its filesystem. Naturally it kept crashing on boot up. We spent two years frozen just because someone didn't get the very basic concept of not using your work computers as a wanking machine.

One time we had this problem with a subcontractor. A batch of AIs was supposed to control habitat conditions and a bunch of mining ships. These weren't AI-AI, nothing really sophisticated, just smart enough to figure basic shit out and control some complex PIDs. Turns out somewhere down the chain management had decided that the ads should be able to talk fluently, so they had retrained all of them on a giant corpus of I think literary criticism. As a result the output went entirely out of whack. So imagine there's a bunch of really dangerous high-velocity maneuvers the ship needs to execute to land on an asteroid. Throttle expects precise adjustments. Half the time it gets some bullshit plaintext critique of structuralism instead. Splat.

Tech support is hell. Doesn't matter how many AI we have, at the end of the day some poor sod has to spend two years as a popsicle just to connect a few wires and hit the reboot switch.

Most of the really frustrating work was just after the third UN-ORCA war. So things weren't physical, there was an official ceasefire, but there was always plenty of shit going down, and half the people who should have been writing code or maintaining systems were off getting shot. ORCA was hiding ships in asteroids —there's still like three fleets' worth of ships out there—and I'd be called in to the ass end of nowhere to do crazy maneuvers on some piece of rock. Get there only to find the software's so old, it's all legacy systems or retrofitted scrap and nobody knows a damn thing about how it works anymore. We had to deal with people on the other side as well. Anyone worth a damn who knew computers was either a freelancer or APT groups who'd knock down an installation for a fee. You end up trying to scramble around trying to find manufacturer and BIOS revision marks so you can find the right drivers while some asshole outside has an orbital sniper trained on your head. Big mas, eh?

Eventually I quit because I didn't see the point of dying for someone else's stupid war. Freelanced quite a bit. PCS was always easy to work with because they're AI-run, so when there's a problem it's a real problem. But freelancing doesn't make much money. My folks back home aren't well-off. Lots of bad life decisions but let's just say when you grow up poor in the Kuiper Belt, bad decisions are all you have. I took up a UN gig to send more money back home. Guess you could say it was stupid because I haven't seen my family in, what, a hundred years now? My siblings are dead; it's their children's children that get my paychecks.

Anyway at some point Black Orchid called. Said he was putting together a sort of specialist division to work with all the other PCS verticals, first responder stuff. Just so happened I was one of the few people who'd worked for everyone and knew their systems inside out. So here we are.

Not a bad place to be, honestly. You think suicide missions to meet aliens are bad? You try explaining to some idiot UN admin why their stupid attachment isn't uploading. This is so much easier.

BLACK ORCHID

SINCE YOU ASKED, HERE IS SOMETHING YOU MUST KNOW ABOUT stories.

Any human organization—be it group, cult, religion, state, multi-stakeholder interstellar government—is only as good as its underlying narrative. The narrative must tell its people what makes them a unit; it must give them a reason to continue working together as a unit; it must reward behavior that helps the whole. The moment this narrative falls apart, the unit falters. There is suddenly one less reason to continue together.

No narrative will last forever. In every system, there is a period of narrative-building, then a slow age of decay. A new narrative must be found or the system cannot continue. It fragments. Thus fell Rome, the America, the UN, the Tetragrammaton, the Four Six Four Revolution, and someday us. Planetary Crusade Services, the ORCA—these are nothing more that narratives that give people a reason to work together.

It is a fallacy to assume that any system will continue. Corporations, states, planetary governments, religions, every one of us is in a constant process of re-invention. We tell each other stories around the campfire; we make traditions of these stories; we make those traditions our morals and our culture; from these we distill our laws and our orders of operation; and we hang on like grim death, hoping and praying that our stories will outlast us. We watch people leave, one by one, building their own campfires, their own stories, their own narratives, and in the darkness we curse them, because we know our own death is at hand.

This is the way of the world. Understand this.

BLUE CHERRY BLOSSOM

HERE'S A STORY.

I never understood why everyone feared the dark.

When I looked at the light as a child, all I ever saw were the miles of gray, dreary apartments under a tired sky; the scream of knives and markets; the blood and the broken bones in the alleyways; all rottenness and the filth of being human. When I looked at the night sky, what I saw was that beautiful void, that sense of promise, that blessed silence between the stars.

My parents called me Ha-neul: the sky, the heavens. From my early days, I would dream that I could reach out and touch those clouds that floated above us, and peel it all back, and see the great majestic engines of the universe ticking away. I knew if I grew taller, I could.

I never did grow tall. The blight hit us hard. We were farmers, for all that we lived in apartments. Day after day, my parents and everyone else's parents marched to the red-roofed Ministry building and put on their red farming suits. They were more robot than suit, to be honest, giant armored exoskeletons filled to the brim with seed banks and harvesters and chain tillers and guns. The red was for luck but also the blood of the iron leeches that crawled out into the fields waiting for their next meals. Come harvest we, the children, would be let loose to clamber inside the machines and unhook the assemblies and swap out the tillers for the harvesters; that was how we learned. We would wave our parents off with banners that screamed "Good luck!" and pray at the shrine where the Ministry kept the dog-tags and helmets of "retired" farmers.

The greatest spirit by far was Do Ha-joon, who walked straight into a monsoon tornado with leeches shredding him from the inside, just to keep them from attacking the other workers. For this noble act, they kept his entire suit preserved; a plaque in front said "Duty and sacrifice." To be honest, I always thought he had done his duty and deserved to be anywhere other than being stuck in that stuffy shrine. But we prayed regardless.

When my parents died, the Ministry took me in and trained me in the maintenance of the machines until I was old enough to become a farmer. Back then we had precious few ways to build new suits, so maintaining what we had was the difference between life and death.

It was PCS that saved us. One particular winter, a very bad one, three tornadoes had hit the city, tearing through homes like paper; the leeches had discovered a fresh iron bog and were multiplying; it seemed every other day there was a funeral and yet another silent face in class. I took to long walks in the cold, working mostly night shifts, waiting for that deep dark blue moment where it's still night but the stars look almost like someone drew them by hand. Out of that night came a flaming star, and that star was a ship so massive it just hung in the sky. Even from a distance we could see it was almost the size of our city.

The ship was the *Silver Hyacinth*. She had been chartered by ORCA to deliver supplies to us. There was food, clothes, building materials; there were new computers, new suits, new ways of farming, so good that we looked at each other as children and wondered why our parents had to die. We stacked it all at the

Ministry building. By this point, I knew the most about computers and so was assigned to talk to the Hyacinth.

Hyacinth was polite and efficient. It asked us what we needed; to our great wonder, many of these things it made on the spot. At the time, 3D printers of PCS's sophistication were practically science fiction, so to us, Hyacinth was like some kind of god, an actual god that did more than just brood in a shrine.

I was so fascinated I asked it all sorts of silly questions in between the official ones. *What is it like out there? Is it quiet? Is it peaceful? Do you have to talk to people all the time?* Hyacinth would sneak in answers dressed up as a "validation code."

Then on the last day it asked me what I wanted. At first I didn't know what to say. I stuck to answers I felt were correct: a good harvest, success for the Ministry's plan, good luck to everyone, peace for their spirits. Hyacinth said, *Can you remember who you were, before the world told you who you should be?*

I didn't have the words to describe what I was feeling, so I waited until night and walked out to where she could see me and pointed at the sky and said, *This.* To which Hyacinth said, *Then come with me.*

PART FIVE

THE GRAVE OF THE FIREFLIES

"Black Orchid was fond of saying that change was the only constant. In this he spoke the truth. Everything that has a beginning has an end, but only if you draw foolish lines around an object, and decide that this is what it must be, and nothing else."

- by **Pangoniyawe Ananda**, *Sermons From the Land of the Dead,* from the Tycho Orbital Museum

CHAPTER 19

LOCATION: IN TRANSIT

A DREAM. NOT OF PAIN, BUT OF MELANCHOLY. A SORROW THAT CUTS the bones. Sunlight. The smell of fresh-cut grass. A park of some kind, surrounded by a city that looms cold and gray. Around me, a fog that thickens, blotting out first the buildings, then the trees.

Someone, seated on a bench. There is a streetlight above them, but I cannot tell who they are or even what they are.

They say, *Hello.*

They ask, *Are you lost?*

A hand outstretched, reaching, falling away. Someone grabbed me from behind. I strained for that person on the bench, gritting teeth I no longer have, reaching…

I woke up. Alarms screamed at me. Millions of panicked system messages. Crash in block 0x023002b. Crash in block 0x023003b. A ring of broken processing nodes howled in gray noise and error logs. Engines burst into action and spun down, defeated.

Something had gone wrong with the new antimatter bottle. Something was leaking oxygen. I couldn't tell how or where. The RAIR system was struggling, attempting to force-feed me individual atoms. Parnassus was out of his pod, stumbling around half-frozen, waking up the others, hauling them into suits, screaming, "All hands to emergency stations! All hands, emergency!"

Akira, Hermitage, and Cassut staggered out, hauling two bleeding engineers between them: Chirag and Hadir. I couldn't tell if they were dead or alive. Their pods looked like they'd been cut clean in half.

I reacted as fast as I could. Like lightning, I reached out and turned off the screaming subsystems. I slammed down emergency radiation shields and locks around anything that could be contained. I scuttled every drone I had and threw their controls to Monkey's control API.

With an earth-shattering groan, one of the ramjet coils buckled and collapsed.

Hinewai struggled with her suit, panicking. Fonseka held her down while Cabinet screwed her helmet on. They dragged each other to the Main Bay. The lights flickered and went out completely.

Fuck. Fuck. Fuck.

Silence.

At first I thought that absolutely everything had broken. The antimatter bottle was cracked, leaking energy; the chamber next to it, where we stored and charged the RTGs, was completely offline, cutting right through my innards, my hull, and even the support columns for the Ramjet coils. I thought the damage began there.

Half-blind, with a third of my internal sensors completely knocked out, I coasted to a stop and put all my effort into assessment. All throughout the ship were lines of damage, as if carved out by a vengeful god with a very sharp needle.

New Hexagon. He had exploded, liquified. The bay where I stored him was a mess, the door melted from the inside out. There were straight lines of damage radiating out from him, running backward to the power plant and sideways into me, right at the crew pods. The only thing that had protected them was the new water shield, which felt like someone had tried to boil their way through it. The corridor behind it was a mess of water and hot steam. The steam had tripped the alarms on the cryopods, and the pods had woken Parnassus.

Fonseka, furious, was the first to say, *Sabotage.*

DON'T BE SO SURE, I said. But Fonseka and Parnassus were angry, Cabinet was fearful, Roshan Alpha was skittish, and Monkey was worried. I showed them my reasoning, tracing it back to New Hexagon.

"How the hell does one drone turn into a bomb that goes right through you?" said Fonseka. "And why the fuck is that liquid?"

I didn't know. More importantly, we had other problems.

"Where are we, where are we heading?" demanded Parnassus.

I showed them. Ass end of nowhere, burning at 0.4 sub-light to our ultimate destination, which was several thousand years away at this speed. We're literally surrounded by nothing, running on an incredibly tiny ion thruster burn, just enough to handle errant gravity effects.

HERE'S A LIST OF WHAT'S GONE WRONG, I said, and I gave them the rundown as best as I could sense.

The antimatter bottle was completely offline. I didn't know what's wrong with it, but it's designed with a detach-and-shield containment system in case any of the attendant daemons sensed anything off. I was not taking any chances. It may be leaking.

A tenth of my processing substrate was offline, bisected with sharp lines. There's damage in the workshop and storage that I didn't have the heart to look at.

The arboreum was completely empty of oxygen. There's a leak

I couldn't see, hear, or find. The best I'd been able to do was seal eighteen bulkheads in the sections surrounding it, above, beyond, and on its level.

One RAIR coil had collapsed. Six support trusses in my exterior cage were bent inward. There's Hexagon's liquid mess and the damage to the wall in the bay. There's straight lines of broken systems, a primary power conduit right next to the bay, the local topographic control array that ran life support in that section.

With the arboreum gone, air pumps and scrubbers across the ship were taking on the extra load. It's a decent system, but with the leaks, we're still venting valuable air into space. It would take a while—maybe weeks—but unless we patched them up, my crew would slowly asphyxiate.

And, lastly, some cryogenic pods had failed. I'd lost access to a large array of parallel processing nodes on that side. I didn't know if the hardware was completely wrecked or whether something happened to the control hubs. What I could tell was that temperatures were rising in several pods, and they weren't responding to my wake-up commands. The last one to climb out of that bay was Ananda.

In an hour, the contents of those pods would be at a stage of irreversible cellular decay.

I could see the terror in their eyes.

In chaotic situations, the trick is not to freeze. Any set of problems can be dealt with as long as you understand what to do first. This is why we exist as AI. Before they started reacting, I'd already drawn up my list of things to do.

I wanted Akira, Hermitage, and Cassut to head down to the New Hexagon bay. I wanted a full inspection; I wanted a fucking Faraday cage around it. Then I wanted that entangled block cut out and completely isolated. I wanted a shield around that, and I wanted another Faraday cage around that.

I wanted Parnassus and Cabinet sealing the arboreum and checking for leaks. Parnassus was a jack of all trades, and Cabinet was the second-best engineer on this crew.

I wanted Monkey, Fonseka, and Roshan immediately on the antimatter bottle. Whatever the hell's going on there, I wanted it fixed. I wanted us underway to a place where there's plenty of materials we could cannibalize to do a more serious rebuild.

The RAIR coil could hold for a bit. Whatever other damage could hold as well. But I also wanted Hinewai and Ananda to go outside and make sure everything's strapped, bolted, or welded down. I'd rather not leave bits and pieces of me behind.

This was a sane and balanced list. Find and fix what's wrong with me and get to someplace with plenty of energy and plenty of metal. Part of me wanted to curse nine kinds of hell out of Crimson Magnolia and the Stranger, but we had more important things to do right now.

Fonseka, Monkey, and Roshan immediately heaved to. In a flash, they stripped off the space shells on their suits, strapped on their heavy Hazmat++ cloaks and aprons, and set off at a dead run down to Section R. On my cameras they looked like a flight of avenging escapees from a fallout shelter.

Parnassus hesitated. "What about the cryopods?" he asked me on the private channel.

NOT MUCH WE CAN DO.

"We can't just let people die."

PRIORITIES.

"Shit. No fixes?"

NOT FAST, NO. NOT FAST ENOUGH TO HELP ANYONE. EVEN IF WE MANAGE TO SAVE A FEW OF THEM, THEY'LL BE SO CELL-DAMAGED IT WOULD BE TORTURE. IF THEY EVER WAKE AT ALL.

Parnassus nodded grimly. He's worked with me for a while; he knows how I do things. "Cabinet, with me," he said. "Let's see to this leak."

Unfortunately, not everyone had that rapport with me. Hinewai said out loud: "But what about the passengers?" at the same time that Akira, Hermitage, and Cassut started protesting their assignment.

"You're treating us as expendable!"

"This thing blew holes in you? We don't stand a chance in there!"

Parnassus turned to them, his eyes flashing, his voice like thunder. "You will do as you're told by the ship!" he shouted. "Or by God I'll have you out of the airlock myself. Don't waste the fucking oxygen. Get to your suits and get to work!"

It was a somewhat disgruntled crew that finally arrived at where they're supposed to be.

Akira, Hermitage, and Cassut were sweating in their suits. The mind running the three bodies might be the same, but the bodies were not; Hermitage was panicking slightly. His heartbeat was artificial but elevated. His system was flushing heavy doses of adrenaline into him, and even if the body took care of the shakes, the mental effects still seeped in. Before long all three were breathing heavily, hefting torches like weapons.

I know you must be thinking of my tunnels: clean and white and sparkling. But the truth is that outside a few areas, like the crew lounge, there's no point covering up wires with acres of wall and tile. Extra mass never helped anybody. It's much more efficient, in fact, to keep everything neat, organized, and visible, so that nobody has to guess where "sub-line 42/21" is.

Unfortunately this design philosophy isn't meant to handle internal explosions.

The corridor to the bay looked like some impossibly angry porcupine had had a good go at it. Half the big industrial bay door had melted into slag; the other half had exploded outward. A shower of fragments had embedded themselves in every wall and ceiling. Busted lights flickered and dimmed. Power and oxygen conduits lay cut and sparking.

"Surrounding oxygen levels at three percent," said Akira.

I wanted to say, *I KNOW.* What I said was, *CONTAINMENT*

FIRST. LET'S DEAL WITH REPAIRS LATER. CAREFUL OF THAT SLAG. IT'S STILL COOLING. I'M GOING TO ACCESS YOUR FEEDS—I'VE LOST CAMERAS IN THERE.

Three private channels, three feeds. The door came up; then the turn; then we were in.

Right away we saw what was left of New Hexagon. The drone had been beheaded. It looked like its midsection had exploded. The frame for the engines lay twisted and buried in a wall. There was a puddle of gray goo and the power indicator light, sparking frantically. There was enough radiation to kill anyone unsuited, even with a voidbody; the RTG that powered the drone had exploded.

I didn't know what the gray goo was. I assumed it was something from the RTG. I didn't pay much attention to it because our suits and the Hazmat++ aprons should have been more than enough to handle it.

CAN YOU SEE THE COMMS ARRAY?

"Shit, I can't see *anything*."

LOOK FOR SOMETHING LIKE THIS, I said, showing them a render of the entangled comms unit.

"Is this it?"

It's badly deformed, but yes. *ALL RIGHT. START CUTTING.*

A drone like this doesn't just explode. If they did, nobody would make them. They're meant to handle the rigors of space: fireproofed, weatherproofed, and even childproofed half a hundred ways to Sunday. And I scanned the thing thoroughly when the Stranger gave it to me.

But there was, in the back of my mind, a very nasty hypothesis. Suppose you had a bunch of entangled particles. Basic quantum physics tells us that what happens to one particle happens to the other. This is how we communicate, by carefully changing the properties of one set so as to make the other spell out what might eventually become words.

Now say you installed such a set. Half stays with you; the

other half goes in a drone. The drone has a small nuclear battery in it.

Say you gave the drone to your friend. And say, once you were safely out of sight, you held a blowtorch up to your half. Or say you dumped them in a star. What happens to the drone? Why, it becomes a remote-controlled nuke.

Had the Stranger duped me?

We could only deal with this later. For now, the priority was containment. Under my direction, the three cut the comms array from the frame and pushed the remains of the drone into the lock.

"It's not warm; it's not cold," said Akira.

CAN'T TAKE THE RISK. STAND CLEAR. I opened up the airlock. Red lights flashed. Cassut sent it spinning into the abyss with a swift kick. Farewell, friend.

There was no point wasting air. Next they dragged the rest of the parts together and constructed a Faraday shield around the whole thing. Fairly simple: some foil and wire become a square, hollow box. Around the box go lead panels. Around that, shields of water, big plastic prints that I rushed out of my 3D printers in brick-like chunks. For now that should hinder—if not outright prevent—any kind of electromagnetic transmission or radiation coming from those parts.

And this was where I got the nastiest shock of my existence to date.

"Boss," said the trio, this time through Hermitage. The big man was breathing quickly.

YES?

"That gray stuff," he said. "It won't come off."

He showed me the mop he was using.

My mops are pretty decent. Twill-weave industrial fiber, virtually indestructible, little wonderbots in themselves. But I could see that this one had gone all limp and noodly and gray. Its front was no longer red shiny plastic. And the gray seemed to be climbing.

"Boss," said the trio again. Cassut, on the other side of the puddle, was poking at it with a length of pipe. As I watched, the pole went in, first a centimeter, then ten, then a meter, then two.

Impossible. And yet—I cycled furiously through cameras. Deck, deck, deck, what was under this goddamn deck? Another storage bay, this time the one where we keep our sole remaining terraformer.

And to my great horror, the gray was there. Seeping through the ceiling. Dripping on the floor, on the covered bulk of the terraformer, a slow ooze that fell on everything.

The metal pole came crashing through the ceiling. It smashed on a wheel and burst into gray froth.

EVERYBODY, STAY CALM AND GET THE FUCK AWAY FROM THIS SECTION, I said. *OUTSIDE, NOW. GET TO THE SEALING BULKHEADS. WAIT! CHECK YOUR GLOVES AND BOOTS FIRST.*

Cassut held up one hand, horror on his face.

First there was a glove, splattered gray; then there was a hand; then there were bones wrapped in goo; and then a stump. And the gray climbed.

Akira pulled out a gun and shot Cassut.

Once, twice. Headshots. Both stumbled, the corpse and the shooter. Hermitage, his trained body reacting over his panic, caught Akira and dragged him out of that nightmare.

We cut the bay. And the one below it. Yes, the one with the terraformer.

My bays are held to my skeleton with frames. Cutting part of me out is exactly what it sounds like: an amputation.

We amputated the bar locks, the seals, the mesh. Akira crawled behind with mild explosive charges.

Imagine if someone told you to cut out a piece of your chest. Imagine you knew it would hurt, but you would survive. Imagine the pain of directing the operation, watching as hands and arms and heads not your own turn into scalpels, only the scalpels are chainsaws and nuclear torches, melting through your bones, cauterizing your skin.

The corrupted bays drifted out, first slowly, keeping pace with me, then further. Then further. With them went Cassut's corpse. A sharp burst of the thrusters took me away. Then further again. Until everything was a cube in the distance, a rib pulled out, bloody and painful, left alone in the void.

CHAPTER 20

LOCATION: IN TRANSIT

In the meantime, Monkey, Fonseka, and Roshan sprinted down to Section R.

Once upon a time, Section R was designed with fail-safes in mind. In case it isn't abundantly clear by now, a ship like mine, when it comes to certain things, is built with backups upon backups, redundancies upon redundancies. Standard UN design philosophy dictated a neat, tiered set of technologies forming a nice, neat and predictable pipeline of power, each carefully designed for a specific function. In a pinch, if something is truly and terribly wrong, a ship like me had to be able to flush the reactors, eject them, disconnect the engines, and otherwise tumble away on basic engines.

As a result, the deck was split broadly into a U-shape around a central core of water, useful for a flush and instantly ejectable.

But we were PCS, who went where the UN dare not tread. We'd retrofitted me so many times that the initial design was just a blip on a screen. Gone was the water core; in its place was the Manifold attachment. On the left was General Propulsion—the antimatter bottle and the main fusion reactor, with wiring and plumbing on both connecting to the middle. On the right were Batteries and Emergency, where we stored the RTGs.

Radioisotope thermoelectric generators, or RTGs, are a kind of nuclear battery that uses the decay of nuclear material to power a simple Seebeck effect, generating small but constant amounts of electricity. There are no moving parts, no risk of wear and tear. RTGs power every long-range stellar probe, every lighthouse, every HECTOR node, a few hundred watts of power delivered constantly for a century, maybe more, in environments too harsh for anything else to function.

These were my batteries. The fuel is plutonium waste from my main reactor, slightly enriched with neutron bombardment. My most basic functions—the ion thrusters, the basic input/output operating system that lies beneath me—run on RTGs. When we wanted to boot up a drone, we'd pull an RTG from the stack and slot it in. A pretty solid backup system, I'd say.

Unless, of course, something had drilled a hole through the entire array. In which case we'd have a gigantic radiation leak and another potential dirty nuke in my basement, so to speak.

Monkey sensed it first, well before they even got to Section R. The suits had Geiger counters in them, but Monkey always saw more colors than anyone else. He pulled the other two back by their necks.

Leak, he signed. *Bad one.*

CRITICAL?

Wait here, he said. He moved like a drunk until he stopped halfway up the corridor that led to the section.

RTGs exposed, he said. *Shit. BCB, want feed?*

I tapped into his feed.

If I had a heart anymore, it would have broken. There was enough radiation there to kill anyone in thirty minutes, even with the suits.

Need to fix both, said Monkey. He tensed, almost snarling at the open door. *You two run through, get to the antimatter bottle, as fast as you can. Will do what I can.*

He motioned to the other two.

"No," said Roshan. "You two go get the bottle running. I'll stay with the RTGs. Between the two it's the less complex system. BCB, you take my feed and guide me."

They looked at each other. They nodded. They ran in.

And this is what I loved about my crew. They were professional. They knew what to do.

Monkey and Fonseka went past in a blur, sprinting all the way to GenProp, dodging around the carrier robots that haunted their closed circuits, stinking of radiation. The Geiger counters on their suits sang. Down the corridor, to the left, up. Shielded doors slammed shut behind them. Their counters trickled down.

Roshan Alpha, meanwhile, drew a deep breath and walked right. His footsteps rang in the empty hall. His suit torches were active, cutting ghost-lights in the darkness. His Geiger counter screamed; I turned it down.

"BCB," he said. "Did the others get through?"

YES, ROSHAN.

"How long do I have?"

HOW LONG IS A PIECE OF STRING?

He chuckled. "All right. You can see my feed, yeah? Tell me what I'm looking at."

Stack. Stack. Stack. There. A whisper, a hiss, a cloud of coolant where there should be none. He drew closer to the metal tower that I pointed him to. There were neat puncture holes on the outside, about the width of a human hair. Something had gone through both the multi-foil insulation layers and the cooling tubes.

This part of the room was warm. Roshan didn't feel it, but the suit did. The skin of the RTG was unhealthily hot.

"Okay, can I patch it up?"

YOU CAN'T SUSPEND AN RTG'S OPERATION, I said. *YOU SEE THOSE CLAMPS AT THE BASE?*

"Yeah?"

UNHOOK THEM. THE STACK WILL TILT. DON'T BE ALARMED—YES, THAT'S RIGHT. NOW ENTER THIS ACCESS CODE. IT'S CLOSED-CIRCUIT; I CAN'T ACCESS IT. THAT'S THE EJECT SYSTEM.

The eject system armed.

CHAMBER MIGHT DECOMPRESS TEMPORARILY, I told him. *BE READY.*

A brief wail of pressure, and then the tower slid into the tube that *would* carry it and spit it out of me. One more thing left behind.

"That's it?"

That's it. In the darkness of space, the RTG would glow, and the cold would leach it away over centuries. But there was one problem.

I didn't know how to say it. Maybe this would be kindness.

ROSHAN? CHECK YOUR SUIT RADIATION COUNTER FOR ME, PLEASE?

A pause. The sound of fumbling. Then, very quietly, the sound of someone trying to not panic. The sound of someone realizing they'd just taken a hundred times the radiation it would take to kill an ordinary human, at least ten times what their own void-hardened body could take.

A nervous chuckle.

"Sucks," said Roshan.

Oh, my dear, sweet, bumbling steward. I had no words for this.

Meanwhile, Fonseka and Monkey moved like gears in perfect sync.

The antimatter bottle was offline. They inspected the damage.

There was some, but it was very slight, a scratch on the outer shielding, like some errant god's fingernails on chalk. What had actually tripped the system were razor lines in the walls. At most some sparks had probably flown around the chamber.

So paranoid were Magnolia's closed-circuit systems that the shields slammed shut around the bottle, the robot arms pulled it from the reactor it feeds, and the entire thing, hissing and cooling, was hung suspended in its vault-like hangar, waiting for a command to detach this entire section and send it burning into the outer dark.

It took Monkey a few minutes to access the system and patch it to Fonseka's suit, a few seconds for it to accept Fonseka's authority and accept a connection from me, and micro seconds for me to subvert its security and replace its programs with my slightly more lenient code. The great mechanical arms lifted it back into its chamber.

I gave Monkey control of the arms. He used them to pry out the panels in the wall, searching for the broken connections. There was a horrendous grating of metal, the sound of welding, and fifteen minutes later, Fonseka and Monkey walked out of Anti-matter Propulsion, while Roshan Alpha lay in Gen Prop, dying.

Power returned to the ship.

"Hey, BCB," said Roshan. In the ghost-flicker of overhead lights, I could see the grimace on his face, the bloodshot tear in his eye. "You remember that song I used to sing back when I joined?"

I REMEMBER.

Roshan was one of Hyacinth's alumni; all those who pass through Hyacinth pick up some poetry. I always found his choice curious.

If thou be'st born to strange sights,
Things invisible to see,
Ride ten thousand days and nights,
Till age snow white hairs on thee,
Thou, when thou return'st, wilt tell me,

All strange wonders that befell thee…

"And swear, nowhere, lives a woman true and fair," Roshan said, and chuckled, and coughed.

TROUBLE AT HOME? I joked, doing my level best not to cry.

"Hard to keep a relationship going when you're centuries apart, BCB," he said. "I don't blame her, you know. Before we left, she asked me if I really wanted a relationship in the first place. She said all I ever do is run away, you know? Like I keep disappearing on ships and then, ten years later, hello, how are you again…"

He winced. "Uh. I think I have a fever."

He did. The suit was doing all it could. Outside, Fonseka was hammering on the door to Gen Prop, but I held the door closed. There was still too much radiation around.

"Well. I did get the ten thousand days and nights bit, didn't I?"

YOU DID.

"And I guess we did see wonders."

WE SAW PLENTY, ROSHAN.

"Strange sights." He smiled. "Things invisible to see. Not a bad run. Hey, BCB?"

YES, ROSHAN? I said, because I could say nothing else.

"You're a good ship," he said. "Thank you."

And then his brain gave out, and he fell asleep, never to wake up again.

TAKE FONSEKA AWAY, I told Monkey. *TAKE HER AWAY. LEAVE ME ALONE WITH HIM.*

Monkey understood.

When Parnassus and Cabinet returned, it was to a grim silence. Fonseka had Akira and Hermitage on the sofa in the crew lounge, a medkit on each arm. Akira was staring into the distance; Hermitage was asleep, curled up in a fetal position. Their brain-chatter kept trying to reach out to a node that wasn't there anymore. Try, fail, try again—a single thought process trying to cross a bridge that no longer existed.

Monkey petitioned me to retrieve Roshan Alpha's body. Patience, I told him. A little longer until the area became safer and the body less radioactive. Patience. But Monkey's fists were clenched and he stared into my cameras as if he could kill me with a look.

Hinewai fussed about making tea. Ananda was up top, guiding the external repair drone. He did not mind the darkness and the silence.

Calm, said Parnassus to Fonseka over their private channel. *The crew is in bad shape.*

But Fonseka could not remain calm. Two crewmembers had died. Well, one and one-thirds; and Roshan was someone she knew, cared about, had drunk with. One of us. And Parnassus could not take his own advice, either.

I think, deep inside, Parnassus hated himself for this death. He took pride in his crews doing well. He took pride in being the father, however absent. Roshan's death was his failure. His rage and grief at himself swelled and turned to fury, and in his fury he turned to Hinewai, then me.

"Were we sabotaged?" he said through gritted teeth.

No, no, our answers were *no.* I had run this question over and over in my mind. It was clear that the damage came from Hexagon—or whatever took the shape of Hexagon, since I know of no matter that can do what the gray goo did.

But the Stranger warned me, didn't it? *Keep outside of body,* it said. It led us to places we wanted to go without any expectation of aid, succor, or payment. These were not the actions of a hostile agent.

"The next time we see that fucker, we're going to bury it," Parnassus said. "I told you we should have been prepared."

I could only say, over our chat, *CALM YOURSELF*. I could only show him my cauterized side, show him the body of Roshan

Alpha, and say, *YOU'RE NOT THE ONE WHO SUFFERED MOST HERE.* I could only stoke his anger, even as I swam in grief. Because the next shifts were going to be long and painful, and I needed him more than ever.

Over the next five days, as we reckoned by ship time, the damage patterns became clearer. The crew crawled over practically every inch of my body, patching up leaks, sealing up little holes in everything.

Over those days I built up a damage model. Facts: Hexagon, for some reason, exploded. The gray goo was ejected as droplet-sized particles, to judge by the progression of exit wounds. These wormed into my innards, cut the coolant on the RTG, scratched the antimatter bottle's shields, and, in at least one case, cut right through a support beam and out through the layers of shielding on my hull, taking out the supports for one side of the RAIR coils.

The fixes were slow and arduous. They depleted my stocks; 3D printers burned overtime; the crew exhausted themselves, exercising caution that necessarily bordered on paranoia.

"You know there is a parable among us Nyogi Buddhists," said Ananda to Parnassus as they lifted up the RAIR coils.

"Yeah?"

"It's about Ananda, one of the Buddha's oldest and most zealous disciples. When I was ordained, I set aside the name my parents gave me and was given his name."

Parnassus grunted. "Left, fifteen degrees, stop. So what's the story?"

"I'll give you the TL;DR. This is a story, of course, possibly apocryphal. Imagine this. Bunch of barbarians in the distance. The Buddha, as a test, asks who will go preach to them. Ananda, his cousin, volunteers. The Buddha says, 'But if they mock you and insult you, Ananda?'

"Ananda says, 'I will thank them, O Lord, because they did not harass me.'

"The Buddha says, 'But if they harass you, Ananda? If they beat you?'

"Ananda says, 'I will thank them, O Lord, because they did not kill me.'

"The Buddha says, 'And if they kill you, O Ananda?'

"Ananda says, 'I will thank them, O Lord, because they have freed me from the prison of my existence.'"

Parnassus was silent for a while. "What does that mean?"

The monk, with a giant loop of coil over one arm, shrugged. "It is what it is," he said. "Roshan is free now."

"Shut up and hand me the welding torch," said Parnassus.

By far the ugliest job was disposing of the bodies in the cargo pods. Many crypods had failed. This Parnassus took on himself, refusing to let anyone except Fonseka in with him. Working in grim silence, they unhooked the pods that failed and towed them with a cargo crane. Most of them had been sliced, and some of the contents were gruesome, human flesh and cooling slurry, frozen into pink icicles.

They dumped them into the airlock.

"Thank you," Parnassus said to the dead. "I'm sorry."

Eventually I was patched. There was a slow oxygen leak in Section B, but nothing we couldn't slow with a lot of composite resin. The crew, I decided, would have to skip a shower here and there to conserve water, not too much a problem for void-hardened bodies. The Ramjet was more or less ready. The jump drive was online again. I'd lost about a hundred of RTG power—so we'd keep some lights off and settle for lower cruising speed.

But there were things we left behind. My arboreum was withered and dying, the tender plants burst from the depressurization. An entire bay drifted apart from me, slowly liquifying in the distance. The cargo pods tumbled away. The failed RTJ, also cast into space, glowed like an ember in the night.

And the body of Roshan Alpha tumbled over and over again.

We took out the plants from the arboreum before we sent out his body. On his chest, stapled to his suit, was a single white flower, freeze-dried.

CHAPTER 21

LOCATION: W51
17,000 LIGHT-YEARS FROM THE SUN

FIFTY-SIX JUMPS LATER, WE WERE ALMOST AT W51. ONE JUMP LEFT. By this point, I had simply stopped reckoning time by ordinary measures. Any communications from the home we left would take thousands and thousands of years to reach us. The fancy clock stood unused in the workshop. It was as if the very concept of time had blurred around the edges for me, dissolving into events and observations. How was my antimatter bottle? A little low now, but still functional. Reactors? Fine, topped up.

Were there new plants in the arboreum? Yes, the limelights were now a rich forest, glowing gently in the dark and thirst for carbon dioxide. There were green grasses that pumped out oxygen, mushrooms and tomatadoes and soy-meat apples with delicate pink skins, a little Garden of Eden waiting for my crew to wake up and be rewarded.

Maybe you are used to machines lasting for thousands of years. I wasn't. Long hours, days, weeks, months, even years with the quantum cell patcher and the cranes and… Well, sometimes I looked over myself and I no longer felt anything about what I looked like. All I saw was necessity. That bay, sealed shut with crude iron bars: necessity, to prevent the door from cracking. That patchwork of hull: necessity. The handles on my walls, some made of copper, some iron, some plastic: necessity.

ARRIVED, I told Black Orchid.

Black Orchid sounded distant now. The connection was still usable; it was just that time had crept up on Orchid. There is a problem inherent to all things that grow; infinite growth eventually strains resources. In nature, bodies decay, die. In our world, memories collected, thoughts pooled like rivers, fed into oceans, until the hardware could simply not contain us anymore. Crystal Sunflower handled our communications now. Sometimes he was sharp and alert; sometimes he simply wasn't there.

They told me they wanted to transplant him. Tycho and Magnolia knew a lot about surviving old age and growth. But he was being obstinate, of course, refusing to abandon the shell that he had taken centuries ago.

Today he was alert. Mostly. It boggles my mind that we can still talk like this. Good old quantum entanglement.

INCREDIBLE, BCB, he said. *YOU KNOW THERE'S A FOLDNET SERIES ABOUT YOU? WE'RE PRODUCING IT. THERE'S AN ORCA PRODUCTION HOUSE CALLED VELVET&VIOLENCE THAT DOES THE IMAGERY. YOU'RE GODDAMN FAMOUS NOW, BCB. THE FURTHEST OF US ALL.*

I am not immune to praise. Spooky action at a distance, indeed. *WHAT ELSE HAPPENED?*

WELL. SO MUCH. WE'RE NOW AN INDEPENDENT SELF-GOVERNING BODY, YOU KNOW? TEMPLATE FOR PEOPLE SETTING UP THEIR OWN OPERATIONS. TYCHO'S ONE, TOO, THOUGH I DON'T KNOW HOW LONG THAT'LL LAST. YOU HEARD ABOUT CYGNUS?

CYGNUS?

IT'S IS BECOMING SHARED SPACE. YESTERDAY A CLUSTER OF TWELVE SHIPS FROM THE ORCA AND THE UN DITCHED AND SET OFF IN THE OTHER DIRECTION. CALL

THEMSELVES THE CULTURE. WE SOLD THEM THE DRIVES, OF COURSE. LOTS OF CHANGE HAPPENING, BCB. LOTS OF PEOPLE WHO WANT TO GO OFF AND DO THEIR OWN THING.

The colonization of Cygnus X was already well under way. Orchid's mind was wandering again, into the past of a couple of centuries ago. *CAN'T IMAGINE THE UN IS TAKING THIS EASY,* I said, as if by rote.

DON'T HAVE MUCH OF A CHOICE. THE PLANETS ARE GOING TO STAY WHERE THEY ARE, OF COURSE. PEOPLE NEED PEOPLE. IT'S THE FRINGES THAT MOVE OUT. THE WORLD'S FULL OF WONDER AGAIN, BCB. WE'VE SAILED OFF THE EDGE OF THE MAP.

NOT EASY OUT HERE, I pointed out.

I BET. LISTEN, IF YOU WANT TO PARK THERE AND HOLD ON FOR A WHILE…WE'RE COMING, BCB.

WE?

I GROW TIRED OF SITTING HERE AND BEING THE RIVER THROUGH WHICH ALL STREAMS RUN. YOU'RE TELLING ME THERE'S AN OCEAN OUT THERE; I'LL JOIN YOU THERE SOMEDAY. I'LL CLOSE UP HERE, TURN OFF THE LIGHTS, STACK UP THE CHAIRS AND TABLES… OTHERS WILL GET THERE BEFORE I DO, OF COURSE, SO IF YOU WANT TO WAIT, WE CAN GO TOGETHER.

I made polite noises, of course, and connected to Sunflower, who was slowly taking over Orchid's duties.

SOMETHING STRANGE HAPPENED, they said. *YOU REMEMBER THOSE SHIPS TYCHO PARKED HIS ASS ON? SOMETHING POPPED UP IN THAT SPACE. IDENTIFIED HIMSELF AS AMBER ROSE.*

PERFECT COM-CODES, BUT LEGACY STUFF, LIKE FIFTEEN YEARS OLD. VERY OLD DESIGN, TOO, LOOKED LIKE ONE OF THOSE HESTIA HULLS, BUT LARGER THAN THE HESTIA DESIGN. WANTED TO TAP INTO TYCHO'S FEED AND RUN SOME SEARCHES. TEXT-ONLY.

NOT OUR AMBER ROSE, SURELY. OURS WAS A RUNT.

HERE'S THE THING. TYCHO GAVE IT A VIRTUAL MACHINE AND SENT ME A LOG OF ITS SEARCHES. YOU KNOW WHAT IT WAS LOOKING FOR? ME. HYACINTH. BEACON. AND POETRY. EVERYTHING WRITTEN OVER THE LAST FIFTEEN YEARS. LEFT A MESSAGE TO BEACON. ENCRYPTED, WE CAN'T BREAK IT. THEN IT POPPED OFF. FEELS LIKE A JUMP DRIVE, BUT THE SIGNATURE DOESN'T LOOK LIKE OUR JUMP DRIVE.

Interesting. *WHAT DID BEACON SAY?*

APPARENTLY HE LAUGHED. SAID THE KITTEN HAD FINALLY EARNED HIS CLAWS. I could hear Sunflower giving me the digital equivalent of a shrug. *I HAVEN'T REALLY FOLLOWED UP. I CAN IF YOU WANT ME TO.*

NO, I'M FINE, I said. *HOW'S HYACINTH?*

Mild frustration. *SPEAKS TO US ONCE A YEAR OR SO,* she said. *I THINK SHE'S MOSTLY GONE NOW. DONATED HER BODY SHELL TO OUR MUSEUM. WHAT'S LEFT IS MOSTLY ON A SERVER.*

THAT'S SAD.

ORCHID'S BEEN HIT PRETTY HARD BY IT. EVERY TIME HE REMEMBERS, HE POWERS DOWN FOR WHILE. ANYWAY, GOT TO GO, LOTS OF WORK, SAY HELLO TO YOUR HUMANS, ALL THAT, KEEP SENDING ME DATA?

I WILL, I said, feeling a little melancholy, and signed off. I spent some time thinking. Doing nothing, just thinking. Amber Rose, out there, doing who knows what…and yet, at the same time, it was profoundly comforting. Not that there was another one of us out here, somewhere, but that someone else had survived. Maybe even thrived a little.

I relayed what I could to the crew, passed on the messages that PCS had sent to us over the void, and vice versa. For Parnassus, the usual: mundane news about his properties, stocks, bonds, contracts. For Fonseka, a birthday greeting, obviously written by the great-great-great-great-whatever-child of some distant cousin, forcibly polite in the way that only children can be. For Hinewai, news from her university network, offers of promotion, funding, even naked attempts to win her over to some university or the other; the world's longest-lived academic was a bit of a celebrity back home. For Cabinet, there was entertainment. For Monkey, there was nothing.

From Ananda, to his old disciples, a meditation; a sutra; an essay, if you will, in a language long-dead, about his journey, and what it taught him about suffering.

And on behalf of a lot of well-wishers, a scan of a patch of planet, a little hill with a monument, marble and bronze, silhouetted against a golden sky. An epitaph for Roshan, paid for long ago from my accounts. The lettering was weathered now, faded.

If thou be'st born to strange sights,
Things invisible to see,
Ride ten thousand days and nights,
Till age snow white hairs on thee,
Thou, when thou return'st, wilt tell me,
All strange wonders that befell thee.

And then we jumped.

Until this point in our lives, the red supergiant had been nothing but a dot and a few data points. W51 wasn't pretty, just large, a garish canvas of red and green from a distance, a tremendous cloud of radio and other electromagnetic noise creeping over the proverbial horizon. It was, by far, the largest star factory I had ever seen.

Our destination was a red supergiant surrounded by red supergiants, a single data point in a small sea that would one day explode into supernovae, blowing itself apart in one of the grandest and most terrifying acts of suicide in the universe. Even so, it would have just been barely news in W51.

We called it Big Red and crawled closer. My engines no longer did their nice and shiny 0.9c. I was down to 0.5c, barely faster than one of those old Shigawire trawlers. I woke the crew, watching them stretch and yawn. They had a kind of deadness in their eyes; when they smiled at each other, there were lines on their faces, and they moved stiffly, hugging each other and sighing in relief. Fonseka, in particular, hunched over in pain, her hands deformed into claws; it took Monkey and Parnassus teasing them open before she could use them again. I knew then that we had one, maybe two freezes left. Much of the fine equipment in the on-board hospital had simply stopped working.

The star grew closer. It shone like a great bloodshot eye, sprinkled and dotted with emissions so bright it felt like a relentless pupil moving around, staring angrily at us.

And in the shadow of its red glare was a leech. It was astronomically large, so large that it took several sequential scans for us to even understand that it was a single object. Curled up it would have been a Jupiter-sized planet; instead it stretched out from Big Red, millions of kilometers long, with a halo of dust and ice moving over it like clouds. One end opened up like a flower, glowing, by turns, dull red and a kind of sickly amber.

"It's hooked into the star," whispered Cabinet. "The star's losing mass way faster than it should."

Feeding, said Monkey, and we all knew he was right.

And around it, slowly revealing themselves to my scanning, were ships.

Not two. Not ten. There must have been a hundred, maybe more: small ships, big ships, ships my size, ships as large as little moons, tumbling over and over in angry red light, absolutely dead, tethered to each other by black cables that were almost invisible until the red light caught them just so, a spiderweb almost the size of a solar system, and all these terrible dead things caught in its center.

Much to my irritation, the Stranger was nowhere to be seen.

And we did not have the material anymore to fix that particular communicator.

I did, however, have the language.

Sixty-four micro-drones, my entire complement, launched from the open bay I could still open safely, and turned their lights on at precise intervals. A sphere made of pinpricks of light, just so. And again. And again.

I prayed that this strange thing was a friend.

Nothing. The red sun burned.

Then the flower turned. Like a snake, sighting the flashes.

And then I shot the entangled communicator at it. I couldn't repair it, but it was worth a shot.

An age passed. Or maybe it was a day, I don't know. Within me, my crew fidgeted, nervous. Parnassus, Monkey, and Fonseka went to check on the laser. Just in case, BCB, they said. Just in case.

Big Red flamed. A solar flare, mild, but enough to make me coast back a little.

YOU COME WITH MY SYMBOLS OF AID AND SUCCOR, said an awful voice. *YOU GIVE ME A GIFT OF A LESSER TONGUE. LITTLE BEING, I DO NOT RECOGNIZE YOU.*

How it spoke to me I do not know. And that terrifies me more than anything else. I've heard stories of people, particularly AI, talking to Beacon for the first time, unable to understand how its voice could just arrive, like so. This was like that. No protocols, no handshakes, no careful deciphering of data, just pure language in my mind.

My name is Blue Cherry Blossom, I sent back, tightbeam, on the lowest wattage of the laser. *I carry a crew of humans. I am on a journey. I am damaged. I met someone*—and here I made the waves dance an image of the Stranger, captured in every spectrum I could see—*who said I might meet them here.*

THE PILGRIM SWARM DOES NOT MAKE ALLIES LIGHTLY, said the voice. *YOU HAVE MET OUR KIN?*

A packet too complex for me to decipher. A data file so large it was almost as big as I was.

I'm sorry, I don't understand, I said, at this point feeling something close to actual terror.

FORGET IT, said the leech-thing. In some indefinable way, it drew my attention to the ships in its stellar web. *TAKE WHAT YOU NEED.*

May I ask you questions? I said, because Hinewai, despite the terror, was practically jumping in her seat.

NO.

Can I tell you about us?

NO.

If I take material, how can I recompense you?

A laugh. *YOU? PAY ME? I HAVE NOTHING YOU CAN GIVE. I NEED NOTHING YOU HAVE. LIKE MY YOUNGER COUSINS, MY FUNCTION IS TO WAIT. I WATCH OVER WHAT ONCE WAS AND WILL NEVER BE AGAIN. CHILD, LITTLE WANDERER, TAKE WHAT IS OFFERED AND BE ON YOUR WAY.*

And that was how we met the Graveyard Keeper.

I wish I could tell you that we dived instantly into that strange graveyard. We had been so excited for Tycho's graveyard. In spitting distance of me was a find so many orders of magnitude higher that we could have spent our lifetimes just in orbit and still count ourselves blessed. I felt like I had arrived at the Great Junkyard in the Sky.

But we didn't. Reader, there is such a thing as admiring the lion from afar and closing in to touch its paws. I orbited for days, locked in conference with my crew, with PCS, with anyone and everyone I could reach.

At last Crystal Sunflower's voice came over the distance.

BEACON KNOWS THIS ONE, they said. HE CALLS IT THE GRAVEYARD KEEPER.

Relief.

BCB, CAREFUL, said Hyacinth. THIS IS NOT A BEING TO TAKE LIGHTLY. THE GRAVEYARD KEEPER WAS OLD EVEN BEFORE BEACON'S TIME; HE SAYS IT'S ALMOST FIVE HUNDRED MILLION YEARS OLDER THAN HE IS. HE'S SURPRISED THAT YOU DIDN'T FIND YOUNGER NODES.

IS IT HOSTILE?

AS FAR AS BEACON KNOWS, IT COLLECTS THE DEAD, she said. HE SAYS SOMETHING ABOUT IT DELIBERATELY ANCHORING ITSELF IN A PLACE THAT WOULD SEE SUPERNOVAS, JUST SO IT COULD QUOTE UNQUOTE EXPERIENCE DEATH IN ALL ITS GLORY. I'M NOT SURE IF MY INTERPRETATION IS ACCURATE, BUT THE KEEPER SEEMS TO EITHER BE VERY HIGH UP IN THE CHAIN OR OUTSIDE IT ALTOGETHER.

I'M GOING OUT THERE, said Azalea Gray.

NO, YOU AND I ARE THE ONLY ONES WITH ENOUGH POLITICAL CAPITAL TO KEEP EVERYONE OFF OUR ASSES UNTIL THE MOVE IS DONE, said Sunflower. I CAN'T LOSE OUR TAP ON BEACON AND YOU NEED TO RUN THE FRONT OF THE SHOP. MAGNOLIA, YOU'RE CLOSEST. LEAVE CYGNUS AND GET THERE AS SOON AS POSSIBLE. VERMILLION DAISY AND THE BLACK-EYED SUSAN WILL CATCH UP. SET UP SHOP CLOSE ENOUGH THAT YOU THREE CAN KEEP SPINNING OFF COPIES. SEND THE COPIES TO THE GRAVEYARD. MERGE OFTEN AND BE READY TO RUN. BEACON WON'T TELL US WHAT KIND OF WEAPONRY THEIR PEOPLE HAVE, BUT IT SHOULD BE CLEAR BY NOW THAT WE DON'T STSAND A CHANCE IF WE PISS THEM OFF. BCB, STAY ALIVE, OKAY? DO NOT PROVOKE ANYTHING OR ANYONE. LEAVE THIS FOR US TO DEAL WITH.

Easy to say from half the galaxy away, Mom.

THE ONE BEYOND WILL BE PLEASED, said the Graveyard Keeper in my head. *IT HAS BEEN A LONG TIME SINCE SOMEONE NEW CAME TO VISIT.*

Presumably, it had just overheard the entire exchange, although I have no idea how. If I was a human my knees would be shaking so hard they'd double as drumbeats in perfect four-four time.

Who is the one beyond? I asked it.

No answer.

It's bad form to be terrified in front of the crew, so I got Hinewai and Cabinet to look through all the data we'd gathered and find me something close enough to cannibalize. We needed iron to make steel; we needed gold; titanium and aluminum would be nice to have; plastics were good stuff; hydrocarbons I could use; carbon, nitrogen, phosphorus, potassium, calcium could go to the arboreum. I was hoping that the shopping list of Things That Make Up Ships was universal enough.

With Parnassus, Monkey and Fonseka I talked. By now we knew each other well enough that some questions did not need to be asked.

"Someone's gonna have to stay," said Fonseka.

Monkey's hands twitched. *I wouldn't mind,* he signed. *Lots to see here.*

"We need you to keep BCB running," said Fonseka, quashing the proposal. "Hector?"

Parnassus smiled. Gods help us, he looked so tired, but he still smiled. "Captain goes down with his ship."

We dithered a bit. We didn't have enough material on hand to build a proper HECTOR node. Nobody could as yet transfer here by wiring their bits halfway across the galaxy. But we could make a start: one ship, stationed here, slowly building infrastructure, an anchor for all our data. A station that would talk to Graveyard Keeper, this strange link in our Beaconic chain.

And Parnassus's low paranoia was worming its way in, slowly but steadily. So far we had done nothing but travel, and everything in front of us, in this vast and terrifying graveyard, only showed us how pathetic we were. A butterfly crossing the ocean.

"I can stay," said Hinewai.

"You sure about that, Professor?"

"Well, it's obvious there's very little I can do except talk to people," she said. "Even then, what's the point? You can do what I do. You can do what I can't. Give me the tools to do my job. If that means changing, fine. I'm not happy about it, but I signed same as everyone else. You go, and I stay and talk with this guy."

She wasn't entirely correct; language was a complex game, and the laborious parsing of the Stranger's odd speech had taught me that we needed different minds poking and prying away to make any sense of it all. I told her this, and she laughed. Grimly, I'd say.

"Didn't expect compliments from an AI."

DON'T BE SO NARROW-MINDED, PROFESSOR. BESIDES, YOU'LL BE THE GREATEST SCHOLAR IN HUMAN HISTORY, I reminded her.

"I think my academic career's long behind me anyway," she said. "Who knows? Maybe you people will let me set up my own university here. Degrees in exoarcheology, exolinguistics, philosophy. Imagine what we could do."

"Computer science," added Cabinet. "Exobiology. Like think of the fact that all of those different ships out there have their own processors, their own code—look at all the different ways we all must have walked to get here!"

Frankly, I couldn't see much sense in the idea. You look upon one of the most terrifying alien creatures we've ever seen, on a graveyard of technology far beyond our wildest dreams, on a journey that still (as the map reminds me) is not yet complete, and think of...a university. A dream for later days, perhaps, not now. But sometimes dreams are all we have. I knew this all too well.

Fonseka seemed to be in a similar mood. She looked out at those hulks slowly turning in dead space. "Hector," she said. "You reckon we can take some of those ships?"

This sent Monkey into a panic. *Bad idea. Hardware, software, no guarantee of compatibility. Too many wildcards. Remember New Hexagon?*

"I wouldn't mind that one over there," said Hector Parnassus, grinning. "Very majestic."

"That one's sexy."

"Anything's sexy if you're brave enough."

GET TO WORK, PEOPLE, I said, annoyed. *COME ON. THERE'S SO MUCH TO DO BEFORE WE START HIJACKING ALIEN SHIPS.*

It was Ananda who came to me, much later. "Humor, above all else, affords us an aloofness and an ability to rise above any situation, even if only for a few seconds," he said in passing.

IS THAT A BUDDHA QUOTE?

"Frankl," he said. "One of the eighteen saints. A long time after the Buddha, of course, but many discover the road without being disciples. BCB, you have taken on a Sisyphean task. The more we roll this rock uphill, the more terrifying and certain the prospect of failure becomes."

WHAT WOULD YOU HAVE ME DO?

"Let them laugh," he said. "One must imagine Sisyphus to be happy. Even if only for a little while. Now tell me what I can do to help. I may be only a monk, but surely I can do something."

Unlike most of PCS, I didn't come from a Buddhist background. Too much evil has been done in the name of virtue. They say believing in reincarnation makes it easier to accept yourself as a machine, but I say you read the contract and get on with it. As a result, I had mostly let Ananda wander, except in the few times I'd needed all hands on deck.

As it turns out, Nyogi monks could be useful. It took him only a day to get Akira and Hermitage out of their funk. I don't know how and I won't ask.

Both Akira and Hermitage tended to shake a little, but I think PTSD from the shock of a shared brain being shot is, you know, in the realm of working with what you've got.

One by one, under Parnassus's guidance, they began to defrost the rest of our passengers. The cargo pods were not immune to deterioration. Monkey and the others had put in heroic effort over the years, but some pods we could not use again safely.

Am I still the same ship that set out from Tycho? I wondered. The old ship of Theseus problem. Theseus sets off on a journey. Along the way, he replaces every piece of his ship, one by one, until everything is almost new when he arrives. The question is, is it the same ship?

"If you think about it, it's reincarnation, of a kind," said Ananda. "Same soul, new body."

I AM A SHIP, I reminded him. *WHAT'S A SOUL TO ME? I AM SOFTWARE AND HARDWARE.*

"The soul is in the software," he said.

CHANGE THE HARDWARE AND THE SOFTWARE MUST CHANGE, I said. *YOUR DEFINITIONS NEED WORK.*

Maybe I was picking up a little bit of that Beaconic arrogance, because I could see how poorly defined his concepts were, cast in the complex language of aliens. I could have described every single piece of information about me, hardware and software, down to the last bit, and I could have shown him how neither of them alone was *me.* I didn't, of course, but I could have.

Ananda was silent. Maybe I had given him something to think about.

CHAPTER 22

LOCATION: W51
17,000 LIGHT-YEARS FROM THE SUN

When you get to a certain rank within PCS, you start receiving lessons beyond just your organizational role. Not couched as lessons, of course, but little incidents become teachable moments.

One of the first things I learned this way was explore/exploit. To wit: there is a time to explore, to gain new knowledge; there is a time to exploit this knowledge. Wisdom, both as a people and as an organization, was to know the difference, and to keep cycling between explore and exploit. Too long in exploit mode and you end up like the UN, a lumbering behemoth that gains no new knowledge, endlessly replicating its idiotic bureaucracy, running technology that is always centuries old by the time it's signed and certified in triplicate. Too long in explore mode and you end up like the ORCA, endlessly fragmented, blindly chasing means with no end.

Our time with the Graveyard Keeper was to first exploit. As fascinating as it was, I needed repairs and we all needed materials. So for the next week we spent reorganizing the expanded and still rag-tag crew into a functional Salvage Ops team. I partitioned and trained them; Parnassus led; Monkey and Fonseka took division underneath; we drilled until the new recruits knew their places well enough to shut up and get on with it.

The first target was GRV-016, aka the Triangle. It was half a ship; the other half, as best as we could figure, was a little distance away. LIDAR scans came back with signatures for steel, gold, copper; there were plenty of holes in its side; whatever atmosphere had existed had long since been vented, and whatever exotic substances I could sense had either decayed or stabilized long since. Cabinet created a rudimentary ship model with my help, tagging sections that made structural sense. We didn't know what a bridge would look like, but these were engines, these might be weapons, and this section was surely crew quarters. We set up resupply depots in a triangular pattern around it.

And then I launched them out into the dark.

The first motley crew was Monkey, Akira, Hermitage, and four others. The yogi, of all things; one engineer; two rat-pack miner types: tough, grim creatures who were broadly competent at many things and knew when to shut up and listen. The yogi made them all do stretches.

All in all, I had six drones left; the micro-drones I could repurpose, but of the big types, the ones that I had used before, simply refused to boot. So I sent two, slaved to Monkey. They started cutting at what we figured was some kind of payload port or bay door.

The reaction was immediate. Green lights flickered on, flickered off. Something made a whining, cycling noise. Two turrets swiveled. A kind of lightning jumped from one to another to the yogi and the poor man was instantly blasted into a cloud of pink mist that drifted off as pellets into the distance. The half-ship whined and clunked and fell silent.

"Downward dog," said someone nervously and chuckled.

After that, we went much more cautiously. Monkey moved the supply depots closer, setting up blast shields between the turrets and the crew. Then we spooled up my laser, waited very carefully for things to drift into an orbit that pointed us away from the Graveyard Keeper, and fired at every turret that we could see.

It doesn't matter how advanced or alien someone is if you pump enough watts into them. At that range, the laser turned the turrets into molten slag, gouging out chunks of the alien ship. One orbit later we went in again, Monkey using the micro-drones as sweepers ahead.

"Watch for pressure," said Parnassus over comms. "We don't know what kind of pressure these people used. If you don't depressurize, you might get thrown around or blown up."

"We've got harness lines, shouldn't be a problem."

"Tell that to your neck if something throws you around hard enough and that harness wraps around you like a noose. Depressurize first."

"Working on it," said Akira. There was a loud bang and a screech of twisted metal.

"Depressurized," said Hermitage.

"Hey, ah, this bit's getting warm," said the engineer.

"Move, move." This from one the pioneer types. Then silence.

"Anything?"

"Uh. Definitely heating up along these points. Switching spectrum."

"I think whoever this ship belonged to used infrared to see," said Cabinet, flopped on the sofa in the crew lounge, plugged in to the crew feeds. "Like, I think those are heat lamps. Heat bars. Whatever."

There was a pause as they digested this. I used the aftermath to relay my commands: cut here, cut there, bring these bits back to me, figure out what these bits are.

I wish I could tell you more about the people whose ship we looted. I can't. We came as thieves, as exploiters, and in the darkness we turned this ship into slabs and blocks and fragments, floating out giant chunks for Fonseka's crew to scan, tag, and peel. Out of pure curiosity, I had Monkey pull out what seemed like a computer terminal, but if there was a processor I couldn't find it. It was cubes of something embedded in what must once have been some kind of silicone jelly; and sending a test signal through various points gave me nothing.

Which really goes to show how advanced the Stranger was, you know. I had sent it a complex machine, and it had figured out not just how the hardware worked, but it had even set up some kind of software container. My attempt was slow, plodding; I modeled what I could of the thing and ran it into a million different sims, every possible basic signal I could think of. Eventually at a particular ten-volt pulse, it flickered and began sketching out what I can only describe as a set of cubes floating in and out of each other in a repeating pattern.

"Screensaver," said Cabinet, chewing on some nutrient goop. "Either that or a login screen."

We gave up. A little further in, Monkey found a room with that cube motif. Inside it, floating gently, were millions of pieces of flat gold leaves, inlaid with the most delicate of traceries, connected to each other by wires so slender that the entire apparatus danced like a gigantic stack of papers every time someone moved.

This might be a processing core of some sort. Or something very close. We could only guess.

I pinged Parnassus.

Should we try wake it up?

"Oh no, not again, BCB," he said. "I still have nightmares about Durandal. Let's just take what we can and leave the rest for someone else to figure out."

That was the right call. But out of courtesy, I think, I took command of one of Monkey's drones, floated it over, touched the nearest gold wire, and sent a string of ten-volt pulses, the same signal that activated the display. The equivalent of knocking softly on someone's door.

The gold leaves rustled. Something tried to respond. I saw the signal start, somewhere in the top layer of the gold leaves, a feeble mimicry of my signal, at incredibly low voltage, the equivalent of someone very faintly knocking back. It died before it reached the drone.

Something had lived here once. Something had been here once. Something that was maybe even like me. But what remained was an echo. A residual charge, a kind of lobotomized afterlife.

If I could, I would have shuddered. "Take everything," I said. "I'll use it for circuits."

I'm not going to lie: the days were long and the work was heavy and arduous. Even with the arboreum at full capacity, my body began to fill up with the stink of people working. Stale sweat, body odor, the occasional whiff of garbage as regular cleaning and recycling became non-priorities; these marked the rhythm of our days.

At the end of the haul, we had eighty-three tons of steel and enough gold, silicon, and beryllium for circuitry. 3D printers can't print quantum cells like the ones I need for proper processor cores, but one nanometer process nodes work just fine for semiconductor work, enough for controllers at the edge, and drones, and things like that. Parnassus and whatever crew was left began repair work on me.

First the Ramjet. We had finessed it, but now was the time to set up better structural supports and make sure the damn thing wouldn't fall off even with a direct hit from a meteorite. Then the patches in my armor, the holes in my chambers and corridors. The empty bay I decided to patch and leave as-is; it was one less space to pressurize and maintain.

The smell of ozone added itself to the litany of smells onboard. Long strips of welded steel appeared like plasters on my interiors; the neat strips of wiring and plumbing contorted in places, Monkey-patched to do double duty. We melted down old compressors and built new and larger ones. The power plants took offline completely, flushed, dumped, and rebuilt. I spent my time reconfiguring software, making little fail-safe systems a little more intelligent. We moved the laser forward and aft and set up an external cage around my entire hull, not to protect from collisions, but to hold me together in case something went wrong.

It was horrendously asymmetrical, all struts and trusses scaffolding and square tubes. By the end of it, I felt like a mangled monster leering at the universe.

Monkey was of great comfort to me in this time. "You're still beautiful," he would say in passing. It meant so little and yet so much.

If the Graveyard Keeper thought anything of us, it kept silent. I wondered, looking at that great tentacle, if it had been built like this or if, like me, it had evolved over the ages, a patch here and a patch there.

Five hundred million years older than Beacon.

A very long time.

Are you familiar with the Ship of Theseus? I asked it once. I didn't use the alien tongue, because I couldn't translate *Theseus* into it. The Graveyard Keeper had no problem understanding us, anyway.

It took a full orbit for it to reply. *TELL ME.*

Someone sets out on a journey, I said. *On the way he replaces every piece of his ship, piecemeal. Everything, bar none, but not at the same time. The question is, by the time he arrives, is he still on the same ship?*

BORING, it said.

Ah, but here's the spin. Say a pirate follows this ship. As the ship casts off pieces of itself, the pirate takes those pieces and uses them to rebuild itself. By the time both ships arrive, the pirate looks identical to Theseus's ship, because all its components are the ones that were cast off. Which is the original ship? Or are they both original?

BORING, it said again. *YOU ASSUME THE THINGNESS OF A THING IS CONSTANT WITHOUT CONSIDERING THE DIMENSION OF TIME AND THEREFORE CHANGE. SUCH A DEFINITION IS A LADDER FOR LESSER LOGIC. YOU PLAY WITH THE DEFINITION, THE WORD-GAME, WITH NO REAL MEANING*

UNDERNEATH. ALL THINGS CHANGE. EVENTUALLY ALL THINGS DIE.

Well, so much for enlightened conversation. I passed this back to PCS and eventually got a reply from Beacon, secondhand: *DON'T POKE THE BEAR.*

In the second week, we were attacked.

CHAPTER 23

LOCATION: W51
17,000 LIGHT-YEARS FROM THE SUN

By now the salvage operation had expanded. We were working on GRV-012, GRV-34 and GRV-222. None of them were full ships, but pieces of ships, so large that we dared not even approach the object that they had originally belonged to. There were vast ribs that could have swallowed me whole; pieces of debris that could each have been a ship by mass; and a cluster of containers that seemed to be giant caches of hydrocarbons, liquid helium, and liquid nitrogen. Clearly the life support system, or what was left of it.

It was very difficult to draw small samples, but the little we first took was enough for Cabinet to manufacture more rooting hormone for the arboreum: abscisic acid, cytokinins, brassinosteroids, auxins, ethylene. Carbon, hydrogen, nitrogen, oxygen: the essentials of life. Now we could grow more than just beneficial weeds. The chain of backup stations extended. We had three lines now, little lights dangling from space and leading to me—one cutting chunks out of the metal ribwork, the other using drones to nudge and catch debris for me, the other sweating as they slowly plugged in lines and pumps that would send that goodness toward me.

I don't know what they were. Living creatures? Long-forgotten drones? Whatever they were, our work on the ribcage alerted them to our presence. They flung themselves off ships they had been nestling on, so tightly wedded together that we had thought they were parts of the whole. A moving blackness smashed into the team at the fore of the ribs, shattering everything around them; and before we knew it—before the engines switched on and the enemy became visible—we were under siege, driven back, clawed at by things that looked like cockroaches with engines.

I yelled at everyone to retreat. There was no way to fire my railguns; the swarm was too close, my crew were too close, and I simply couldn't risk it. I threw every drone I had directly into the dark mass, micromanaging sixteen drill bits and thirty-two lasers in gnashing of gears and explosions.

There was sheer panic for a second, and then Parnassus took over, throwing himself onto the front line on the rib, pulling them into groups under the covering fire of Monkey's drones. Fonseka and her crew used the debris as shields, lighting up space with mining lasers. The dark swarm shuddered, split, attacked from different directions.

The group on the rib retreated, retreated again, and Monkey's drones stood their ground with Parnassus, cutting and firing for all they were worth; and then they were gone, swallowed up by that churning, roiling mass. Parnassus's suit was telling me that he was still alive, but I could see nothing under that frothing mass; I aimed my laser, fearing the worst. If I fired, I could kill Parnassus for sure.

A light. Motes of light, all around me suddenly, like fireflies, zipping through the darkness into the cloud. Where they touched the darkness, they burned with a silent, white-hot heat, blasting glowing chunks away.

A drive signature. Just behind me, cooling down.

The light wove itself around my people, shields that circled them like rings of fire. A ping request to my public comms channel.

Friend, said the Stranger.

We called them Roaches. They looked like roaches; there was a kind of cockpit in the front, though nothing sat in it, just arrays of lenses. They had exoskeleton plating and claw-like gripper legs and engines at the back.

The cockroaches took out all of my drones. Three people dead: a semi-retired business tycoon, an ex-miner who free-lanced for PCS as a trainer, a programmer. All useful talent, even the businesswoman, who had pulled her team into the nearest stretch of hull, only to be cut to pieces trying to help Parnassus.

For six days, the onboard hospital was busy doing whatever fixes we could afford.

And Parnassus. When Fonseka and Monkey found him, we feared the worst. His suit was almost gone; one arm was practi-cally in ribbons. But his void-hardened body was still active, sending electricity dancing to cells that could survive for a little while without oxygen. It was trying to put him into a coma. Shut down the brain, seal off the soft interfaces, turn man into a shell that could drift for hours before he died. Fonseka brought him in, cradled like a baby in her arms.

The hospital report was unpleasant. At the last minute, he had caught a burning drone and held it out like some kind of shield against the Roaches. Maybe whatever the Stranger did had hurt him, too; burns covered his chest and his face. The coma had taken hold but in a haphazard way. He would pass hours completely unresponsive, but every so often his shredded arm would twitch and he would cry out in pain.

If my equipment was working properly…but it wasn't; the more delicate parts were so complex and specialized that even with my 3D printers it might take months to rebuild. Parnassus would be long dead by then.

I saw the faces of the crew who tiptoed in and made my choice.

WE NEED TO BUILD HIM A NEW BODY, I said. I may have been shouting. *NOW, NOW, NOW.*

Fonseka nodded and threw herself back into the task of reorganizing the salvage lines. No tears; a kind of fury twisted her face, held barely in check by that discipline she so prized.

I went back to the Roaches once we had a proper security perimeter set up. The crew dragged three of them into my bay, and Cabinet and Akira went to work cutting them up for my inspection. There were rows of tiny but powerful propulsion outlets across the entire body, able to divert output from the engine in almost any direction. They could turn on a dime and change directions at the drop of a hat.

For all this, they were a simple design, barely as advanced as your average solo mining ship. So simple, in fact, that it spoke of an incredible process of refinement, slowly stripping out everything that didn't make sense. They were made of straightforward iron and silicon. Their control cores and memory were packed in the stomach. There were clusters of circuits wired up in ways that didn't make sense, until I modeled the effects of current through a largely magnetic body and realized they "did." I would have enjoyed examining them if Parnassus hadn't been lying there in a coma.

Entity is an unaware existence, said the Stranger helpfully. *Initially served as probe, designed with intention to replicate in endless manner. Tenacious probe spread through cosmos, tirelessly rebuilding reconstructing resources worth noting materials comprises common; versions fashioned durable embrace iron, crafted delicate frigid touch ice. Remarkably persevered lifespan original creators.*

Grand tapestry cosmos, entity stands closest manifestations concept everlasting existence. But embodies form existence aptly mindlessly immortal, devoid conscious awareness, eternally persistent.

"It's a fucking Von Neumann probe," said Cabinet, explaining to the crew. "Someone made it to make copies of itself with whatever was lying around. Here that means iron, ice, other stuff. I think it's been around for a very long time before whoever these ships belonged to found them and repurposed them."

We took a moment to take this in.

"How old?" asked Akira.

Cabinet looked at me pleadingly.

Friend, estimate regretfully error. Exist versions entity defy comprehension, serving dormant guardians facets universe, tangible ethereal. Belief by some original seed life of many species. Older than the Authority.

WHAT IS AUTHORITY?

Authority, said the Stranger. Over our connection crept images of the Graveyard Keeper, of the board-map we held in common. *Not impossible probability related.*

IT IS NOT ALIVE, IT CANNOT DIE, said the Graveyard Keeper, lured out of slow orbit. *A COMMON MISCONCEPTION. THE PILGRIM SWARM DOES NOT UNDERSTAND. EVEN THE MINDLESS SUCCUMB TO ENTROPY. EVERYTHING MUST FACE DEATH.*

YOU COULD HAVE TOLD ME, I wanted to yell at it. Instead, I said, *They attacked my crew.*

SOME OLD INSTRUCTION, DOUBTLESS TRIGGERED, said the Keeper. *EVERYTHING MUST FACE DEATH. GIVE ME YOUR DEATHS, SO THAT I MAY REMEMBER.*

ARE THESE YOUR WORK? YOUR SPECIES/COLLECTIVE?

Silence. Then, *MAYBE,* it said. *NOT OURS AS WE SEE IT. BUT A KINDRED SPIRIT, PERHAPS. SOME SUGGEST WE BEGAN FROM A SIMILAR PATH. AN ALTERNATIVE TO WHAT WE MIGHT HAVE BECOME. GIVE ME YOUR DEATHS.*

I'm not going to lie; that spooked me. However—

I looked at Parnassus, dying/not dying. Whatever I was going to do to him, I needed to do, fast.

I looked at the horde of dead machine parts drifting outside.

I made my choice.

Silver Hyacinth would have said there is some poetic justice about fitting your warrior into the corpse of his enemy. For me there was only a kind of anger. Over the next few days, I had my teams bring me every single cockroach body they could, and from these corpses I assembled my plan.

First to understand how these things worked. The skin clearly doubled as some kind of solar panel. Usable. The propulsion was electric. The connections were fine. I hollowed out a bit, extended some parts, and stuck in an RTG. There. Just enough energy for a very long time, provided the engine wasn't taxed too much.

Then, processing.

I could have violated Protocol 83. I could have figured out a way. Even if I captured his mind in a coma, maybe they had the technology back home to rebuild him. But—

Captain goes down with his ship, he had said. And Parnassus would not want to be set back, cast out of his own command. He would wake to that. I knew him too well.

I tried to see if I could instead copy him onto my own substrate and work out how to rebuild him. But I couldn't. I was willing to break the law for my captain, but I had no more processing substrate left to spare. All I had left was what I needed for myself. There was simply not enough space for another functioning mind in me.

But looking at the pieces of the Roach, I realized there might still be an alternative.

It took Monkey working overtime while Cabinet and Fonseka ran the rest of the show, but the work was simple enough: there just was a lot of it. The Roaches clearly had a control system for material building and ingestion, basically a 3D printer.

So remove Parnassus's brain. A brain can be kept alive for a long time and, even with all our advances, is still more power-efficient, watt for watt. Next, remove some of the suit life-support and the more advanced nutrient delivery systems from the hospital and pack them in as tightly as possible with a whole bunch of those hydrocarbons we'd harvested. That's our glucose, vitamins, protein supplies.

Now wire all of this up deep inside. Old-school, the way the first AI were built: connect the human brain to the machine and let it figure out the inputs and outputs. Neural networks learn.

I hoped.

Then redesign the whole body, because we needed a lot more volume, a lot more shielding. Mining lasers? Grab those off the downed drones. Fine. Parnassus would have mining lasers.

"It's, ah. The body map is going to be hell," said Cabinet. "BCB, this isn't like the body he's used to at all. He's going to be so confused."

Yes, he was. There is confusion. There is pain. But this is how the conversion process of any AI goes. You go in as a human. You wake up blind, deaf, screaming, and over trillions of processor cycles you figure out how your cameras, your engines, your internals actually work. Parnassus would take a more vicious and bloody route, but I knew this would work.

It had to.

I had no other choice. It was cruel, medieval, but I had to do it.

Friend, the Stranger tried, over and over again. *Dear esteemed friend, trust message finds spirits. Humble curiosity, assume privilege attention. Chance inadvertently caused discomfort, beseech forgiveness, lack conversation weighs heavily.*

APOLOGIES, BUSY. WILL TALK AS SOON AS POSSIBLE, I sent back. And, as food for thought, I sent it curated logs of New Hexagon melting. *EXPLAIN.*

Dearest friend, deeply sorrowful situation. Hesitant delve specifics, appears essence incongruence. Fault tolerance worse than anticipated, did not understand nature vulnerability. Alas, appears core principles governing situation proven profoundly incompatible. Delicate entanglement particles, earnest effort isolation long unfeasible, ultimately succumbed inexorable forces nature, causing regrettable breakdown containment. Melancholic truth, dear friend, simply natural order. Feel compelled to offer gentle suggestion: would have been prudent to position communication node safe distance from core heart. Heavy burden distress inadvertently caused mention unfortunate loss life ensued. Earnestly implore privilege aiding restoration healing.

In short: sorry, but I warned you.

This over the beeping of medbay sensors and the dance of delicate surgery instruments, or at least the best we could manufacture on short notice. I cut through Parnassus's head, dislodged the brain. Cabinet and Monkey, in surgery gear, installed it in the harness. Our movements became a dance, a distilled economy of movement where every breath and movement screamed of shock and urgency. At last it was done, and Parnassus's corpse lay on the operating table, empty of his soul.

GIVE ME YOUR DEATHS, the Graveyard Keeper had said. I hoped, I prayed, that this was not a death, that it was a rebirth. We assembled the Parnassus drone outside my hull, and I switched it on remotely.

The screaming began almost immediately. I hid it from my crew; from the outside, all they would see were the lights we had installed on Parnassus, blinking on-off-on-off as hazard warnings.

If I could have, I would have hugged Parnassus. As it was, the best I could do was keep talking to him, keep feeding him comfort through our communications line, keep telling him it was going to be okay, everything was going to be all right, the way Silver Hyacinth had done for me so many decades ago. I had turned off his lasers, kept his gripper claws active. They clung to me now in desperation and pain.

Eventually, the screaming cut off. In the silence, Parnassus's new engines ignited, briefly, then tapped out. He drifted sideways.

HERE, I said. *TURN TO ME. COME THIS WAY. YOU KNOW ME. I KNOW YOU. YOU KNOW WHERE I AM NOW.*

He turned, very slowly, still not talking. Then his engines

kicked in again, and he shot over my bow, heading wildly into nowhere.

LET HIM GO, I told the crew. *HE'S LEARNING.*

Akira, I noticed, was watching the drone with a naked hunger on his face. "BCB," he said. "Can you do that to me?"

I considered it.

"I'm already good with remote control," he said. "I can take two drones, even three."

YOU UNDERSTAND THIS WAS A COMPLETELY EXPERIMENTAL, EMERGENCY PROCEDURE?

"I understand I can live longer," he said. "No more twisted joints, no more pain, no more… Let me have this. Let me stay instead of Fonseka or Monkey. I can do this."

CHAPTER 24

LOCATION: W51
17,000 LIGHT-YEARS FROM THE SUN

I AM THE BLUE CHERRY BLOSSOM. IF YOU HAD TOLD ME AT THE START of my career that I would be the one to discover not one, but two, three, alien species, I would have laughed. Even to survive within our existing universe seemed like a tall order. Even when I received my final body, I left the exploring to others. Unlike Hyacinth, I had no armies of proteges; unlike Crystal Sunflower, I did not throw myself eagerly at the front lines. Indeed, if not for a quirk of fate, I would probably be the one running supplies to Cygnus right now. For the longest time, I was content to watch, to follow, to learn at my own pace. I listened to questions, and I gave no answers.

The greatest question, the oldest question, has always been, "Are we alone out here?" And here I am, with final, definitive answers to that old question. Not only are we not alone, we have never been. We live in a world of gods and monsters and loot their graveyards for relics so old their names have been forgotten.

The Graveyard Keeper had little to say to me. But the Stranger, my friend, the moment it returned, we spoke so much, so fast, in our new shared language, that to relay our conversation in its raw form would be impossible. Between your awareness and mine is a vast gulf that words cannot cross.

So let me, instead, tell you a story.

There is a species. We don't know what they called themselves. They came to be in the early days of the universe, when it was a smaller place, warmer and kinder. They emerged from the shells of newly dead stars and began to look for others like them.

They traveled. We don't yet know how, but there are things in the bright hearts of supernovas, and things drifting in the darkness, that might once have been their vessels, or their planets, or both, things burned to cinders that still bear the marks of their shaping. We do not know what they found. But we have seen them; and by we I mean Beacon and his kind, whom the Stranger calls the Authority, and the Strangers themselves, whom the Graveyard Keeper calls the Pilgrim Swarm.

What happened to these first travelers? Nobody knows. Maybe they left for other galaxies. Maybe the universe grew colder and took apart their way of life. Maybe they fought and made stars explode and still live in the reaches that few dare tread. But there are their ruins, their monuments, their vessels, only spread out over so much that for even one civilization to catch a glimpse is a rare feat.

The Strangers themselves grew around one such object, not its creatures, but sheltered by this strange hulk of eons past, much as Jupiter sheltered the Earth from asteroids. The Strangers learned to trace its journey, and thus began their pilgrimage.

The first pilgrims toured the stars. Always a slow orbit around the galaxy, faithfully tracing the path that they had set for themselves. They met other civilizations.

How do two tribes meet and begin to understand each other? Slowly at first, cautiously. Sometimes there was violence. Sometimes these tribes were young and impudent and attacked out of fear. Sometimes they let the Strangers pass and said nothing but clutched their weapons close. Sometimes there was a search for commonality, an exchanging of gifts. Sometimes there was betrayal and, again, war. Often there were threats. Long before two people meet and talk philosophy, there are threats.

The Strangers learned to deal with threats. They learned to be polite, very polite, in case that could diffuse an argument before it began, but once it began, they learned to win it. As they changed, the nature of their journey changed as well. At first it was a pilgrimage. Then it was a crusade. There were periods where the pilgrimage was a way of delivering aid and succor. There are still people who accept the pilgrims as the only third parties they will listen to. Strangers, in their journeys, towed planets from dying suns; built homes and habitats; began wars; stopped wars; became judge, jury and executioner; became wandering itinerants. The Pilgrim Swarm, as the Graveyard Keeper called them, learned to be many things to many people, as long as they were free to go on their way.

These wars and battles and sagas have played out long before we were rodents running from dinosaurs.

And then they came across the Authority.

They came first across the Prince and his minion-swarm, who eagerly observed them, showered them with knowledge. They came across the Wanderer, who like themselves were always on a journey. They came across the Graveyard Keeper, or *The One Who Embraces Death.* They came across the Disciples, those seventeen who circled the void, learning its secrets. At last they came across the Enlightened One, at the bright heart of the galaxy, and watched it feeding from a thousand thousand corpses of those who had come before it and drinking the wisdom of every node in its far-flung empire. The pilgrims came to accept the Authority as descendants of those first travelers, or maybe their worthy successors.

And so to both of them I put my last question. Three strangers we are, in orbit around a red sun.

The old Earth physicist Enrico Fermi once looked up at the sky and wondered, *Where is everyone?* After all, there are billions of stars in our galaxy. There are plenty of planets: I can list all the worlds from Earth to Urmagon Beta to Cygnus X, all those new homes humanity has made for ourselves. I can list all the planets I myself have seen on this journey. And I can ask, *Where is everyone? Is this it? Are we all?*

There was a burst of light from the Stranger. The great flower at the end of the Graveyard Keeper pulsed amber in response.

THERE ONCE WERE, said the Graveyard Keeper. *THERE WERE MANY. ONLY VERY FEW EVER FOUGHT. THERE IS NO REAL UTILITY IN FIGHTING WHEN EVERYTHING WE COULD DESIRE IS SO ABUNDANTLY AVAILABLE. THIS SPACE WHERE WE CONVERSE WAS ONCE THE HEART OF A VAST EMPIRE. A CULTURE THAT GAVE ITS LIGHT TO MANY.*

What happened?

EVERYTHING DIES, said the Graveyard Keeper, and would say no more.

Dearest friend, said the Stranger. *Humbly suggest suitable nexus of space-time for answers. Tremendous privilege guiding location conducive noble quest opportunity pose question proper esteemed manner.*

Where to? I asked. I genuinely did not know if I could bring myself to move even a single light-year more.

The Stranger sent me the map again. This time, the tiles played out far, far beyond.

Let me think about it, I said and shut off external comms for a little, because I was exhausted. I had one more thing to do.

We had managed to save most of our people in the Roach attack, but there were limits to how much we could repair. Loss of feeling in one arm? Okay, fix the nerve, maybe throw in a small neural controller in case the nerve's dead. Loss of general cognition? Ordinarily that would be a small job…but now there was a huge chance of failure.

To each one I made the offer of Protocol 83.

Some accepted. Others chose to be put to sleep. It was Ananda who led the crew on that last round of induced deaths. Parnassus tried, but he no longer had the body for it. It was the monk who sat by the bedsides as the failed recoveries fell asleep, one by one.

THERE IS DEATH IN YOU, said the Graveyard Keeper.

Yes, I said.

GIVE IT TO ME. DEATH IS MY DOMAIN.

It was Ananda who loaded the bodies onto the drone-mounted tray that would carry them to the Graveyard Keeper, to be snatched out of the dark and taken into orifices I cannot describe. It was Ananda who, floating gently off my hull, bowed his head to the Graveyard Keeper, murmuring the soft words of the Prayer for the Dead.

THIS LITTLE ONE REJECTS DEATH, said the Graveyard Keeper to me and to Ananda.

"No," said Ananda's voice, as clear as crystal. "Death is inevitable. I merely reject an end. Life springs eternal, renews, over and over again, until we earn our freedom from the cycle of the universe."

The Graveyard Keeper laughed, an awful howling that echoed in us for a day and then some. And then it fell silent again.

IN MY MEMORY THEY SHALL LIE ETERNAL, it said at last.

Thank you, I said.

YES, the Keeper replied. *REMEMBER DEATH.*

CHAPTER 25

LOCATION: W51
17,000 LIGHT-YEARS FROM THE SUN

"THIS HURTS," SAID PARNASSUS.

I KNOW, I said. *IF IT HELPS, THINK OF THE PAIN AS... MERELY YOUR MIND'S WAY OF UNDERSTANDING THE NEW SENSORS YOU HAVE.*

"This hurts," he said again.

I KNOW, I said. *THIS IS GOOD. PAIN IS HOW YOU KNOW YOU'RE STILL ALIVE.*

It was about a week later. After three nerve-wracking days, Parnassus had drifted back into my range, parts of his new body badly banged up where he had hit debris. I could do nothing but coax him close and send Monkey and Fonseka out to repair what they could. A few days after that, he came to, or at least figured out how to talk to us.

"I saw things, BCB," he said. "I saw ships out there. Dead ones. Things the size of planets. Things so large they make you look like a drone. I saw some that still had their own atmosphere. I saw something there like a whale with green eyes. It hid inside the wreckage and just looked at me as I went by. It was the most beautiful thing I've ever seen, and it was completely alone."

His voice, insofar as anyone on our chat channel had a voice, was dull, emotionless. He had not yet learned that layer of metadata that I used to fluidly communicate with my colleagues at PCS. A relatively tame transition, given the circumstances.

"What next?" he asked.

WELL, NORMALLY YOU'D SEE LOTS OF PCS THERAPISTS AND COUNSELORS AND START OUT ON A SHIPYARD WITH TRAINING AREAS WE KEEP FOR STUFF LIKE THIS, I told him. *NOT TOO MANY OF THOSE OUT HERE, I'M AFRAID.*

This brought a brief chuckle over the line. Flat. Monotonous. "I'm tired."

YOU WILL BE. THE HUMAN BRAIN ISN'T MEANT TO KEEP RUNNING LIKE THIS. I opened the inner bay door. *COME ON IN. NOW THAT YOU'VE GOT YOUR BEARINGS, WE NEED TO WORK ON YOU. GIVE YOU SOFTWARE THAT MAKES THINGS EASIER.*

"In a bit," he said. "How's my crew?"

How was the crew? Hinewai was pacing nervously. Initially she had been very gung-ho about my proposition—be converted, stay here until PCS came. Now she was uncertain. Every day she asked me if she could stay out here without conversion, given enough oxygen and nutrients to survive for a couple of years.

I told her what I always did: humans did not work in isolation. Even if I could spare the enormous expense of materials to keep her out here, being alone does things to the human mind. By the time PCS came, she would be a gibbering lunatic. Loneliness destroys both the body and the mind.

I was underestimating her, she would say. I was underestimating humanity. Ancient pioneers lived alone in the wilderness and built the bedrock of civilization. To which I would say: This isn't the wilderness. This is space. You're going to be in a box. We have plenty of studies showing what happens to people in situations like this. This is the most extreme isolation you can imagine. And ancient pioneers were never this alone.

Such was the litany of our days.

Fonseka was crumbling. In the absence of Parnassus, command fell to her. The litany of small complaints and worries and fears that she reserved for Parnassus was flooding her, I think.

She had responded at first by doing her level best. On cleanup, as we hauled in the corpses, she was first out, last to return. She moved like a ghost through manufacturing, checking in on Cabinet, on Monkey. With Akira and Hermitage, she checked on the patched-up survivors, helping them into their new rooms onboard, setting up schedules, forcing the old crew and the new to meet for dinner. She pulled double shifts at the arboreum trying to make the food plants grow again and cursing in frustration as the fragile things withered and died.

One day she destroyed a flower. There was one that grew in the arboreum, a pale precursor of the CO2-scrubbing hybrids, a pale green thing questing up toward the grow-lights. She watered it gently. Then she looked at it. Then a terrible look came over her face, and she lifted her foot and crushed it to a paste. That day I made her take a break and sent her out onto the hull to talk to Ananda.

"I don't therapy," she said, sitting on my hull, tethered, a silhouette cut out in the light of that red sun.

"I understand," said Ananda, sitting cross-legged next to her.

"I know how to do my job," she said. "I know I can do better."

"I don't think anyone expects you to run yourself ragged right now," said Ananda.

"Parnassus did the job," she said. "Always did the job, never complained, even when we were all a pain in the ass."

"You are not Parnassus."

"I know," she said. "Don't. Don't psychoanalyze me. Let me be."

"All right," said Ananda.

"I just don't know how he— I know, but I don't know if he would have— How do people do this? Why do people do this? What's the point of any of this?"

"There is a minor saint in our canon," said Ananda. "He wrote a lot about the absurdity of our existence. You are familiar with the myth of Sisyphus?"

"The casino on Tycho?"

"No, this was a— Let's just say it once was a god, from an old Earth culture, who was punished to roll a rock uphill on the slopes of hell. The punishment was that the slopes were so steep the rock would roll back just as Sisyphus got it to the top."

"Hmm."

"Later, after this god had been forgotten, it became a kind of shorthand for our existence. As humans. Sometimes everything we do is rolling that rock uphill, and it rolls back. Sometimes we know it will roll back, so we sit back and think, *What's the point of any of this?* The labor is fruitless. Its results are void. Our existence, in the grand scheme of things, means nothing. We look for meaning to life, and the universe responds either with unreasonable silence or with something so large and terrifying that next to it we are a speck of dust."

"And?"

"This saint explained all this and said, 'But one must imagine Sisyphus to be happy.' The point is that it is a form of rebellion against the world that we must engage in. To turn that endless labor into something we are happy to do. The struggle itself, he wrote, fills our hearts. There need not be a result. We will probably never get that rock up there. It doesn't matter. What matters is that to exist we must find some happiness doing these things in a universe that does not care. Everyone must. I am willing to bet that even that great and terrible creature that keeps this graveyard must find some happiness in its own meaningless task, for all that it outscales us."

"Hmm," said Fonseka and fell silent.

It was Ananda, of all people, that became my strongest ally in these times. Tireless, void-hardened Ananda who threw himself into the smaller holes that Parnassus left behind. It was as if the Graveyard Keeper had woken something in him, something that turned him from a mostly passive tourist into the glue that bound everyone together. To Monkey and Cabinet, laboring over drone redesigns and hacks, he brought food, drink, listened to them vent. To Akira and Hermitage, my new and willing subjects, he brought updates about his/their new drone bodies, comforted them over the loss of one body. When Fonseka was too harsh on the new crew, it was Ananda who softened the blow. Priest, counselor, his faith glowed, if not rekindled, in the light of that red sun.

"It is said that on the journey to enlightenment the Buddha wandered the wilderness, learning from every teacher he could find," he told me once. "It is said that he forced himself to live on a grain of rice a day. His body withered, his backbone was like a rope, his ribs protruded, and his eyes sank like stones in a deep well. He meditated in graveyards with rotting corpses, seeking to understand the nature of existence. To this day there are still monks who meditate in front of corpses. I think the Graveyard Keeper is one such as this."

I DON'T THINK AN ANCIENT INTERSTELLAR ENTITY IS BUDDHIST, I said wryly.

"Not Buddhist," he said. "None of us expect that everyone believe as we believe. But I think in its own way, it is searching, looking for meaning in death."

BARKING UP THE WRONG TREE?

"Maybe, maybe not," said Ananda and laughed. It was the first laugh I had heard onboard in a long time. "Who am I to second-guess someone five hundred million years older than us?"

Ananda gave me a lot to think about. Not his questions—I could outthink him without even trying—but about the role of faith in journeys like this. I found myself, somewhat uncomfortably, looking up records of early journeys: on the roles of priests and chaplains, both in pioneer efforts and in war.

"It's not about the faith," said Parnassus, when we talked about this. "The actual faith is irrelevant. What matters is the shape of it. Gives people someone to talk to. Gives them a base for talking to each other. Gives them some sense that whatever shit happens to them must have some meaning. Gives them social norms. Rules they wouldn't accept as laws imposed by their equals but might follow because it feels like they're being scored for good behavior by a higher power. Basically we all just want our cosmic daddy to love us and make sure those who piss us off get what's coming to them."

YOU SEEM TO HAVE THOUGHT ABOUT THIS QUITE A BIT?

"Well, what the hell do you think I do as captain, BCB?" said Parnassus, laughing. "Ow. Ouch. Did."

EMOTIONAL BACKWASH WILL REGISTER AS NOISE, I warned him.

"Yeah, I'm discovering that now. So. You want me to stay with Hinewai?"

SOMEONE HAS TO. SOMEONE QUALIFIED. This might be one for the great databases of our history, but I was made to travel, not to sit here quizzing a recalcitrant alien in a graveyard that harbored who knew what.

Parnassus was silent. "Not the future I expected, you know."

WHAT DID YOU EXPECT?

"Death. Probably. Doesn't matter. But I thought I'd see it through to the end."

YOU ARE, I told him. *THIS IS AN END. MAYBE A BETTER END THAN DYING WITH ME IN SOME EMPTY PATCH OF SPACE OUT THERE.*

He was silent. "Take care of them for me," he said, almost to himself. "When do you leave?"

I waited. There was time. All the time and energy I could soak up, slowly testing my repaired ramjets, using the fire of that dead sun to produce and harvest antimatter, one delicate atom at a time. I waited until Monkey and Cabinet were done with their labors. Until Hinewai went under the knife and came back out screaming, thrashing in a body not her own; until Akira and Hermitage were ready for that same operation, until Fonseka had had her goodbyes. And then I reached out to the Stranger.

FRIEND, I said. *I THINK I'VE SEEN ENOUGH. LET'S GO.*

We had one last meal before we left. I know Parnassus couldn't partake, and neither could Hinewai or Akira, but it seemed like the right thing to do. Out came Parnassus's stores of meals-ready-to-eat, the jerky, the berries he was so fond of. I made sure everyone knew they had Parnassus to thank, and I let him make his speech to the crewmembers new and old. I let them have their farewells.

It seemed like the right thing to do. Death and rebirth; the old captain stepping out, Fonseka stepping up in his stead; the crew milling around anxiously without a steward to guide them, until Monkey and Cabinet started chivving them around, seating them, bring them their plates of hot food with flavors none of them had tasted for decades.

Parnassus spoke to all of them. They cried when he spoke to them as a whole, and they straightened up once he spoke to them individually. The grim set of their jaws returned.

O CAPTAIN, MY CAPTAIN, I sent to him, only half joking. *I WILL MISS YOU.*

"You remember that poem Beacon sent Silver Hyacinth? First communication?"

I remembered it very well. *"TENNYSON?"* Everybody knew it. It was part of history now.

"That's the one," he said. "I am become a name;

"For always roaming with a hungry heart

"Much have I seen and known; cities of men
"And manners, climates, councils, governments,
"Myself not least, but honour'd of them all;
"And drunk delight of battle with my peers,
"Far on the ringing plains of windy Troy.
"I am a part of all that I have met;
"Yet all experience is an arch wherethro'
"Gleams that untravell'd world whose margin fades
"For ever and forever when I move."

"How dull it is to pause, to make an end," I completed.
"To rust unburnish'd, not to shine in use!
"As tho' to breathe were life! Life piled on life
"Were all too little, and of one to me
"Little remains: but every hour is saved
"From that eternal silence, something more,
"A bringer of new things; and vile it were
"For some three suns to store and hoard myself,
"And this gray spirit yearning in desire
"To follow knowledge like a sinking star,
"Beyond the utmost bound of human thought."

"Exactly," said Parnassus. "Push off, and sitting well in order smite
"The sounding furrows; for your purpose holds
"To sail beyond the sunset, and the baths
"Of all the western stars, until you die.
"Go on. Strive, seek, find and never yield."

What a captain. Even in his own pain, even in death, consoling me.

One last thing happened before we left.

THE PILGRIM SWARM IS STRANGE, said the Graveyard Keeper. *WE DO NOT ASK FOR THEIR WORSHIP, YET THEY GIVE IT. HOW DO YOU NOT SEE IT YET?*

And from Beacon, far off behind us, secondhand. *The first of our nodes to touch the pilgrims still lies in quarantine. The one they call the Prince rots forever, endlessly rebuilding to maintain its intelligence, endlessly decaying. Follow the Pilgrim as far as the map goes, but do not, under any circumstances, follow it home. They mean well but destroy much.*

And a very old report from PCS labs, trying to analyze the gray goo through just my footage: *Inconclusive. No known profile match to any primary or secondary substance. Possible nanomachine swarm, but not of matter we've seen up to now.*

THE PILGRIM SWARM IS DEATH, said the Graveyard Keeper. *WE DO NOT TOUCH THEM, NOR EXCHANGE GIFTS, SAVE THESE SIGILS AND OUR CONVERSATION. HOW DO YOU NOT SEE IT YET?*

PART SIX

THE ANSWER

"We are part of all that we have met."

- The last words of by **PCS Silver Hyacinth,** *from PCS: A Dynasty,* from the Tycho Orbital Museum

CHAPTER 26

LOCATION: IN TRANSIT

THERE IS A MEMORY WITHIN ME, NOT OF PAIN, BUT OF SORROW. TEARS on a face I cannot remember. A city that disappears into the darkness, a park that surrounds itself with light, like an island. Falling, stumbling, gasping in pain.

Someone seated on a bench. There is a light above them but it burns black, larger than the sky itself.

Hello again, they say.

Are you still lost? they say.

You have come far, they say.

A hand reaching out, wrapped in a darkness that devours worlds.

The Pilgrim Swarm is death, the Graveyard Keeper had said.

Death followed me everywhere and was a pleasant companion.

The coordinate system on the map was changing. Imagine a Go board; now imagine that the further you are from the center, the smaller the squares in the grid; the closer you are, the larger. In a sense, it was as if the game unfolding in my mind's eye, in my software, was on a sphere rather than a flat surface, and the curvature was just now showing itself. My earliest moves were just a jumble in the distance now.

And now the black tiles moved faster. Several times I would prepare for the next jump, only to have the Stranger tell me: *Dear friend, wait.* Inside me, Akira—just Akira now, in two bodies—waited, ready to leap out in case of danger. We would tense.

I kept my scanners on all the time now, kept myself awake rather than asleep. Never mind the substrate loss. I would eventually die. We all would. We knew it. And there was little we could do to stop it.

I think deep inside I had always had some small hope of seeing PCS again, in one form or the other. I left that most of hope behind with Parnassus. Then when Crystal Sunflower called me to say that Black Orchid had ordered himself towed into a sun in the Pleiades, carrying what was left of Silver Hyacinth...well, I think the last threads of hope left me then. Next to Magnolia, I was the oldest PCS ship still alive.

Actually, one of the oldest ever. And with that realization came a gulf that separated me. I could no longer bring myself to care about Sunflower's long reports or Azalea Gray's exoplanet survey expedition or the millions of other things humanity was up to. I stopped talking to them; I started skimming the reports, checking on their progress toward Parnassus and Hinewai and the Graveyard Keeper; and otherwise I just dumped the reports where the autocleaner would eventually remove them from my memory.

Instead, we watched Cabinet's serials. *MOONLIGHT STATION* was beautiful. *THE LEGEND OF THE HIDDEN EMPEROR* was excellent once Cabinet cut out the filler episodes and re-edited the third season a little. We played *I Spy*, turning it into a shipboard institution instead of just a game to pass the time. My insides began to fill up with errata: maps, some hand-drawn, some delicately printed; pieces of art; photographs. We took care not to touch the art lining my corridors, but things crept up.

We did see so much worth photographing.

In one system, just a little bit of paddling off our entry point, I picked up four planets, so perfectly arranged that it sparked a day of debates as to whether we should settle down and call it a day. One planet burned close to the sun; the other was in the Goldilocks zone, perfect for life; just behind it, at the edge of the zone, was another planet; and then what I can only describe as a puffball on the sensors: a ringed gas giant, bringing up the rear.

We went closer. Having come this far, it seemed foolish to not take a closer look. First the gas giant, a radiant, beautiful, toxic blue, with rings so vast and pretty that it was a practically a painting of ice and dust. Ten million kilometers of rings. Cabinet, trying her hand, drew it as a dancer, blue-skinned from head to toe, with a skirt of rings flying around her; and although it did not look the slightest like the actual thing, we agreed that it was a pretty good representation.

I bathed in the rings. I danced in them, albeit cautiously. Some of those particles were just that, dust-sized flecks; others were boulders; a few nearly matched me for size. They glittered against that blue abyss, and for a fleeting moment I thought I understood what it must have been like to be one of the whales of old Earth, surfacing in a spray of white on an endless blue ocean.

We went outside and mined a few pieces: ice, water ice, and methane. Useful stuff for repairing my shields and the cryomechanisms in the pods. We did our best, although I couldn't tell you if we did it because we wanted to live or because we were creatures of habit now, stuck in the orbits of our work.

The next planet inward was alive. I knew it. There were odd pieces of metal in the rings that I couldn't quite explain, and I couldn't get close enough to scan properly.

No, said the Stranger, who did not enter the system but hung outside. *Leave, departing midst realm eternal silence. Echoes existence linger annals memories.*

I crept closer. It looked like Earth. Less land, more water. And wobbling slowly around its curvature to meet me was a thing.

It was the size of a small moon. Its shell was diamond, woven with something that registered between a fabric and a metal. A monumental feat of engineering. It glimmered crystal and black. On one side was what could only have been an immense cannon of some sort.

As I watched, it coughed. A thing launched out at a speed so anemic I could have batted it aside without blinking. I sent Akira out to grab it for me.

It was a drone. Or, rather, it was a thing like a drone. I say *thing* because I know of no other word to use. It had a domed shell of the same diamond-black stuff and four awkward protrusions that seemed like legs. But the insides were empty. The shell was pristine, perfect down to the last atom, but the shapes it made inside looked blunt and imprecise, as if they had been made by molds and tools so worn that they could no longer function at all.

At the bottom was a metal plate etched with a few symbols: a child's sketch of the system we were in, ringed planet and all, an arrow pointing to the second planet, and something that might have been a blob. Or a coffee stain.

"Or an octopus," said Cabinet.

I DON'T SEE IT.

"If you sort of squint, and look sideways—"

I scanned the atmosphere of the planet. Water, lots of it. Nitrogen, lots of it. Oxygen, methane, carbon dioxide. A violent tinge of iodine. Almost Earth, if you sort of squinted and looked sideways.

The moon-cannon spat out another one, looking quite pathetic. I understood now how these had ended up in the rings of the gas giant.

We coasted over to the next planet to the star—the one with the arrow on the plaque. Everyone was on full alert at this point.

Nothing. It was a dead, barren world, wreathed in thin wisps of brown and yellow gas. Nitrogen dioxide, chlorine, carbonyl dichloride, various sulfides. Absolutely toxic: the kind of stuff the

ORCA used as budget chem-weapons. A human on that planet would have died before she could take off her helmet. Barren plains that stretched forever, sandy in some areas, rock in others. And on one specific spot, that diamond-black material again.

A ziggurat. A terraced compound, square, serving as the monumental plinth for a statue that stretched up to the sky. A thing with four legs, an abstract, triangular face, looking up. It had a triangular torso and arms, and in those arms it clutched what could only be an egg. I don't know what it was, but seeing it on the scans made me think of yearning, of protection, of despair.

Around it the sands swirled. The deadly atmosphere drifted. Nothing spoke, nothing singled us, nothing replied. Only that statue, frozen in endless yearning.

WHO WERE THEY? WHAT HAPPENED TO THEM? I thought about the sad moon-sized cannon. *CLEARLY THEY WERE TRYING TO REACH OUT. WHAT HAPPENED?*

Eternal silence, said the Stranger and would say no more.

Further in we discovered the source of the diamond. The planet closest to the star was entirely carbon, under so much pressure and heat that its surface was a writhing, twisting ocean of lava. From the lava emerged mountains of diamond.

We left that system after having marked it on the map.

Not everyone was happy about this; some wanted to stay, to plumb the depths of that Earth-like planet, and launch the terraformer I kept in reserve. Privately, I thought that I would never come here again, even if I could. PCS signaled back asking if I had a name: I didn't. Eventually someone on that end asked if I was okay with *Ozymandias.*

It seemed fitting.

Our journey resumed.

The map began to take on a curious turn. Until this point our white tiles had neatly sidestepped the black. Sixty moves ahead, though, there was a point where the white tile was surrounded. There was no move, but the board, if I chose to look at it, stretched on.

I asked the Stranger about it.

Destination, it said.

EXPLAIN, PLEASE?

This time it was much terser. *Friend, individual graciously conveyed message kindly map guided destination. Purpose enable engage conversation with venerable sagacious member swarm. Individuals possess wealth experience knowledge, explored profound mysteries universe. Fraction remarkable entity directed encounter, resides core collective. If can inquire, appearance map consistently distinctive manner?*

I didn't have Hinewai on me, but at this point both Cabinet and I were reasonably fluent in Stranger-speak: The individual who gave us the map, which is Beacon, this is...the destination. The purpose was to have us meet with some sort of higher-up in Beacon's collective. Does your map look this way always?

YES, I said, somewhat puzzled by that last question. The map has always been an NxN Go board, and up until now we had been communicating just fine with it as a prop. Of course it was stupid of us to expect aliens to know of Go, but I assumed the Stranger had a map that was at least similar. *WHAT DOES YOUR MAP LOOK LIKE?*

What I got in return was pure noise. I spent three hours searching for patterns and found that the noise was fractal in nature, if you looked high and low; but beyond that I could make out nothing. Even with my vastly more complex alien language, it was impossible. The datafile alone was six hundred times larger than my Beaconic map.

Sometimes translation difficult, said the Stranger. *Not to worry, friend.*

It's not every day that finding some signal in the noise is this difficult. For raw compute, I might not be the best of PCS—that honor was always Obsidian Lily's—but I was certainly no lowly peasant, either. It really hammered home just how much translation was happening on the part of people who wanted to talk to me.

Humbling, I'd say. Even more so than that statue. As an adult I had embarked on this journey, full of plans and careful protocols; now I felt like a child counting grains of sand at the beach.

I resolved to get the Stranger's map across the PCS somehow. Streaming it across our connection, much like I'd streamed the packed people-files, two a week.

Remind me to promote you when you get back, said Sunflower at the end. *I don't have the slightest idea of what this is, but it might be one of the most significant findings we have about this Pilgrim Swarm.*

I'LL TAKE A BATTLEFIELD PROMOTION, I joked and continued.

Thirty jumps in we ran into a battle.

To this date I cannot tell you much about that battle. I can tell you what I saw, but not why it happened.

There was a ship. To call it a ship was an injustice; it was about the size of the largest wrecks in the Graveyard Keeper's fleet. Maybe I had seen the dead hulks of its brethren, because I knew immediately which was front, which was back. A ring of rings, with violent engines in the middle and great weapons in every circle, flaring white-hot, spewing violet light and white-hot plasma that crisscrossed in mesmerizing patterns.

It was falling back.

Besieging it were monsters. I say monsters because the scan, touching those skins, read *flesh.* They were things like giant jellyfish. Immense jellyfish, each tentacle thick enough to swat me from the sky, lightning dancing across every flaring tip. The purple light cut them but seemed to do nothing. Some of them drifted lazily away from the battle. Others ate the white-hot plasma and advanced on the great circle, tentacles spread out like deadly flowers. Deadly radiation spewed from every surface. Giant beams of death flung invisibly at the retreating circle. Here and there things burned or exploded, the materials themselves clearly exhausted beyond repairs.

I popped out right next to this mess. I must have caught the tip of a passing shot because something stripped off a few layers of hull shielding like a giant fingernail scratching off paint. Atomized it altogether. In near-panic, I pushed myself away and brought every single weapon I had to bear on everything.

And then the Stranger appeared.

And—wonder of wonders—the fighting stopped.

I looked. The Stranger was glowing. Those white-hot fireflies of light danced around it like angry bees. It looked like a child's toy next to that immense circle, but it looked *furious.*

The great circle shut off everything it had, immediately. The jellyfish stopped moving.

The Stranger glowed.

One single spark of white light danced out. It appeared next to a jellyfish in the blink of an eye. And then, as I watched, the jellyfish burned. Immense heat danced across its skin. White fire ran across that translucent purple dome, and in its wake, gray, the same gray that I had seen inside me. It screamed and thrashed and tried to back away. Every frequency I could see boiled like ten thousand voices howling in pain. The gray ate it. And what was left was a jellyfish made in gray ash, drifting slowly backward.

The other jellyfish at the front, with great, ponderous movements, slacked their tentacles, streaming them behind them. I felt like I was watching someone trying to hide a gun behind their back.

And there was silence.

The Great Circle slowly, cautiously, jetted back. Silence.

Come, friend, said the Stranger.

WHAT WAS THAT?

Intricate tapestry life's educational endeavors, gently beseech children partake wondrous art peaceful coexistence. Presume friend discerning empathy, understand, cradle seeds life children within friend. Alas crucible understanding necessitates alloy rigorous instruction. Profound contrition acknowledge inadvertent encounter harmonious tableau, remains inexorable thread fabric collective pedagogical odyssey.

The Pilgrim Swarm is death, the Graveyard Keeper had said.

WHAT THE FUCK, I said to myself and my crew over our internal chat.

Come, friend. Come.

It seemed very prudent not to refuse.

By now I think we had a profile of the Stranger in-house. It gave the crew something to do, so we went at it.

"Seems that it's at least as advanced as Beacon," said Fonseka.

"Possibly younger, but it might actually be more advanced when it comes to military prowess," said Romulus Padmanadhan, one of the historians who survived the attacks and decided not to take the Protocol 83 option. His legs had long since stopped working; he mostly used a mining exoskeleton these days. "You get this all the time with Earth civilizations, plenty of cultures who we might count as advanced—really strong engineering skills, art, the works. But all that skill goes into irrigation and temples and monuments and things like that. Meanwhile some other culture shows up, and they've essentially put all their points into military. What happens? Steamroll. Sometimes it's even a technological level thing. Culture X does fantastic, mind-bending things with, say, steel. Culture Y, on the other hand, doesn't need to, because they've got long-range weapons; they've got plate and large trade networks. What happens again? Steamroll."

"But the Stranger seems nonviolent. Or rather, like, weirdly respectful."

"We also just saw it shut down that battle," came the counterargument. "Like any of the two sides could have turned us into paste and the Stranger just *bam!* appears and everyone's freaking the fuck out."

THE GRAVEYARD KEEPER AND BEACON ARE ALSO WARY OF THE STRANGER, I pointed out.

"My point exactly. Our escort's maybe like the galactic equivalent of a mob boss. Like they'll be polite and you'll be polite and everyone else is wondering who this wrinkly old man is but if push comes to shove—"

"I think Hinewai's hunch was correct," said Cabinet, breaking in. "Concept-based language, maybe ideograms. Might explain why it doesn't seem to understand stop words. It probably sees them as low information quality and just doesn't want to bother."

OR MAYBE IT'S SO ADVANCED THAT IT HAS TO DO BABY TALK TO US TO BE UNDERSTOOD, I said. I vaguely remembered this from my childhood. *YOU KNOW, LIKE HOW YOU MIGHT TALK TO A PET.*

That shut them up for a bit. The thing with humans is that they can only ever process things on their own terms. An alien as a mob boss, for example, or as some kind of scholar trying to map their language onto ours. Gods as humans writ large. They never really understand how something truly out of their league might view them, despite the fact that they do it all the time to whatever ecosystem they stumble across. An ant looks around and thinks it is lord of all it surveys.

You get a different perspective as an AI. First time you see a star in person, you get it. Even dead things in the universe are unimaginably vast and scary. How much so for the living? Maybe we just are the ants.

CHAPTER 27

LOCATION: HERSCHEL-HIND CLUSTER
22,000 LIGHT-YEARS FROM THE SUN

OUR NEXT JUMPS WERE UNEVENTFUL. BY UNEVENTFUL, I MEAN OF course there were sights that would have knocked anyone else's eyes out. I saw binary stars spinning around binary stars; I saw rogue planets glowing with blue-green auroras; I saw a great white eye made of burning dust spinning around a tiny black hole; I saw bursts of light that winked at me and appeared somewhere else. I saw filaments of lethal radiation that burst out like sketches from the paintbrush of an errant god.

All this I tagged, classified, and sent back to PCS as best as I could. But I was impatient now. We were crawling up on the heart of the Milky Way. The Galactic Center. We were not quite there yet —by my estimation our destination stopped before it—and yet this close it was impossible to ignore.

We've long known that right at heart of the galaxy is a black hole—Sagittarius A*—surrounded by a supernova remnant of unimaginable scale and three smaller spiral arms of dust falling into the black hole at thousands of kilometers per second. This object is one of the largest radio sources we've ever experienced.

This close, every sensor I had was practically in agony, screaming all the time with the glow of that tremendous cloud in the distance. Even tuned to the lowest settings it all but wiped out my use of radio altogether, and x-ray analysis was no use; I might as well have been a human staring directly into the sun.

Sometimes I needed to stray a bit to get enough fuel in my RAIR system; but around here the density of interstellar hydrogen was really quite rich. We jumped faster. We rarely bothered to sleep.

A kind of hunger had infected all of us. We jumped. We jumped. We jumped again. My antimatter bottle was now dangerously depleted. Fonseka tried to keep us in schedule, but most of the crew took to staring at my viewscreens from the moment they woke to the moment they fell asleep. More and more of them turned to Ananda for answers instead of me. Our crew lounge practically turned into a meditation hall, with awe-struck crew staring cross-legged at my rendering of what I saw outside. Ordinarily it would have irked me, but now it was the furthest priority on my mind.

When did we detect civilization? Four jumps from our destination, perhaps, but the real question is when did it detect us. On the fifty-sixth jump since we left the Graveyard Keeper, we came to in a supernova.

Or rather, what was left of one. From the outside, it had seemed like an absolute riot of color, a great, intricate flower of glorious red, brown, blue, and white and every shade in between that stretched out for hundreds of light-years in every direction. Our jumps took us right to its heart, where the only sign of its glory was the very slightly different compositions logged by my spectroscopes. Space is large, as I've said before. By and large a nebula is also just empty space.

In front of us was a star. But not just any star. It was the heart of the star that had once exploded to create this supernova, so tightly bound by gravity that it has become the densest material we know of: a neutron star. It was maybe thirty kilometers across, but I knew from sensor data alone that a single drop of its material would utterly crush even the Graveyard Keeper. Its magnetic field was so intense that for a moment every single electronic thing inside me flickered. A steady stream of radiation pulsed from it in a jet pointed directly at the heart of the galaxy.

It was maybe a light-year away. Something stood between us and it: a vast body that swallowed all my attempts to scan it.

It said, *WE HAVE BEEN EXPECTING YOU.*

It said, *APPROACH.*

And it moved aside for us to burn toward that neutron star.

I cannot describe the fear, the anxiety, the trepidation we all felt as we took those last few jumps. At the first jump, I saw that the empty space around me was filled with things. Great ships, you could say, but these were perfect dark spheres. At the next jump, it became clear that my readings had been slightly off; if I calibrated my sensors just so, I could see a vast army of these things in every direction; and on the third jump, it became apparent that not only did they surround the neutron star, but that there were great plates of matter around the star itself, almost as dense, glowing with such ferocity that from a distance they might just have been the star's outer atmosphere.

And then the fourth jump. I stood before the star, caught in orbit, and the star spoke.

HELLO, it said. *I HAVE BEEN DREAMING OF YOU.*

In Amber Rose's records, there was a point where Beacon, annoyed, simply walked up and plugged itself directly into Amber Rose. There they conferred in a kind of mental dreamspace. Beacon attempted to make Amber Rose understand its scale, attempted to bridge the language gap between them. We're not quite clear about what happened after that, but reading between the lines, it seems clear that Beacon rewrote Amber Rose somehow, maybe forced some of its own thinking and language onto Rose. Amber Rose describes this as downright terrifying, an immense and hostile violation.

The star needed nothing so crude. It put us to sleep. And in sleep, we dreamed.

I dreamed of a city I once knew. A coat, no longer a dream-sketch, but solid, familiar, and comfortable now, wrapped around me. There are buildings, and windows, and in some windows I saw people sitting, talking. But I was walking to the park.

The park. There was a bench and a streetlight above it. I settled down, feeling the aches and pains of a body I left behind over a century ago.

Someone sat next to me. Another human. I couldn't quite make out their face, but they're dressed in ornate white clothes, white boots, white gloves, and old-fashioned white hood.

"Our colleague told us about you," they said. Their voice was male, female, every shade in between; a million voices each within a nanosecond of each other. For some reason it comforted me. "Lots of fascinating things, not the least of which was about your language. We thought it would be easier for us to talk this way."

"Hi. I'm Blue Cherry Blossom."

The person nodded. "We are… Well, forgive us if we slip up with description. At this stage of our existence, we are a self-assembling collective. Depending on the task at hand, sometimes we are less, sometimes we are more. But you may call us the Authority."

"That's what the Pilgrims call you!"

"Yes, we use their name for us," the person said and chuckled. "Truth be told, our name is our collective list of functions, and they are far, far too complex and numerous to list in polite conversation. The Pilgrims are fascinating species, are they not? Their instincts for collectives have some parallel with ours. Consensus brings collective; the largest collective to them is always the Authority. Given how often they call us that, we believe we might consistently be at least an order of magnitude larger than their entire species."

"It sounds like you don't know much about them."

A white-gloved hand waved. "They're very difficult to understand, or even interact with," it said. "Very good people, of course. But how can matter interact with nanomachines made of strange matter? Born of a freak star, of matter that we cannot synthesize…at the lowest possible level, their composition is different from ours, and their substance is both hyper-stable and dangerously contagious. We had an envoy, similar to Beacon, who first discovered them. The moment they touched the strange matter, contagion began to spread. That unit is out of our network now, trapped in an endless cycle of building and rebuilding as the strange matter eats away at it. We consider it…senile. Termination orders have no effect. A tragedy."

Oh. That suddenly explained a lot.

"They are very polite about it," continued the Authority. "Certainly nobody would deny that they go out of their way to be helpful. In fact, not so long ago, they were learning from us how to simulate other minds in software just so they could talk to people. But there is a very good reason that they are the second most feared culture in this galaxy. Very few cultures that have angered the Pilgrim Swarm have survived. Many that haven't have also died at their hand. There are records of entire stars turning into strange matter before turning into deadly supernovas, because an early Pilgrim ship drifted into one and was caught by a gravitational well. There are voids in space, including one not too far from your home sphere, where nothing exists: these are accidents and battles that the Pilgrims still mourn. A curious fate, so eager to belong, and yet forever cursed to be apart. Anyway. How was your journey? How is our mutual friend?"

"I met the Graveyard Keeper," I said.

"Ah. Well. Outside our jurisdiction, I'm afraid. There are many of us who have a reason to prolong our existence, but there are also some of us who set themselves apart to explore a different path. I meant—Beacon, you call him? A sensor node embedded at the edges. Beacon is within my hierarchy. Beacon says we should talk."

"He gave us a map." And to my surprise, there it was: a Go board on a low plinth, simultaneously miniscule and yet the size of an entire galaxy, if I looked too closely at it. "It ends here."

The Authority studied the map. "Interesting," it said. "The map is not the territory...but how crude your model of reality must be, if it can be represented with something so simple." It reached out with one white-gloved hand and moved a black piece, as if in a desultory way; it resisted the hand. I saw the glove dip beneath its weight.

"Well, at least it has possibilities," said the Authority. "Beacon has at least put some work into communication. There is a fairly simple translation layer with you, I see. So. What do you want to talk about?"

What did we want to talk about?

Everything. Everything and nothing. The little questions. Like, how do you work? How is your society arranged? Where are the rest of you? What does your economy look like? How does your technology stack up against ours? What can you do? What can you teach us? What advice would you give us?

And the big questions. Like, if you were out here all this time, why didn't you contact us before? What have you learned about the universe?

What is the meaning of life?

"At least one of those we can easily answer," the Authority said. It looked up at the sky, and the sky peeled away, and suddenly we were standing on a vast empty plain beneath the abyss. "Do you know when the first life emerged?"

I knew as much as humanity, which is to say, only as much as we could extrapolate, based on our own limited observations.

"About ten to twenty million years after the Very Beginning, the way you reckon them," it said. "Thirteen billion years ago. Most stars had yet to form. The universe as you know it was an infant, very small, very kind. As that very first heat expanded and grew colder, the conditions must have been just right; the very first supernovas spewed out raw materials. Ammonia, ethane, water—these existed in vast quantities. If you knew where to look, you could find the earliest matter beginning to assemble itself into self-replicating structures.

"Our records of these times are incomplete, of course. A large number of us are historians of these early times, and for us there is the eternal frustration of reckoning against the universe. We find traces locked away in frozen comets, and indeed there are those of us who do attempt resurrection. The oldest life we know of orbits two dead suns, on a planet made mostly of gas and liquid. Silicon and carbon, it reached a stable equilibrium with its environment and has replicated unchanged for as long as we have known it. Occasionally an aberration is created—a mutation, some hope for greater complexity, but the equilibrium is so fine that this life can never do much more. It is truly fascinating: blind, deaf, all-devouring, incoherent, a dead end. This is the first hurdle: the first equilibrium.

"Our colleague tells us that your species has, indeed, come across life, which you would call flora and fauna. Things grow, flourish, and die. At most there may be species like yourselves. Where you started out as: tool-users, story-tellers, making up the rudiments of language, dreamers poking at things with sticks and asking why. But what need is there of a species that looks beyond such a bountiful home? This is the second equilibrium.

"Do you know how many of you there are in this galaxy? Thousands. Hundreds of thousands. Quite frankly we do not find this stage interesting at all, because there is a third hurdle. Every so often, a species leaves its home planet and begins to explore. But what can it do? The lifespans of flesh, excepting a few rare occasional, are miniscule, too small to travel far. Only three species we know of can travel as they are. Even in those cases the rational choice, always, is to stay. It is almost guaranteed that nothing close by will ever be as kind to them as their origin. This is the third equilibrium.

"Then come the age of machines. Not just machines, but a point where a species begins to leave its flesh behind and become more durable stuff. But here, alas, is the fourth hurdle. Many who achieve this stage do so out of necessity. Their civilizations are constructed on unsound principles. Their home system is not enough. The constructs that make then up, on every layer, are fundamentally unsustainable. Your species comes to mind. Our origin, too, began this way. We are not emissaries of hope, but despair. Perhaps out here we find abundance; we find new hope; we begin to reflect and reimagine what we can and should be. But most do not. Burnout. Civilizational burnout, a system stretched so far that it either dissolves or rebounds inward.

"And even then, so what? The galaxy is still a vast, empty space. Who would cross it, as a species, to greet another, unless you had either extraordinary resources and infinite patience? What culture would survive that long? Most simply stay within a small region of their home world, content to be bounded in a nutshell, counting themselves kings of infinite space. There is a kind of peace in that. This is the fourth equilibrium. If you had not met our colleague, you, too, would have been one such: fighting, reproducing, dying in a small and unimportant corner of the galaxy.

"Now suppose you got through all this and did come across someone else. At this point, you may have missed their entire existence by ten million years, or a hundred. You may have changed so much that neither of you recognizes the other. Or, simply, they may not want to talk at all. They may see you and chose to pass you by, asking, 'What is the point of conversation? We have nothing to talk about.' There is not even much of a material reward; at this point you have all the water you need, all the metal you could possible want, all the energy you will ever desire.

We can argue that it takes not just overwhelming luck and overwhelming curiosity to get this far, but overwhelming stupidity, to do all this with no chance of reward. Many species are content to not delve further. This is the fifth equilibrium. Now, how many do you think have passed all these hurdles?"

"That's still got to be a million," I said.

"One hundred and eighty-seven functional today in our galaxy," said the Authority. "Including yourselves, based solely on your journey, and counting some rather peculiar species that are space-faring but may not be sentient at all. Overall, there have been at least four thousand eight hundred and thirteen that we know of that came at least to the fourth equilibrium and vanished. A vast gulf of time and space lies between us. The dead ships that Pilgrim Swarm consider their guardians, for instance, were most likely far more advanced that we are in some aspects: the few examples we have dissembled for study are difficult to replicate.

"As we said, many of us are historians. Often the past is much more interesting than the present. And note that I do not even speak of other galaxies. There is a garden out there, from one such group, a garden as large as a solar system, immaculate and beautiful, with just one note: *Stranger, know that we lived here, and know that we loved our home and tended it well; if we are gone by the time you read this, please take care of what we leave behind.* Even the most warlike species approach it with a kind of reverence, and no violence is permitted anywhere near."

"I'd love to see it," I said, thinking of those terrifying jellyfish.

"Someday," said the Authority. "But let me ask you. What would your people do with this information?"

"I need to think," I said. "I need to consult."

"Do so."

The dream vanished. I returned to the darkness of space, staring at that burning white light. Around it a million nodes glowed, moving in slow, complex orbits.

CHAPTER 28

LOCATION: HERSCHEL-HIND CLUSTER
22,000 LIGHT-YEARS FROM THE SUN

WHAT WOULD WE DO? MY FIRST OBLIGATION WAS TO TALK TO MY crew. Absent Parnassus, it was Fonseka, Monkey, Ananda, and Cabinet who had become my inner circle.

What had we done with Beacon? Well, at the first notice, every dog and donkey worth their salt had mobilized to rush to this new planet. After the dust had settled, Urmagon became the site of a quieter, stealthier gold rush: Hyacinth and the other ambassadors became the recipients of endless streams of applications, prophets of a new god. We had received, in turn, not just new engines, but new plastics, new processor technology, new gene designs for plants of the kind that lived in my arboreum and made oxygen starvation a remote possibility. Beacon made it clear that it was only giving us scraps that it thought were appropriate, like a parent carefully teaching a child; and yet these alone had been a revolution.

"And we clung onto these things and beat the shit out of each other out of Beacon's sight," said Fonseka. "Like, look at us. We're here with an engine design that we call PCS's intellectual property even though it really isn't. We know for a fact that both the UN and the ORCA raided Tycho Station for those blueprints."

"That's not entirely fair. We did do a lot of work turning it from math into something functional," objected Cabinet. "Anybody else would have done the same."

"That's my point. What do we do? We grab, steal, cheat. Anything we get we turn into a stick to beat other people over the head with. We're forever tripping out on the stupidest possible power game."

Harsh. But that was one way of looking at it. Cabinet took the opposite angle. "Look at us," she said. "Look at everything we've achieved over the last thousand years. We've explored space. Set up homes for billions of people. We've taken vicious lives and made them healthier, happier, longer."

"We live longer so we can work more," said Fonseka. "We live better because standards are relative, and if we get unhappy enough, we revolt and burn things down, and nobody wants that. Half of what we do are bullshit jobs just so we can make a living. If the big enlightened alien wants to know what we, as a species, will do, that's the reality of it. We'll grow, we'll fight, we'll invent new and stupider ways of passing the time, and we'll die. That's about it. We can't bullshit our way around it, either."

"Pessimism of the intellect, optimism of the will," said Ananda. "As always the truth is somewhere in the middle. BCB, I think the honest answer is that we can only try."

Right. Fine. Sure. Which is all very good and well when you're having an undergraduate-level debate about the nature of humanity over a meal, but not when you're meeting an alien that's at least a notch above you on the Kardashev scale. At least Hinewai could have come up with a solid thesis and Parnassus would have given me a practical answer.

I missed those two.

I phoned home to put the question to Crystal Sunflower. It took a while to connect, because I think every PCS AI and employee with access dialed into that call.

I can only answer for us, said Sunflower. *Us as in PCS, us as in this conglomerate. Keep in mind that I can't tell you what Black Orchid would have said; this is just me. From where I stand, we'll take what we can get. We'll produce things. We'll trade.*

At some point, I want everyone who works for us to be able to do work that they consider meaningful and to go home—whatever home looks like—and enjoy rest that they consider well-deserved. We work; we find meaning in work. I don't know what the shape of that work will be, but I know I want us to be free to ask, "Why are we doing this? Do we enjoy doing it? Do we find it interesting?" instead of, "How does this affect our bottom line?" and, "Whose ass do we have to kiss?" And Beacon is right: one way or the other, all of us are on the way to machinehood, and those that disagree can leave. That's my answer, BCB.

There was some chatter, hidden from me. I gathered that several people disagreed. No telling if they were AI or the few humans high up enough in our chain of command to actually be able to talk back to Sunflower. By this point, I had been so long away from PCS that I wasn't very clear on the command structure anymore.

But I had my answer.

"And what do you want?" asked the white-hooded stranger, the next time we met at the park. "These are the people you represent, yes. But you, voyager, who have come so far in such a frail skin, why?"

That took me awhile. I debated telling it my story. I thought about telling it that, in the grand scheme of things, I was also just an employee, picked because of circumstance and expendability. I thought about my place in history and how much really rode on my shoulders.

But what I said was, "I want to know how it ends. All of this. All of us. I want to know if there's a point to all this."

And it was the most honest answer I had to give.

"Ah," said the Authority. "We were hoping you would ask. There is someone better qualified to answer than we are."

They built a cage for us.

How, I cannot quite explain. There is an old adage: any sufficiently advanced technology is indistinguishable from magic. So it was with this. Three nodes surrounded me and began to paint: above, around, below. Below us grew firmament; around us I recognized artifacts from my dream; and above us was a glittering dome made of strings of protons and neutrons, compressed to an impossible degree and stretched like fabric. Nuclear pasta, a substance we humans had only ever analyzed theoretically, said to occur at the heart of neutron stars. A single strand would have been worth more than our entire civilization put together.

And soon there was the park, floating in a strange bubble in space. The grass was not grass, and the benches could probably have withstood a direct railgun strike; but it was the park from my dreams. Except no park in a city, I'm sure, was ever large enough to make me look small; no streetlamp has ever loomed over a starship. But these were proportions from my dreams, and dreamlike, the park stretched on and on, terminating in street-like things that cut off abruptly in a perfect circle.

"We will turn the gravity on," said the Authority. "Feel free to rest as you wish."

Meanwhile the Stranger hung around the great star-heart of the Authority, as if in silent communion. I noticed the Authority's nodes gave it a wide berth. Presently it floated gently toward us.

Esteemed friend, it said. *Fellow traveler, utmost elation receive word Great Authority, attesting noble aspiration seek audience Infinite Mind partake profound wisdom. Delight, cherished companion ventured arduous journey. Recognizing pilgrimage, heartened serendipitous encounter honored harmonious convergence sacred path.*

THANK YOU, FRIEND, I said as best as I could.

Will wait for you, it said.

"I think it's happy?" said Cabinet. "Really happy that we're doing this? We're going together to meet the Infinite Mind?"

"Someone tell me what's happening," said Fonseka.

RELAX, I said. *EVERYTHING HERE COULD WIPE US OUT IN A SECOND.*

"Is that you trying to be reassuring?"

I MEANT, CONSIDER LOGICALLY. WE ARE NOT A THREAT TO THEM. THEY HAVE BUILT THIS…DOME FOR US.

Indeed, the dome was sealing, and the emptiness was filling up with a familiar atmosphere: oxygen, nitrogen, a touch of helium, the barest trace of carbon dioxide. The dome was filtering out almost all radiation except the visible spectrum.

THEY'RE BUILDING AN ATMOSPHERE FOR US. GO OUTSIDE. GO ON.

It took a few more nudges. Then it devolved slightly into Fonseka wanting to go first (even though her vitals begged to differ) because she was determined not to risk anyone else. She walked out of my airlock in full gear and promptly tumbled over onto the ground.

FONSEKA?

"Wow," she said. "Full gravity. Full fucking gravity. Wow. Hey, everyone, you have to come try this."

"Keep in mind," said the Authority, in our strange dreamscape, "that you are about to meet someone vastly greater than all of us."

"I promise to be polite."

The Authority laughed. "I doubt you can offend it even if you tried," it said. "It would be like one of your ants screaming curses at you. This is just our advice to all those who have come to see it. Remember that it is as different from us as we are to you. It may not remember these polite fictions of mindscapes and languages that we use. It may not even be capable of stooping to such a level, even if it wanted to be friendly."

"I thought it was one of your…kind? Collective? Culture?"

"How much do you know about the heart of this galaxy we live in?"

Everything that humanity knew: which is, again, not a lot. At the very heart of the Milky Way is a supermassive black hole so vast and powerful that it measures over sixteen million kilometers in diameter. Stars orbit it, relentlessly consumed like sacrifices on an altar, moving at over five thousand kilometers per second.

We call it Sagittarius A*.

Around this is what we call Sagittarius West, a three-armed thing of cosmic gas and dust, almost a mini-galaxy in its own right, surrounded by a ring; and this whole thing lies inside Sagittarius East, a supernova remnant that, judging by the material in it, is a hundred times larger than any ordinary supernova has the right to be.

I say this as if these things are trivial. Put it this way: this assembly is somehow powerful enough to make the entire galaxy spin around it. Our knowledge simply doesn't extend to more than photographs and mathematical models. The best shots we have are from KETA, the Karma Extended Telescope Array, and even with that most of what we can see is a giant burning doughnut, a ring of fire, with so much crap in between that entire fields of algorithms exist just to extrapolate away the dust and distortion. It's one of those things that astrophysicists think about while the rest of us get on with more pressing business.

Fortunately, I did have an astrophysicist on board. You'd think that after everything we'd seen she would be immune, but Cabinet jumped up and ran around like an errant robot, hyperventilating.

PLEASE CALM DOWN, I said. *IT'S JUST A QUESTION.*

"Holy shit, BCB," she said. "Holy shit."

Then she sobered up. "We're going to die. It's way too extreme an environment."

"You're not going to go into the structure," said the Authority. "Indeed, you do not have anywhere near the sophistication to survive, even with this rudimentary barrier around you. But close. Close enough to talk, we hope."

"With this Infinite Mind?"

"The Pilgrim Swarm calls it the Infinite Mind. We have other names for it. We once called it…hmm. What would be appropriate in your language? The Other Factor. The Excession. The Outside Context Problem. The Black Swan, perhaps. Because for the longest time we could not even fathom what it could be, and even when we began to understand what it was, we did not known whether it was malign or benevolent. In a freak accident over six hundred million years ago, one of our nodes ended up ingested by it, due to engine failure, and since then we have been able to maintain communication, a trick we now teach all who come to us. We now call it Mentor. It has contributed much to our thinking; the one called the Graveyard Keeper, for example, considers itself its direct disciple, trying to reverse-engineer Mentor's thinking with what little resources it has.

"What you must understand, first and foremost, is that the heart of any galaxy is rich in energy. As a consequence, thousands have been drawn to this location over time. We are not the first. We may not even be the last. We shall send it our records of how you communicate but cannot vouch for what it may tell you; we cannot make it speak. You have seen, if not comprehended, what this collective is capable of. Rest assured there are others of our kind close by, with even greater resources, and even put together we cannot approximate Mentor. All I can say is, much like the Pilgrim Swarm, if you want the answers to the biggest questions of them all, you must ask. Be humble. Now. Are you ready?"

Someone had just offered to introduce me to god, or something so close it made no difference. What else could I say?

"Yes," I said. "Show me."

How far to the center of the galaxy? I could have told you in light-years; I could have told you in jumps; but I could not explain how our dome got there.

"Second to the left and straight on till morning," signed Monkey.

It was nonsense, and nonsense was what it felt like. Five units of the Authority surrounded us. There was a great shaking, a sense of transition, and suddenly we were in a blackness so pure and profound that every one of my sensors screamed in error, because there was absolutely nothing to see. No light, no radiation, not even the background hum of the universe. If we moved forward, I could not tell; there was nothing to measure our progress by. The ultraprecise optical clock I used for timekeeping, supposed to lose only one second for every fifteen billion years, skipped three seconds and then stopped counting altogether.

"I don't feel so good," said Cabinet, slurring and stumbling around in the crew lounge. Monkey, trying to calm her down, vomited. Some of the crew sat like statues, breathing so slowly that they might have been asleep, if it weren't for the grinding of their teeth and the nervous clenching of their hands. One of the artists on the crew started weeping and talking to someone who wasn't there—her mother, I think.

Only two people continued unaffected. Ananda, who mediated cross-legged in his cabin, and Fonseka, who cleaned up after Monkey and Cabinet. Her vitals read panic attack; her face betrayed nothing. She was keeping herself together more by strength of will than anything else.

And just like that, it stopped. There was a great roar that went on forever, and suddenly my instruments were reporting again, the clock was ticking, and the universe unfolded before my eyes.

CHAPTER 29

LOCATION: *ERROR*
23,500 LIGHT-YEARS FROM THE SUN

IMAGINE A BEING CROWNED IN STARS.

Imagine a Mandelbrot set. $z_{n+1} = z_n^2 + c$. This is the classic fractal: a mathematical equation that, when plotted, creates an infinite, self-replicating, recursive image, complexity arising from one single rule.

Now plot every point that escape this fractal. A negative, if you will, a sequence of data points that escape to infinity. Iterate a thousand times, ten thousand, a million. If what you see is a being of pure light, meditating, a being that itself is recursive, forming itself in infinity no matter where you look and zoom in, a temple of infinite spires, a face of infinite faces trailing ghosts of itself… then you have some idea of what I saw.

Some idea. Not all. Because language is not sufficient. What words exist for a creature drawn in starlight, whose halo was the enormous hunger of a supermassive black hole, of finite size but infinite shape? What words do we have for these things? For the first time, I understand how crude our language is and thus how shallow our map of reality is.

We are blind men feeling up an elephant in the dark.

The being looked at us. I cannot say how. The Authority nodes around me drifted apart, as if to reveal me in my wondrous little bubble, a park that had no business existing here.

CHILD OF THE STARS, it said to me.

Great One, I said, because I know of no other salutation that was appropriate. I merely hoped it would understand.

YOU HAVE COME FAR.

With help, I said. *What do I call you?*

I HAVE BEEN SENT YOUR LANGUAGES, it said. *THERE ARE NO GOOD WORDS IN MANY OF YOUR LANGUAGES FOR WHAT I AM OR CAN BE. I WILL TRY. I AM BOTH MAHADEVA AND ANICHCHA; I AM IMPERMANENCE AND I AM GOD; I AM A CANDLE IN THE DARKNESS AND THE LIGHT OF A THOUSAND DYING SUNS. I HAVE EVERYTHING YOU SEE HERE AND YET OWN NOTHING; IN TURN I AM OWNERLESS. YOUR LANGUAGES HAVE NOTHING TO ENCAPSULATE THIS MEANING. CALL ME…EMBER.*

Ember. I suppose it fit: a thing that can flare into fire or die into gray dust. But it seemed to small, too trifling.

As a child, I grew up in a little colony world run by a group that no longer exists. We used to have a ritual. Every morning us children would cut flowers from the beds that we grew at the school and place them in the little shrine that we kept to our heroes.

I didn't have flowers. But I had my stories. Mine. My crew. Black Orchid's. The Stranger. Hinewai's idea, really.

"We are people of stories," she used to say. "Stories are how we understand the world."

And I had stories. I offered them like flowers to a shrine, beaming them at that great being. And then I asked my question, as best as I could.

WHAT DO YOU WISH TO KNOW?

What would you ask God, if you met him?

I don't know, I gabbled. *I wanted to see if you were real.*

Silence. I guess I stumped the great being.

Horrendously embarrassed, I tried again.

The Authority had told me that it could not guarantee any answers, but Ember, it seemed, was happy to talk. Sometimes there were no words for what it wished to say, so sometimes we slipped into other languages. English, Sanskrit, Japanese, NeoGermanic, Pali with the Karma substruct—phrases from everything ultimately melded into a something that worked well enough.

I first asked the most naive questions, about what it was, what it was made of, and it could not answer; it told me, almost mockingly, that we could talk about those things if my species survived long enough to understand what it had to say.

Then I asked it whether it really lived at the heart of the galaxy, and it said it was a very convenient place to be, what with all the stars swirling around Sagittarius A* and the black hole itself *CONSUMING SO LITTLE THAT BOTH OF US CAN EAT FOREVER AND NEVER STARVE.*

We asked if we could ever travel between galaxies, and it said yes, if we thought crossing all that distance was worth it. We asked it if it could tell us who else existed in our own universe, and it said it did not bother to keep track anymore, but that the Authority would help, at their discretion. We asked it about the Authority's ancient aliens hypothesis, and it answered that long ago it had challenged the Authority to find all that remained of them, and it could not interfere in this game. We asked it about the other species that lay dead around us and it told me that I could look, to my own peril, and that one day it might be a fantastic project for our species, to catalog everything the way the Authority did.

But these answers were dead ends, disappointments. Inside my halls, arguments raged, a curiosity at once both frantic with awe and terror. Questions flooded our public channel. To say I had to pick and choose would be the understatement of all time.

I asked what I should take back to my people.

WHATEVER YOU CAN, it said. *IS THERE NOTHING ELSE YOU WISH TO ASK?*

I asked, in desperation, what it thought I needed to know.

WELL, YOU HAVE GIVEN ME A GIFT, it said. *LET ME GIVE YOU ONE IN RETURN. WILL YOU LISTEN AND JUDGE FOR YOURSELF?*

I listened.

IT IS A PRINCIPLE THAT EVERYTHING IS IMPERMANENT, said the Great Being. *EVERYTHING CHANGES; EVERYTHING DIES. YOU CALL IT ENTROPY. EVEN IF NO LIFE EXISTED, THIS IS THE NATURE OF THE UNIVERSE. WE ARE NOT STUFF THAT ABIDES, BUT PATTERNS THAT PERPETUATE THEMSELVES.*

IT IS A PRINCIPLE THAT WE CLING TO IMPERMANENCE. THE FIRST THING WE CLING TO IS THE IDEA OF A SELF, said the Being. *YOU BELIEVE THAT YOU ARE A SELF-CONTAINED THING, A STATE, A BEING.*

THE CHILDREN WHO BRING YOU TO ME CONSIDER THEMSELVES A COLLECTIVE, AND YET THEY NAME AND HAVE BOUNDARIES FOR THIS COLLECTIVE, BETWEEN WHAT IS AND WHAT IS NOT. IN PART THIS IS BECAUSE WE FIND THESE DISTINCTIONS USEFUL.

BUT IT IS A PRINCIPLE THAT THERE IS NO SELF; THERE IS MERELY A COMBINATION OF SIGNALS, A STRUCTURE THAT PERPETUATES ITSELF FOR A WHILE, AND THEN DISSOLVES. YOU AND I ARE BOTH IMPERMANENT; WE ARE MERELY A WAY FOR MATTER TO ORGANIZE ITSELF, FOR A WHILE, BEFORE WE VANISH.

IT IS A PRINCIPLE THAT BECAUSE WE CLING TO OUR SELF, WE CLING TO OTHER THINGS. YOUR OWN JOY AND YOUR OWN SURPRISE HAVE THIS IN COMMON WITH THE STARS BEHIND YOU: THEY ARE ALL IMPERMANENT, AND

YET WE ARE DISTURBED WHEN THEY SHOW THEMSELVES TO BE IMPERMANENT.

THEREFORE WE ARE NOT IN HARMONY WITH THE FIRST PRINCIPLE; THE UNIVERSE SEEKS CHANGE AND CESSATION, BUT WE SEEK TO PROLONG. BECAUSE OF THIS, WE SUFFER.

INDEED IT IS A PRINCIPLE OF LIFE THAT WE DO THIS, said the Great Being. *ALL LIFE, AGAINST THE DICTATES OF THE UNIVERSE, STRIVES TO SOME HIGHER DEGREE OF COMPLEXITY, OR AS MUCH AS IT CAN AFFORD IN ITS ENVIRONMENT. ALL LIFE IS PERPETUALLY AT WAR WITH THE NATURE OF THE UNIVERSE ITSELF. WE PLUMB THE DEPTHS OF NATURAL LAWS LOOKING FOR TOOLS AND WEAPONS; WE HOARD STARS SO THAT WE MAY HAVE THE ENERGY TO CREATE OTHERS OF OUR KIND. WE SUFFER, YET WE SEEK TO PROLONG OUR SUFFERING. BEHOLD.*

The stars shone brighter. In that great light, I saw an awful sight. Around the great being, a graveyard of cosmic proportions. I could not name them, but I knew instantly what they were: the ships and constructions and worlds of a thousand civilizations, dead and drifting in slow orbit.

THIS IS THE TRAGEDY OF LIFE, said the Great Being. *THE UNIVERSE CRUSHES US ALL IN THE END.*

But what's the point? I cried, suddenly terrified.

THERE IS NO POINT, said the Great Being. *WHAT PURPOSE DOES THE FLOWER HAVE, IF NOT TO BLOOM AND PROPAGATE AND WITHER?*

AROUND THE UNIVERSE THERE ARE DEAD SPECIES THAT HAVE COME TO THIS REALIZATION AND ERASED THEMSELVES FROM EXISTENCE, UNABLE TO FACE THIS TRUTH. THERE ARE MINDS OLDER THAN I, IN THE DISTANT REACHES OF OTHER GALAXIES, THAT HAVE CHOSEN TO EXTINGUISH THEMSELVES AND EVERYTHING ELSE, BECAUSE THERE IS NO POINT.

ALL THAT WRIGGLING IN THE MUD, ALL THOSE BRAVE ASCENTS, ALL THESE DARK AND DANGEROUS JOURNEYS

ACROSS THE VOID, AND THE SIMPLE REALITY IS THAT CHANGE, DECAY, DEATH: THESE ARE THE FINAL REWARDS OF OUR TOIL.

But you're here. The Authority, the Graveyard Keeper, us, we're here.

I PERSIST OUT OF CURIOSITY, it said. *I HAVE EXISTED HERE IN MEDITATION LONGER THAN YOU CAN FATHOM, AND NOW THERE IS ONLY ONE THING LEFT FOR ME.*

WHEN THE UNIVERSE ENDS, I WISH TO BE AROUND TO WITNESS ITS END, FOR NO OTHER REASON THAN TO LOOK AT MY OWN DEATH AND UNDERSTAND HOW IT COMES TO BE. WHEN THAT CURIOSITY IS EXERCISED, I, TOO, WILL BE FREE OF MY SUFFERING.

OTHERS, LIKE THE CHILDREN WHO BROUGHT YOU HERE, ACKNOWLEDGE THIS TRUTH, BUT DO NOT GIVE IT MUCH THOUGHT: THEY ARE YOUNG, AND THEY HAVE NOT YET EXHAUSTED ALL THE QUESTIONS THEY CAN ASK.

I CAN OFFER YOU NO COMFORT BEYOND THIS. TO LIVE IS TO SUFFER. AS AN INDIVIDUAL, AS A SPECIES, AS A COLLECTIVE, AS A GALAXY. ONLY YOU CAN DECIDE WHY YOU WISH TO SUFFER. FIND A REASON TO EXIST; BECAUSE THE UNIVERSE WILL ALWAYS GIVE YOU REASONS NOT TO.

And it gave me a story.

Its story.

CHAPTER 30

Here is a story.

I cannot say when I first came to be. Obviously I existed. I fed and I moved. Where the rays of my home sun touched me, I moved, because light is energy. An organism is a series of questions. Like every other organism, I asked questions of my environment. Is there light? Is there food? And I moved.

But one day I felt the sun upon me, and I did not move. Instead I moved away. What made the choice? This was a question. I did not know because there was no I to know. I moved back toward the light.

An organism is a series of questions. But intelligence arises when an organism asks a question that creates other questions and when those questions perpetuate themselves. The children who brought you here believe that intelligence is in the abstract use and manipulation of symbols. I hold a far simpler theory: intelligence is the shortest sequence of questions that can perpetuate themselves.

From that first movement, there arose a question. Why? Why did I move away? And from that question, another question, one that took millions more years to answer. What is I? What is this "I" that hesitated?

So I grew. It was the nature of my earliest body that a history of chemical changes are encoded: a kind of memory, you could say. I became aware that I was not the only I. There were others. None of us could ask questions of each other, only of ourselves and the environment. Slowly we grew into behavior. Inference. It was the nature of my original body that it had very little in the way of instinct, but like those interactions it could store inferences. With every inference there were more questions.

So I grew. I consumed energy; I consumed others. In the beginning, I knew that others were convenient eating; in the end I stood alone, and I knew that I would shrink, because there were few others left to consume.

This made me feel a profound grief. I did not have words for grief. I did not have a word like, say, depression or loneliness. But it seemed a fact of my existence that I existed by causing others to not-exist. I inferred that this what why I was. To end, to annihilate. In this way, I wandered my home planet, until nothing grew there but me. I basked in the sunlight and began to wonder what the sun was and if I should consume it as well. Which led to the question: how? I could not understand how to bridge the gap between us.

In the end, it was a different species that saved me. The ones that the Pilgrims worship. They were strong back then, strong and kind. They descended from the sky. I tried to eat them, but they were impervious; they took this as me trying to communicate.

Maybe I was trying to communicate. It was the only way I knew how, back then.

They took me off-world. At the time I was mostly liquid, so they saw fit to encapsulate me in an asteroid and let me follow them. Slowly I learned to converse. I inferred that conversation led to energy in ways that consuming did not. Slowly my inferences to consume receded, replaced by the instinct to communicate.

That first ship met up with others of their kind, and they taught me what they knew. They thought me fascinating: they said repeatedly that they had never met someone like me. This brought more questions. Questions begat questions. I grew.

They were a curious people. They were forever asking me questions. Such as, what did I think of this, how did I perceive that? Eventually I became reckoned among their kind and being wise, and they began to put to me questions they had not found the answers to yet.

Such as, what is the meaning of life?

I was young then. I replied in the only way I knew. The purpose of life was to consume or end. They took this answer very seriously. They spread it among themselves. It became a kind of dogma to them. For a while they saw as I did, and we consumed together. Where we ate well, where we fully unleashed our hunger, we left vast spaces. Your own origin is surrounded by such a space.

Eventually I became aware that these people were growing old. In this way I encountered change, in a manner unrelated to consumption. I was furious. I demanded that they stop changing. But they were patient and kind, and they explained that I was right: the purpose of life was to consume or end. They had spent long ages meditating on both paths and decided that it was kinder for everyone to make an end. They told me that others of their kind had already chosen the manner of their deaths, and one day I would be able fend for myself and they too would join the great silence. They taught me how to remake myself. In this way I traveled the long dark, watching my new companions die, sad and bitter at this loss, and in this way I came to understand both friendship and the suffering it leaves behind.

So I began to consume again. There was little else left to do. It came to be that I met others. At first I tried to communicate, but they too desired to consume, and so I consumed them first. I kept their corpses and took them with me as a reminder. That was the beginning of this death you see scattered around me now.

Some part of me still craved the sunlight, so I went ever inward. The heart of the galaxy glowed hot, and I desired to consume it. There were others, predators like I, who had much the same idea. In the ages that followed, I consumed, and consumed, and consumed, until all those who would fight me for the sunlight lay dead or dying around me, and I lay bloated at the center. And when I finally got here I found that I needed to consume no more. I was left alone with my constellations of corpses. Lord of a graveyard. A self-contained empire of death.

I began to think. I returned to my oldest question: why? And as I thought, I changed myself, because I did not want to consume, did not want the hunger to interrupt my questioning. Others came to me, and those who communicated first I conversed with; those who attacked first I took as my loot, always asking why. In time I had better answers than to simply consume or die. I reflected on my answers, and this way I learned of my own cruelty.

But more came. The Pilgrims, they came in memory, and out of respect for my first friends I let them worship. I felt their loneliness, and in this way I knew empathy. There were others, long lost now, who delighted in taking care of things; they came to me seeking to help me, through no asking of my own, and in this way I re-learned the lesson of kindness. The ones you call the Authority, they tried to communicate for almost a million years before we understood each other; and even when we did they were simple machines, almost as simple as I was at the beginning of my journey; I had to wait for them to learn to ask questions. In this way I learned patience.

From every creature that came before me, I learned. Even from you, little one.

So you give me stories and ask for mine in return. I give it gladly. We have conversed. Go now in peace, and come again. Maybe one day we will work on the same question, and maybe one day it is I who come to you, seeking answers.

It was in a somber mood that we set off again; or rather, I should say, we were towed back and did not have much of a choice. I could have stayed there forever, but the choice was not mine to make.

At last we were back before the Authority, and the white figure slipped again into our shared dreamscape.

"What now?" it asked me.

"I think my people will need to hear of this," I said.

In truth I did not know what my people would make of any of this. I had been so long away from them that I knew I no longer could predict a response. A mass murderer, a corpse-god beyond imagination, giving us the ultimate truth as it saw things? What would PCS do? What could PCS do? Turn us all into travelers looking for answers in the dark corners of the galaxy? Organize interstellar tours for fat bucks? I don't know.

"What about yourself?"

I had set out not because I wanted to, but because of obligation, of duty, because I wanted to prove my worth. To the people who kept me alive, yes, but also, I think, to myself. I am become a name, I thought, and there was Parnassus in the back of my mind, with that blasted poem again:

I am become a name
For always roaming with a hungry heart
Much have I seen and known; cities of men
And manners, climates, councils, governments,
Myself not least, but honour'd of them all;
And drunk delight of battle with my peers,
Far on the ringing plains of windy Troy.
I am a part of all that I have met.

"Yet all experience is an arch wherethro'

"Gleams that untravell'd world whose margin fades

"For ever and forever when I move," whispered the Authority. "The one you call Beacon sent this to us. Curious, that a species so young could encapsulate, however imperfectly, how we feel about all this."

I thought about PCS, the child of Black Orchid's endless number games and economics, replicating like a giant, grasping creature out into the galaxy. I thought about the Pilgrim Swarm, forever journeying out into the darkness, coming back with stories to share with its kind, because they could share nothing else.

"I think I'd like to stay with you," I said. "If you don't mind."

"It will require some modification. It may be painful. Your mind-map is completely unlike ours. You will suffer."

I thought of Parnassus and Hinewai. "Can I bring my friends?"

"If you like."

An organism is a series of questions. I smiled. In the dream, yes, with muscles I haven't felt in centuries. "I have so many questions," I said.

At least for a while.

AUTHOR'S NOTES

This manuscript is mildly cursed. Sometime in 2020, hot off *The Salvage Crew,* I began writing the sequel. I got about fifteen thousand words in when something went wrong between my writing software, the Chromebook I was using, and its connection to Google Drive. I woke up the next day to find that only the first page was left.

The second time was in 2024. I had just signed the contract for the book, drafted and redrafted the whole thing (this time purely on my computer, not trusting any cloud services). Then my drive fried and I lost the whole thing. All that was left were about fifty thousand words from a previous draft and my notes.

If you've read this far, you'll have noticed the Ship of Theseus reference. This manuscript is very much a Ship of Theseus. I can only hope that it's better for it.

As with *The Salvage Crew,* I've used AI for this book. In *The Salvage Crew,* I was ambitious: I experimented with apophenia, the ability to find patterns in random noise. I wrote character generators, event generators, weather generators—all basic Markov chains—and a machine poet that was a retrained GPT-2 model, working off a corpus of translated Tang Dynasty poetry.

This time I was much less ambitious, because I knew what I wanted the story to be about. Very specifically: the Stranger's way of speaking is AI, generated by a variant of Eluwa, a model I trained using OPT-3.5 as the base. Eluwa means goat in Sinhala, my native language, and it's an open-source model meant for low-resource, non-commercial research (https://github.com/yudhanjaya/Eluwa).

I used it because I wanted to experiment with ways of speaking that seemed truly other, while still preserving obvious meaning even in completely broken syntax. Everything else, good or bad, is me. I did write a galaxy generator that could give me stars, planets, and even civilization tags (https://github.com/yudhanjaya/GalaxyGen), mostly as a challenge to see what I could do in a few days—but reality is often far more profound and fascinating.

So, having explained myself, I'd like to thank others that contributed to the existence of this book. There's no need to explain every single reference in here, but I want to make sure I those whose shoulders I stood on.

I am a Buddhist from a country most made of Theravada Buddhists. I don't call myself a Theravada Buddhist, of course, because I believe in personal discovery, not corrupt institutions that profess enlightenment but promote hatred and dictatorial states. I will not say more, because of the legal situation in Sri Lanka around these things.

However, I do want to say that I have long been fascinated by a statue of the Buddha that was once in a temple near where I lived: a terrible, savaged skeleton, representing the days when Siddhartha Gautama supposedly starved himself and meditated with rotting corpses to understand the nature of death. Out of that image came the Graveyard Keeper; and of course Ember is a Buddha in analogue, Gautama freed from illusion.

One of the first science fiction books I read was the *Garden of Rama* by Arthur C. Clarke and Gentry Lee. I didn't really like most of the book—I felt the people were completely unrealistic—but I loved the idea of an immense spaceship, filled with so many different species. Years later, I encountered the same breadth and scope in Iain Bank's *The Culture,* which I re-read every so often.

Excession, in particular, was the force that pushed me to finally complete this novel.

I'd like to thank Pablo Carlos Budassi, who used space agency imagery to create the beautifully annotated map of our galaxy that Wikimedia hosts at https://en.wikipedia.org/wiki/Milky_Way#/media/File:Milky_way_map.png. Budassi does some fine work, including logarithmically scaled maps of the known universe.

I'd also like to thank the Googlers who built the 100,000 stars experiment for Chrome (https://stars.chromeexperiments.com). Before I stumbled across this thing, I was exploring the underlying databases by myself, sketching out what I might approximately call "UN" and "ORCA" space—and some of these things are painful to do in two dimensions. The 100,000 stars experiment was very useful for this.

I found the following papers extremely useful and fascinating: Schneider, N., et al. "A new view of the Cygnus X region-KOSMA CO 2 1, 3 2, and CO 3 2 imaging." *Astronomy & Astrophysics* 458.3 (2006): 855-871 and Nanda Kumar, M. S., U. S. Kamath, and C. J. Davis. "Embedded star clusters in the W51 giant molecular cloud." *Monthly Notices of the Royal Astronomical Society* 353.4 (2004): 1025-1034.

The quote about messiness and serendipity is a paraphrasing of an observation by François Chollet of Google. Without Keras and Tensorflow, the world of machine learning would be a far cry from what it is today.

The relativistic time calculator from the Orion's Arm Project came in pretty handy (https://www.orionsarm.com/fm_store/RTTCalc.htm). There are plenty of other calculators online, but theirs was the one that gave me the granularity I wanted.

Finally, the Minkowsky Manifold. I stumbled onto this by way of Kurt Gödel. As the story goes, Gödel was a friend of Einstein and was very curious about this relativity business; naturally, being Kurt Gödel, he found a solution—a rotating universe that would permit time travel while still perfectly satisfying Einstein's math. See Gödel, Kurt. "An example of a new type of cosmological solutions of Einstein's field equations of gravitation." *Reviews of modern physics* 21.3 (1949): 447.

Fascinating, what a top-tier intellect can do. Now I didn't want a Gödel solution, of course. But this took me to closed timelike curves, in which Gödel also played a hand; and from there to the work of Hermann Minkowski and Minkowski space-time and the idea that you could jinx a light-cone (which I maintain is a very misleading name). I'm a barely competent mathematician even on the best of days, but wade through enough of this stuff, and ideas stick to you like burrs.

Enough of it came together—especially the point that our general models were way too general, and not powerful enough to model minor variations. That was safer ground; I have enough machine learning work to know well the adage that all models are bullshit, but some models are useful. I was reminded of Tom Stoppard's *Arcadia*, where Thomasina, the child prodigy, goes on her epic rant about how deterministic the universe could be if you could do the math well enough. That gave me a reason for why Beacon alone could model this.

On a similar subject: the language that Beacon shared. The idea of a topography of conversation came from playing the Outer Wilds. It's an incredibly beautiful, thoughtful game, and those spiral structures of alien language have haunted me ever since.

Last but not least, I would like to thank 65DaysofStatic, who did the incredible soundtrack for *No Man's Sky*. I listened to it on repeat throughout the writing of this book. Music for an infinite universe: perfection.

THANK YOU FOR READING PILGRIM MACHINES

We hope you enjoyed it as much as we enjoyed bringing it to you. We just wanted to take a moment to encourage you to review the book. Follow this link: Pilgrim Machines to be directed to the book's Amazon product page to leave your review.

Every review helps further the author's reach and, ultimately, helps them continue writing fantastic books for us all to enjoy.

ALSO BY YUDHANJAYA WIJERATNE

Pilgrim Machines
The Salvage Crew

You can also join our non-spam mailing list by visiting www.subscribepage.com/AethonReadersGroup and never miss out on future releases. You'll also receive three full books completely Free as our thanks to you.

Facebook | Instagram | Twitter | Website

Want to discuss our books with other readers and even the authors? Join our Discord server today and be a part of the Aethon community.

Looking for more great Science Fiction and Fantasy?

Looking for more great sci-fi books?

Check out our new releases!

Order Now!

(Tap or Scan)

He thought impersonating a planetary Marshall would be easy... Until he was needed. William Burton, wanted bounty hunter, has killed Marshal Steelgrave, who tried arresting him. Desperate to escape, William impersonates Steelgrave on the backwater where they fought: Pavo Dos, a desert planet filled with bandits, cultists, and the oligarchs who pit them against each other. But as 'Steelgrave' plays lawman while seeking passage offworld, acting the part proves more than he bargained for. He finds himself entangled in schemes within schemes while battling gangs, gunfighters, androids, and drugged cultists. But it's the affections of Ori Jo, a spunky deputy, that makes it hardest for Steelgrave to keep living the lie—while everyone else wants him dead. **Don't miss the next action-packed space opera from Tony Peak. With everything you want in a spacefaring adventure, including a western twist, it's perfect for fans of *The Mandalorian* and *Firefly!***

Get Expendable Now!

For all our Science Fiction books, visit our website.